# DEATH IN THE SHADOWS

Karen fumbled for her keys. Something prompted her to glance over her shoulder. She stared across the street into the black shapes of the thick foliage.

There was something. A form . . . Karen gasped. The dark silhouette of a man stood with legs apart, arms folded across his chest, his featureless face directed toward Karen. He took his first step toward her.

"Oh, no!" she screamed, fear urging her to run. She dashed toward a neighbor's door, pounded desperately on it, not daring to look back. Her neighbor opened the door. "What's wrong," he asked.

"There's a man." Karen turned to point to— He was gone.

# PRESUMPTION
## — of —
# INNOCENCE

## DAVE PEDNEAU

AVON
PUBLISHERS OF BARD, CAMELOT, DISCUS AND FLARE BOOKS

AVON BOOKS
A division of
The Hearst Corporation
1790 Broadway
New York, New York 10019

First Avon Printing, January, 1985

# PRESUMPTION
## of INNOCENCE

# PROLOGUE

Gracie Mack owned much of nothing . . .
. . . yet even that was too much.

Her lot was meager. Abetted by her wits and a contemptible contribution from Social Security, Gracie narrowed
the gap between her needs and her resources by baking
pies, apple turnovers and cakes, all of which she peddled at
the local bank or to friends who could afford such luxuries.
She shared her four-room, frame house with a nest of resis-
tant cockroaches and a tenacious den of oversized rats. For
years, both had defied her every effort at eviction and appeared to thrive on the conflict. Gracie had given up.

That day—June 4th—had been a roaster, more typical of
mid-August than late spring. The walls of her house radiated a stuffy, damp swelter. The condition was compounded
because she had chosen to bake most of the day—a couple
of pound cakes—in case her useless son-in-law remained
sufficiently sober to deliver her daughter and grandchildren to Sunday dinner. The kids loved her cakes, and
Gracie loved her grandkids, who made her waning life tol-
erable.

And, as she had suspected, across town her son-in-law
lay stinking drunk. Not that it mattered much in the long
run. Gracie wouldn't live to see the next dawn, much less
her beloved grandchildren and her daughter. It became
one of her son-in-law's more opportune drunks. Gracie was
a proud woman; she would not have wanted her loved ones
to find her the next day . . . not looking as she was to look.

Gracie, just beyond 65 and widowed for more years than
she cared to count, made a fatal mistake that sultry June
night. Just a little thing, but it cost her dearly. Deciding
that the mosquitoes which would surely invade her house

1

were less of a discomfort than the smothering heat, she left open her kitchen window. What were a few mosquitoes to a woman who had grown accustomed to worse vermin? Besides, on many a summer night, she had left open the same window to allow the prevailing westerlies to dispel the heavy heat.

On this night, however, something far more bloodthirsty than the mosquitoes or even the rats lurked in the misty darkness. Not a hundred yards from her open window, a creature called Virgil Sampson prowled the night. Virgil wanted to steal something. Nothing definite . . . just something that belonged to someone else. He hadn't a thing against Gracie Mack—didn't know her, in fact. Virgil, though, got his jollies from other people's misery. Like leeches and fungus and even mistletoe, Virgil was a kind of parasite. Some folks find their niche in the world doing good, others by wallowing in evil. Gracie Mack would be remembered for her savory and delightful pastries, Virgil for his offenses against humanity. They occupied the same world, but lived within different planes of consciousness . . . and their planes were about to intersect.

That evening something more profound than a desire to steal compelled Virgil Sampson. Trailing behind him, in the place where his shadow would have been, had there been the slightest glimmer of light, crept a small boy. He was Virgil's 14-year-old nephew. The boy worshipped this man whom he followed through dark alleys and threatening shadows. The youthful, pimpled face displayed proud and frequent awe over his uncle's constant confrontations with "the law." And, like his uncle (though perhaps not to the same degree), Michael David Sampson, a.k.a. Mickie Sampson, had little use for cops. They treated him "like shit," he decided, because his last name was Sampson.

In just a few weeks, his uncle was to stand trial for murder, and Virgil had told Mickie that he'd "beat 'em again." Virgil was lucky that way. Like when he was arrested for the killing back in December. He'd been in jail less than a week when one of his half-dozen brothers, feeling sorry for their haggard mother, posted Virgil's bail just in time for Christmas. Mickie's father was also one of Virgil's brothers, but he'd skipped town long ago, deserting Mickie and his mother. During the years that followed, Virgil became something of a father figure to the young boy. On this night, the kid was being shown "the ropes."

Virgil didn't deny the killing that had landed him in jail in December. The cops claimed that he ambushed a fellow reveler after a beer joint ballbuster. "A goddamn pig lie," Virgil had said to the allegation of an ambush. "The bastard came at me with a knife. Ain't a man got a right to defend hisself?"

"Damn right," Mickie had said.

Virgil, magnificently wise to the boy who skulked behind him, studied the backs of the houses on both sides of the alley. He halfheartedly swatted at a mosquito which settled to feast on the tough, swarthy skin of his face. "I guess ya think we shoulda gone to the ritzy part of town, eh, kid?" Virgil said. "You'd be surprised. Most of them rich folks put all their money in banks. Poor folks keep all they got at home."

"You ever rob a bank?" Mickie asked of his uncle.

Virgil chuckled. "Not yet, but I'm young yet."

"Bet that gun you got there would scare them bankers into turning over their money," the kid whispered, referring to the monstrous, long-barrelled .44 magnum stuck down in Virgil's belt. The gun, the gain from an ancient house burglary, was Virgil's pride and joy, his "good luck piece." But Virgil was careful. Carrying a gun without a license was a hard rap to beat. Either you had a gun and no license or you had the gun with a license—not much room to maneuver. So Virgil sported the gun only on big jobs—or when he wanted to show off—like tonight.

Mickie, too, was armed. He labored under the weight and bulk of a .12 gauge shotgun which his uncle had given to him "just in case." The boy easily ignored its burden and carried it with a swaggering respect, its hefty presence making Mickie feel "as bad" as his uncle.

"How do you know which house to pick?" Mickie asked.

Virgil, wafting away yet another whining mosquito, shrugged off the question. "It don't really matter. We got as good a chance of finding something in one as t'other."

"What if somebody's home? Shouldn't we wear masks or something?"

Virgil ruffled the boy's long, greasy hair. "You watch too much TV, kid."

3

They slipped farther down the narrow alley, their inky shapes concealed by the row of ill-kept hedges and stacks of overflowing trash cans, which flanked them on both sides.

Light from Gracie Mack's window streamed out into her yard. Virgil saw it first, and he smiled. "Lookee there!"

The boy saw the open window, the yellow light pouring from it. "But that means someone's there!"

Virgil continued to smile, his face now slightly revealed by the window's illumination. "It also means we can see what we're doing."

Virgil slipped through an opening in the hedge and started across the yard. Mickie, his stomach doing funny and uncomfortable things, paused before he followed. He wanted to believe that his uncle knew what he was doing, so he too crept into the backyard.

Inside, Gracie sat in her living room, sipping a beer and enjoying a rerun of *Love Boat*, the opulence of the latter seeming to her a science fiction. Gracie didn't drink too much beer, usually one can a night as her doctor had prescribed, just enough to flush her kidneys and make her sleep a little better. On this evening, because it was so damned hot and because those fruity-looking tropical drinks on the TV looked so good, she decided to have a second can.

As Gracie rose from her chair to fetch it, Virgil Sampson hoisted himself into the open window. Mickie, ready to pull himself inside, saw her approaching shadow flit across a wall as she came down the short hall toward the kitchen.

"Virg!" Mickie cried just as Gracie stepped into her kitchen. The woman's eyes bulged at the sight of them—a young boy framed at that instant in the open window and the strange man standing inside her kitchen. As wide-eyed as she was, Gracie caught only a fleeting glimpse of the long black tube of the gun's barrel swinging toward her. She managed to turn her head. The metal smashed across her cheek and ear, and Gracie Mack, her brain stunned by the blow, slumped down to the floor.

Mickie, by then inside, gasped. "You kilt her!"

"Not yet I ain't." Virgil stood still, stood tense, listening to see if someone else was at home. He heard nothing but the sounds of a television. He glanced back at the kid. "Come on. Let's see what she's got. Not too fuckin' much, I bet."

Starting with Gracie's bedroom, they commenced to savage the house. Virgil emptied every drawer onto the bed. A lifetime of photos—Gracie's most valued possessions—fluttered onto the worn linoleum covering the floor. Mickie emptied the contents of a small jewelry box on top of the contents of the drawers. Virgil, attracted to the shimmering jewelry, joined his nephew to sift through the small collection of trinkets. He pocketed what looked valuable (knowing it probably wasn't) and told Mickie to take whatever he wanted.

After ripping the mattress from the bed to be sure nothing had been stashed beneath it, Virgil directed Mickie back to the living room. The television, still tuned to *Love Boat*, was an old and heavy console model. Virgil punished it for its size by sending his booted foot into the face of a buxom, near-nude *Love Boat* blonde. Sparks flew; smoke gushed from its decimated guts.

Mickie cringed at the suddenness of the sound.

A small, battery-operated radio rested on a metal shelf amid a collection of portrait-type photographs of a young woman and children. Virgil snatched up the radio and jammed it in his rear pocket. As an afterthought, he swept the portraits from the shelf. The glass of the frames shattered one on top of another, all except the last. The glass of the frame holding the portrait of the young woman somehow remained intact.

Mickie couldn't understand the violence. He thought they had just come to steal something, anything that they could sell for money. He stood transfixed in the living room, his attention drawn to the old woman whom he could see from the living room. Most of her body, including her head, was visible, and he could see her bloody face moving slowly from side to side. "She's still alive," he said.

"Huh? What?" Virgil looked back over his shoulder. "Tough old cunt, ain't she?"

He moved on to the fourth room which was cluttered with old furniture and boxes of clothing and junk which Gracie Mack had been saving for a yard sale. She loved yard sales and was a prodigious and shrewd trader. Virgil, with the boy hanging behind him, rummaged through the various boxes. Cockroaches scurried away from his ungentle hands. He paused for a moment over a portable sewing machine, lifting it by a broken handle. "Too fuckin' heavy," he declared, dropping it on a fleeing roach.

"Got 'im!" Virgil snapped. "Time to leave, kid."

"Ain't we gonna take nothing else?"

Virgil, his pockets stuffed with the cheap radio and the costume jewelry, headed back toward the kitchen. "Nothin' worth takin'. Sometimes it happens that way."

Virgil allowed his nephew to precede him into the kitchen. The boy, his eyes averted, stepped over the woman. Blood seeped from a gash which ran from her right eye to her ear. Her head continued to sway from side to side, smearing the crimson gore which gathered in an expanding pool. She moaned softly in a way which made Mickie want to say something to her—that he was sorry, that he wished—

"Lookee there," Virgil said, pointing to a purse which sat on the kitchen table. "You check it out. Maybe she's got some money in it."

Mickie opened the battered leather container and dumped its contents on the table. Perfume rolled to the edge and fell to the floor. Then came a tube of lipstick and a dusty compact. A long wallet was the last item to slip onto the table. Mickie pulled from it a couple of dollar bills, lots of small notes, more photos, and a government check.

"Wow!"

Virgil frowned. "Leave the friggin' thing!"

"What?" The check was for better than two hundred dollars. Mickie did not understand.

And Virgil didn't bother to explain. Instead he said, "Look at this, kid. Her eyes is open. She sees me."

Mickie didn't want to look. While his uncle leered down at the woman, smiling into her muddled eyes, Mickie slipped the check into his pocket.

Virgil kneeled down, placing his knee bone squarely between the woman's large pendulous breasts. He slowly waved the gun in front of her face. Mickie, the check safely concealed, turned to see what his uncle was doing. "Let's—" . . . leave, Mickie had started to say, just before the concussion of the magnum rattled the house, cutting off his speech. It deafened Mickie whose eyes distended as he saw the woman's head explode. Blood, brains and bone sprayed over everything.

Virgil Sampson, speckled by flecks of Gracie Mack and feeling very good about the whole thing, hustled his young protegé from the house into the cover of the night.

6

# PART ONE

"In all criminal prosecutions, the defendant shall enjoy the right to a speedy and public trial . . ."
    —Amendment VI,
        Constitution of the United States of America

# ONE

The Custer County courtroom purred with a muted fervor. Uniformed bailiffs guided three uniformed prisoners into its darkly wooded presence, seating them on a shiny waxed bench to the left of the grand bench which rose center stage. Attorneys, also uniformed in their distinctive fashion of dark-colored, three-piece suits, huddled in cellular clusters, laughing and talking, but always casting an expectant eye toward the door leading from the Judge's chambers. Sightseers—just a handful on a quiet Monday morning—filled scattered seats in the rows of pews which reached far back from the wooden banisters separating the common folk from the court's official entourage.

Ethan "Chip" Roth, uncomfortable in his navy three-piece pinstripe, sat in the front row of benches inside the banister. Beside him sat a portly Arthur King, phantom senior partner in the law firm of King, King, Kiestler and Clausen, Custer County's most prestigious law firm. Chip, too, was a member of the firm—for two hours now. He was not yet, however, a member of the bar of Custer County. That honor was about to be bestowed upon him in a brief ceremony preceding the normal Monday morning routine of Circuit Court.

The past few days had seemed a whirlwind to Chip. On Friday he had graduated from the state's law school. While his classmates prepared for vacations at the beach before beginning their jobs, Chip packed for Custer County. The King firm wanted him to begin at once. On the day before, Chip had moved his meager collection of belongings, including the pinstripe (his only suit), into the small apartment which he had selected the prior weekend. He'd taken the first thing he'd found. The rent seemed reason-

9

able, and the landlord hadn't come on like the commandant of Stalag 17.

He had met Arthur King just moments before they had entered the courtroom. Simon King, lesser of the Kings, had interviewed Chip. And it was Simon King who had phoned Chip at the school to tell him the job was his if he wanted it.

If I wanted it, Chip had thought.

Most of the members of his graduating class had wanted it. Only about a third of his class saw any reason to apply, since interviewing was eventually restricted to those in the top quarter of the class. The firm enjoyed a statewide reputation and handled a respectable number of criminal cases—paying criminal cases. Most of the larger coal companies in the southern portion of the state kept the firm on generous retainers. The dark, dismal, or boring sides of the practice of law—divorces, wills and deeds—constituted a minor part of the firm's gross practice, though Chip for awhile would be burdened with those drudgeries.

Simon King's offer to Chip, who had ranked 15th in his class, seemed a breathtaking miracle (though not financially, of course—it was considered a valuable benefit to have been chosen). Simon had even been kind enough to catalog the advantages which had given Chip the nod over the others. Chip had worked a few years as a reporter before going to law school. Simon wasn't high on reporters ("a generally contemptible breed," King had said), but Chip was older than the majority of his class, therefore more mature. Also, Chip was a local boy, having been born, raised and educated in Custer County. (His mother had moved from the county after his father's death, while Chip was in law school.) Finally, Chip's grades were good if not excellent, and he had done particularly well in moot court, that final year's exercise in courtroom scenarios— "play court" to the glib cynics.

Chip had not been spared a résumé of his deficiencies, at least as Simon King saw them. Chip was unmarried and hadn't the "first iota" of apparent interest in community involvement. The latter deficiency would be remedied by fiat, King had said, leaving no doubt about it; the former— his unfortunate marital status—well, Simon trusted that Chip would meet some nice girl soon enough.

So here Chip sat, by the side of one of the state's most

prominent attorneys, ready to be admitted to the bar as a member of the King firm. It was a policy, a tradition, he was told, that Arthur King, King of Kings, appear with new firm members at the short but meaningful ceremony. After he had met Chip for the first time in the hall outside of the courtroom and escorted him inside, the other lawyers had flocked to greet him as if he were a medieval lord returning victorious from The Crusades. The King, as Arthur was ordained beyond the range of his hearing, spent a good part of the year in a country club residence at Hilton Head, South Carolina. He had introduced Chip as if they were old and dear friends, a conceit which made Chip feel as though a sham were being perpetrated upon the court and Custer County.

Chip had seen the King several times before—never had met him though. Growing up in the very shadow of the courthouse, Chip had spent sizable chunks of his summer vacations watching trials. Unlike movies, the dramas in the courtroom were free and sometimes more interesting—at least to Chip, who saw a future of glory in the practice of law. King had appeared in several trials which Chip had attended.

Chip had told the lesser King of his adolescent interest in the law, but Simon had seemed much more impressed by his local roots than his long-term dedication. "Good for our image," Simon had pronounced. Chip would have rather been employed for his dedication, but Simon cited his excellence in mock court, suggesting quite correctly that it demonstrated an interest in the practical application of the law rather than its convoluted and often prostituted theories. Simon had called law school "a contrivance to keep the supply of lawyers profitably short of the demand."

"Doctors do it better," he had added sourly.

For whatever reason, Chip was a member of Arthur King's law firm, and, while he hadn't said more than a dozen words to King the Elder, he now sat beside him waiting to be knighted. Simon King, apparently not a party to the tradition, wasn't present.

The lawyers, as if prompted by some metaphysical command, started to move toward seats on the long bench which faced the front of the courtroom, the bench on which Chip and the King already sat. Chip searched the front of the room for some evidence that court was about to commence. He saw none and was wondering how his veteran colleagues knew to be seated when a side door opened and in strode one of the most striking women Chip had ever seen. Her spiked heels clicked across the tile floor as she walked in front of Chip and took a seat at the counsel table reserved for the State's attorney. The woman was tall and lithe, her breasts understated in size, but feminine in form. She wore her long blonde hair very straight which gave her an almost adolescent appearance. And her legs—Chip couldn't help looking at her legs. They fell just between thin and fat, that rare form of perfect design which modeled panty hose on television.

Lost to the magnetism which he felt, Chip leaned over to the King to inquire about her. The bailiff saved him by suddenly crying out, in a coarse and high voice, "Silence, all present will rise!"

And all did, which gave Chip more time to appraise the woman's figure. She smoothed her skirt as she stood.

The bailiff continued the opening of court. "The Judge of the Circuit Court of Custer County Roger O. Pinter."

A black-robed jurist exited his chamber door.

"Oyez! Oyez! Oyez!" the bailiff whined, louder now as if to impress his dedication upon the Judge. "Silence is now commanded under pain of fine and imprisonment, while the Honorable Judge of the Circuit Court of Custer County is sitting. All persons having motions to make, pleadings to enter, or actions to prosecute come forward, and they shall be heard. God save the State of West Virginia and this Honorable Court."

Even the King had stood on the bailiff's command. It seemed incongruous, Chip thought—the King rising for a mere circuit judge. The Judge noticed King immediately and smiled. Out of the corner of his eye, Chip noticed the King nod to the Judge.

Roger Pinter had been judge for as long as Chip could remember. Tall and lanky, his face eroded by years of decisions and gallons of bourbon, the jurist nodded and the court's population settled back down, all except King who remained standing.

"Morning, Arthur," Pinter said. "I see you got a respectable start on one of those Carolina tans. It's a pleasure to have you back."

"The pleasure is mine," King said.

Pinter grinned. "I understand we have a young lamb to lead to the slaughter this fine morning."

The courtroom laughed; the blonde turned to look at Chip. She smiled. Chip smiled back.

The King motioned for Chip to follow him. Chip stood, aware suddenly that his knees were weak and his belly had started to cramp.

"I'd like to introduce to this Honorable Court Ethan Roth, Esquire. He is the newest member of my firm. He comes before this bench to be admitted to the practice of law in Custer County and the State of West Virginia. I can and do attest to his character and—"

A squeaking door in the rear of the courtroom opened, and the King, his brow knitted, wheeled slowly and deliberately to see who dared interrupt him. A tall, lanky figure, dressed in denim jeans and a grease-smudged jacket, lumbered into the courtroom, unbowed by all the faces which were turned upon him. He slumped down into a seat in the last row. His heavily stubbled jaws worked viciously on a wad of gum.

"As I was saying," the King said, holding his stare upon the intruder for a moment before turning back to the bench, "I can assure you that young Mr. Roth will be a credit to the bar. For those of you who find such informality acceptable, be it known that Mr. Roth answers to the rather suppressible alias of 'Chip,' I believe."

The King glanced at Chip for confirmation, and Chip managed a weak, "Yes, sir."

The Judge nodded to Chip and—to Chip's astonishment—extended a hand across the bench. Chip reached up and over and shook it, cracking his elbow on the edge of the bench in the process.

"He's a local lad," King told Pinter.

"Roth?" mused Pinter. The Judge's many years of running for office caused him to know—or to think he knew—most everyone in Custer County. "Was your father Harold Roth?"

"Yes, Your Honor."

"Fine man, Ethan. I was sorry to hear about his death. If I remember correctly, your mother left this area not long after that."

"Uh, yes, sir." Chip was impressed with the Judge's rec-

13

ollection. He hadn't even known that Pinter knew his parents. "She moved to Clarksburg to live with her sister."

"Good people," Pinter proclaimed. "Well, Ethan Roth, if you'll raise your right hand, we'll make you a legal party to this little sideshow."

As soon as Chip said "I do," the audience began to applaud. The King nodded to Pinter and turned to leave. Chip started to follow.

"Just a minute, Ethan," Pinter said. Chip stopped. The King marched right on out of the courtroom. "If you'll stay with us this morning," Pinter said, "we'll put you right to work. It's something of a tradition."

Again the crowd laughed. Chip didn't really know what to do. The King was already gone. Chip walked back to the long bench on which the attorneys waited. As he did so, he saw the blonde still looking at him.

Sitting among the other attorneys and without the presence of the King, he felt much less special than he had before. And the woman, whoever the hell she was, had started sorting files on the table.

The Monday morning routine of Circuit Court commenced. Pinter began with the three prisoners who had been waiting on the smaller pew off to the side of the courtroom. First came a motion for reduction in bail for one of the men charged in magistrate court with second offense "driving under the influence." The man's attorney approached the bench with the defendant and explained to Pinter that the man was married with a family, that he worked for a local construction company, adding he was a good candidate for a recognizance bond.

Pinter turned to the woman. She stood, her skirt swishing. A low murmur of approval issued from some of the lawyers as she moved toward the bench. "Your Honor, the State opposes—"

Chip had considered it, but even upon confirmation his jaw dropped in surprise. She was an assistant prosecutor!

". . . a recognizance bond," the woman was saying. "As you know, if convicted, this defendant faces a minimum jail sentence of six months . . ." Her voice was soft but firm. She stood gracefully before the bench, arguing with a gentle sincerity . . . and she lost. Pinter released the man on his promise to appear before the magistrate court assigned to try his case. Chip studied her face as she re-

14

turned to the counsel table to make a note on a yellow legal pad. It revealed nothing, just routine indifference.

Then came a motion for a psychiatric evaluation for the second of the three prisoners, a black male charged with a felony child abuse. The State—the inspiring blonde—had no objection . . . motion granted.

The third prisoner, sentenced to the county jail on a weapons possession charge, was asking to be allowed freedom during the day for a "work release" program. Again she had no objection . . . motion granted.

And the blonde took her seat. Chip wished he knew her name. It hadn't even been mentioned during the three brief matters before the court. And there followed a plethora of minor motions, all involving civil actions. Chip anticipated she would leave since the criminal business of the court seemed to have been concluded. She didn't. She studied a file on her desk.

Karen Kinder, though appearing to review the file in front of her, had not the slightest interest in its contents. She contemplated an upcoming matter for which she had no file—a motion by a defense attorney to be allowed to withdraw from a murder case to which he had been appointed and which was scheduled for trial during the month. The lawyer had a good excuse—he was dying of cancer. The office of the Prosecutor had no problems with the change of counsel, but the State did want the case tried on time. No delays or postponements, her boss had told her. Karen would likely lose the argument, but not because she was unprepared. As the drudgery of the judicial routine carried on around her, Karen—for the umpteenth time—framed her argument in her mind, hoping against experience that Judge Pinter would accept the logic of her position.

Unlike Chip Roth, who sat behind her and whom she had silently admired, Karen hadn't always wanted to be a lawyer. The notion hadn't even crossed her mind until Mrs. Steiner, a high school civics teacher, suggested that Karen would make a fine lawyer. Karen, with amusement, often recalled the woman's exact words. "You have a fine analytical mind and an uncommon grasp of democratic procedures," her teacher had said.

Poor naive Mrs. Steiner. Strongly principled individuals

seldom made it through law school. Law professors, while praising intelligent and analytical thought, practiced a form of learning which rewarded good memory and punished independent thought. Like the system for which they prepared their students, law instructors simply wanted prompt feedback of precedent. Karen had attended one of the more liberal law schools in the country, and even there she found the atmosphere stodgy and conservative.

Even after Mrs. Steiner's suggestion, Karen wasn't really interested in a career in the law. Women became teachers like Mrs. Steiner . . . or nurses and secretaries . . . housewives, sometimes hookers. Karen didn't know a single female lawyer. Sure, she'd seen some on television, especially during the Watergate hearings, but she decided that those women were very special, maybe even a little weird. A teenager then, she never understood why she felt that way toward them and had really never tried to understand why she felt as she had. She just *knew* that women who became such things as lawyers or doctors or accountants were different than her mother, different than all the women whom she had come to know as she had matured. They reminded her of Molly Mason who always made straight A's, never smiled, and never seemed to have any fun at all—just plain weird. Molly, Karen thought then, was the type of woman who became a lawyer.

The women's movement had grown up with Karen, but her eventual decision to go to law school had less to do with women's rights than with the birth of her own self-confidence. By her second year in college, Karen had opted to become a lawyer. Her process of choice had been careful and deliberate, almost cold-blooded. The law offered a specialized education with a multiplicity of alternatives after graduation. She could become a politician (which appealed to her in a strange fashion). Or, she could specialize in labor relations, an area recommended to her by an economics professor. Or she could become just a plain lawyer.

And Karen, by then possessor of what might properly have been called "a drive," vowed to become one of the best lawyers. At the same time, she someday wanted to be a wife . . . a mother. Such seemingly conflicting goals appalled her feminist friends who, one and all, were immersed in the movement and its dogma. Karen supported

16

the movement, but it seemed to have so little to do with her. She knew that she could handle all three roles and wanted to—someday.

So she had become a lawyer, had labored two years as a Legal Aid attorney, and was now (strange fate!!!) an assistant prosecuting attorney. She had no plans to marry, certainly no immediate plans to mother a child . . . but someday . . .

Karen often caught herself planning to be happy. It infuriated her when she did it, when anyone did it. Her mother had frittered away a life waiting for tomorrow, waiting to be happy. Her mother patiently awaited that glorious day "when her boat would come in." She always talked about some point in the future when, given the proper mix of finances and emotions, happiness would settle upon her like a state of grace.

. . . Someday . . .

"Miss Kinder!"

Karen lifted her eyes from the infinity she had found in the irrelevant file. "Uh, yes . . . yes, Your Honor."

"I asked if you would be handling the Sampson matter?"

Karen felt her face warm. "I apologize, Your Honor. I was lost in concentration."

"I know of worse places to be lost," Pinter said without much humor. He then nodded to George Stringfellow, a short and emaciated man who rose to his feet and moved toward the bench. "I understand you have a matter to bring before the Court."

Stringfellow turned and looked all the way back to the last row of pews. He motioned for Virgil Sampson to step forward. With the gait of the coolly unconcerned, Virgil swaggered to the front of the courtroom.

Chip recognized him as the fellow who had entered during the earlier ceremony. He impressed Chip in a most unnerving manner. Bulky yet tall, the man's bearing hinted of powerful and cruel menace. A dark, bristly stubble shaded the lower portion of his face, and his forehead swept far back to a receding hairline. The hair itself, long and shaggy in back and unkempt in general, glistened with oil. The nose, obviously broken—perhaps smashed— in the past, rested at a slant on the man's face. The man's eyes gleamed with an obsidian brutality. They were so

17

dark, so infinite in their savagery . . . almost black and without pupils, like a snake's.

And the odor which shadowed Virgil Sampson enveloped Chip as Sampson walked within a yard of the young lawyer. Chip fought to smother his revulsion.

Virgil Sampson stopped beside his lawyer.

"I have Mr. Sampson present for the motion," George Stringfellow announced to the Court.

Sampson—whatever his first name was, Chip at that time did not know—paid not the slightest attention to Judge Pinter. His lean and wolfish face—its texture dark and roughened by acne—was turned toward the female prosecutor. The evil eyes measured her body, and Chip, though a dozen feet away, saw the woman shudder.

# TWO

While Karen had been assigned the case of State of West Virginia v. Virgil Sampson at least three months earlier, she hadn't until that morning laid eyes upon Virgil Sampson . . . or felt his eyes upon her.

She chilled beneath their bitter pressure. Dan Hemmings, the State Police investigator, had cautioned her about Sampson, but his appearance—his air of truculence—surpassed Karen's anticipation. That leer (there was no other word to describe it) was both threatening and sexual; Karen felt raped by his eyes. He scared the hell out of her.

Stringfellow had already started to address the Court. ". . . as I previously advised the Court, medical problems necessitate my absence from the county for an extended period of time . . ."

For eternity, Karen thought. George Stringfellow astonished her. He was dying of cancer, and he knew it. Everyone knew it. Yet he spoke clearly, dispassionately, without the slightest hint of the emotion which had to underscore his words. She wondered how she would have accepted such a fate. Not nearly so well, she suspected.

"Mr. Sampson's case," Stringfellow said, "comes up for trial within the month, as Your Honor knows, on an indictment alleging first degree murder. My motion consists of two parts." Stringfellow paused to gather his breath. So far the pause was the only evidence of the monster which raged in his guts. "First, I ask the Court to relieve me as defense counsel and to appoint a successor. I cannot give Mr. Sampson's case the attention which it merits, and I don't anticipate being in the county on the date for which trial is now set."

Sampson's eyes held to Karen, scanning her from head to toe, stopping to fondle her breasts, her—

She tried to ignore him, but she couldn't, not completely. She caught herself throwing her eyes toward him, jerking them back to the Judge as his eyes locked onto hers. She shifted nervously, wishing Pinter would see, would do something, anything to get those damned eyes off her.

"Additionally," Stringfellow continued, "in light of the fact that I make this request so near to trial, I would also move the Court to continue the case until the next term so that a new defense counsel may have proper time to prepare a defense."

Stringfellow was then silent, and Pinter nodded, then turned to Karen. "Does the State wish to speak?"

Grabbing the opportunity to escape the defendant's unsettling attention, Karen moved quickly toward the bench. Even there, with Sampson behind her, she could still feel his eyes on her back. It was almost worse.

"If the Court please," she said, trying to keep her voice from cracking, "we, of course, have no objection to the appointment of new counsel for the defendant. However, as to the second part of the motion, the State considers Mr. Stringfellow a highly competent attorney. Few attorneys could improve upon his preparation for this case. We would insist that this matter be tried during this term of court. We stand ready for trial."

With that, Karen turned to look at Virgil Sampson, her own eyes now glaring with defiance.

There, she thought. Suck on that awhile, you revolting bastard.

The defendant seemed unmoved, concealing whatever emotions he felt beneath his blatant ogling. Karen continued her argument, after which Pinter leaned back in his chair. "The Court grants counsel permission to withdraw. I'll reserve my ruling on the request for a continuance to the next term." He scanned the attorneys sitting on the pew, and his gaze came to stop upon Chip Roth.

Chip saw the Judge smile; he knew he was in trouble.

"I told you we would put you to work, Mr. Roth," Pinter said, confirming Chip's suspicion. Pinter's words produced a common sigh of relief from the other lawyers. "I'm appointing you to represent Mr. Sampson. Since you're a

20

little fresh at this, I'll appoint Mario Panzini as co-counsel. You know Mr. Panzini?"

Chip had approached the bench and stood within smelling distance of his new client. "I've heard of him, Your Honor."

"Well, you and Mr. Panzini discuss the matter with Sampson here. Assess your situation. Like Ms. Kinder said, I expect Mr. Stringfellow had most of the case preparation done. Unless you and Panzini can establish mighty good cause, we go to trial on schedule."

"I understand," Chip said. He caught the assistant prosecutor staring at him, the hint of a smile on her lightly tanned face.

"The clerk will advise Mr. Panzini of his appointment," Pinter said perfunctorily.

Karen Kinder whirled and clicked out of the courtroom. Chip followed Stringfellow's lead and headed for the suite of conference rooms located behind the courtroom. Sampson followed. Stringfellow formally introduced himself, offering Chip a hand which seemed to quiver. "You got a good one to start off with," he said.

Sampson, accompanied by his stark aroma, paced the room. He was obviously unhappy. "This here's a virgin," he complained. "I deserve better'n him." Sampson's dark eyes cast bolts of resentment toward Chip.

Chip said nothing. Stringfellow, however, slipped down into one of the punishing wooden chairs. "Beggars can't be choosers," he said. "You don't like who the Judge appointed, then go hire your own lawyer. 'Sides, Roth here's been hired by one of the best law firms in the state. He must have something going for him. If he's good enough for Arthur King, he's damn sure good enough for you. Not to mention Mario Panzini. He's practiced law for 20 years."

"Thanks," Chip said, trying to return his new client's hateful stare.

"You better do right by me," Sampson growled.

George Stringfellow sighed loudly. "Tell you what, Sampson. Beat it. Roth and I will talk. He'll meet with you and Panzini later."

"I got a right to listen—"

"Scram!" Stringfellow said sharply. "I ain't your lawyer

21

anymore, and I'll be damned if I have to smell you any longer."

Sampson came toward the lawyer, and Chip, stunned and frightened, prepared to intervene. Stringfellow just laughed, which halted Sampson's advance. "You'd probably be doing me a favor," Stringfellow said.

Sampson's lips curled. "You fuckin' lawyers make me sick."

Stringfellow laughed even harder, so hard it must have stirred the demon in his belly because his face whitened and twisted into a vision of pain. Chip moved quickly to the man's side and said to Sampson, "Go on. I'll be in touch."

Sampson mumbled something under his breath on his way out.

"You okay?" Chip asked, laying a hand on the older lawyer's trembling shoulder.

"Yeah," he gasped, holding a hand to his stomach. "That guy's real scum."

Stringfellow's pain receded, and some of the color returned to his face. "Pinter zapped you on this one, kid. Sampson's a son of a bitch who deserves hanging."

"Is it customary? Giving a new lawyer a murder case right off the bat?"

The veteran grinned. "Not usually, but murder cases are usually easy. They just get all the attention. You got this one because Pinter can't stand the King. The sentiments are mutual—no matter how friendly that exchange in court seemed. Those two old foes just love to hate each other. Don't worry, though. Panzini's no slouch. You'll do most of the work, but he'll lead you through it. It'll be good for you—get your name in the paper."

Chip laughed. "I'm used to that. I used to be a reporter."

"Now you're on the other end of the spotlight."

Stringfellow seemed almost totally over his discomfort. He pulled several thick manila files from his briefcase and slid them across to Chip. "Here are the files. Statements of witnesses, the police report, the autopsy, and the motions I've already filed. It's ready for trial, and I'll tell you right now you're gonna lose this one."

"Why did you ask for the continuance?"

Stringfellow shrugged. "I just thought I'd buy the sucker who got the case a little more time. Call it professional courtesy."

"It's that bad?"

"Sampson's guilty as hell—first degree murder with no room for argument. He and this other fellow got in a fight in a local beer joint. The guy got the best of Sampson. Sampson waited outside for him. Stuck a knife in his gut just as the guy exited the place. Sampson says the guy attacked him—"

Stringfellow stopped to take a deep breath, then went on, ". . . but none of the witnesses support him. The best service you can perform for Sampson is to stall the case. If you want to do humanity and Custer County a favor, get him to trial in a hurry before he kills someone else. He's another killin' just waiting to happen."

"I'm surprised he made bail."

Stringfellow chuckled. "In Custer County, almost everyone makes bail. Pinter set Sampson's bond at $25,000. Anyplace else it would have at least been double that."

"How did he raise that much?"

"Some brother of his came up with the money or the property. I can't remember which. I wasn't appointed until three or four days after he'd made bail."

Chip eyed the files. "What's the defense?"

"Sampson's argument that the guy came at him with the knife. Sampson says they scuffled and the guy got cut with his own knife."

Chip shook his head.

"You haven't a prayer," Stringfellow told Chip, "not unless Pinter shows up for trial half crocked—which isn't unusual—and commits a string of reversible errors. And one last thing—"

Again Stringfellow paused to refresh his failing body with several deep intakes of air. ". . . Sampson's got a record as long as his pecker, which is said to be mammoth. He just got off probation for maiming. Be careful with him."

"You didn't seem too gentle with him," Chip said.

Stringfellow slowly got to his feet. "What have I got to lose? He'd be doing my family and me a big favor."

Chip didn't know how to respond to that. He was too young to know how to handle death. So he remained silent.

The veteran lawyer sensed the young man's unease. "Sorry, I didn't mean to flaunt my misery like that."

Chip nodded. "What about that female prosecutor?"

"What about her?"

"She any good?"

A wry smile crossed Stringfellow's face. "At what?"

Chip laughed, and Stringfellow said, "Just kidding. She's a fair lawyer for a woman. Never saw a woman lawyer that was very good. Pinter's a little soft on her . . . maybe I should say 'hard for her.' And be sure you strike all the young studs off a jury when you're going up against her. Besides, you'll be going against the Prosecutor himself when this case gets to trial. Nelson wants Sampson bad, and he'll get him this time."

They started out of the room, but Stringfellow stopped. "And in answer to that unasked question, she isn't married. If she's got any serious romantic interests, I don't know anything about them. 'Course I'm beyond caring."

"I bet you're a hell of a lawyer," Chip said.

"Yeah. I am. It's a damned shame I get cancer, and some scumbag like Sampson is as healthy as a friggin' bull. There just ain't no justice. You married, Chip?"

"I'm too young to get married."

Stringfellow nodded knowingly. "Sure, and too damned horny to stay single."

Gracie Mack's daughter didn't get to Sunday dinner. Once, about 45 minutes past noon on Sunday, she had tried to call her mother. She got no answer. Connie Brown assumed her mother was mad at her and just wasn't answering the phone, or was mad and had gone over to spend the afternoon with a neighbor. Either way, Connie knew her mother was mad. So Connie hadn't called back—no sense catching hell. Besides, she was ashamed. Her old man had gotten so damned drunk Saturday night that he'd pissed all over himself. He awoke with a hangover that made him even meaner than usual. He'd decided he felt so bad that he needed another drink. By noon, Eugene was smashed again. Since he wouldn't allow Connie to drive their car, she was stuck and had no way to get her and the kids to her mother's.

So much for Sunday dinner.

On Monday morning, Eugene somehow had managed to get to work. At 10. a.m., Connie dialed her mother's number, prepared to accept the verbal assault which would ensue. Again she received no answer. Connie found that a little strange so early in the morning, worrisome in fact, so she called her mother's neighbor who quickly volunteered to go next door to check on Gracie.

The neighbor found the front door locked. She knocked until her knuckles ached, which hadn't taken long since her hands were afflicted with arthritis. Then Gracie's neighbor, now also very much worried, hobbled around to the back of the house. The back door, too, was locked—from the inside. The kitchen window, though, was wide open.

"Gracie!" the woman called.

A gentle morning breeze brought to her a nauseating response, a gut-turning stench which seemed to come from the open window—so terrible that the neighbor didn't dare investigate anymore. The woman had a horrifying suspicion about the cause of the odor. She hurried back to her house and called the cops.

Just as a baby-faced deputy was dumping the contents of his stomach onto Gracie Mack's kitchen floor, Chip Roth was entering the law offices of King, King, Kiestler and Clausen. The offices, situated on the penthouse floor of the Custer County National Bank, were three blocks from the Court House, two miles or so from the Locust Drive section of Wharton, the "other side of the tracks" part of town in which Gracie Mack had lived.

The firm's receptionist, a matronly woman with the demeanor of a Marine DI, informed Chip that Simon King wished to "confer" with him at once. Chip, his mood chilled by the woman's curt tone, ambled slowly down the long, ornate hall. His feet almost bounced on the thick, wine-colored carpeting. Understated classic murals decorated the beige walls. Somehow, the uptown style of the firm's offices just didn't jibe with the dismal mantle which had draped Chip since his encounter with smelly Virgil Sampson.

Carrying the thick manila files under his arm, Chip knocked on Simon King's door. A deep, coarse voice bid him enter. The earthiness of the voice belied Simon King's appearance. Unlike his elder brother, Simon was a mousy man, slight of build and frail of frame. Wrinkles etched his artificially tanned face, and he sported a much too dark, shaggy wig. The toupee, obviously an expensive one, would have looked fine on someone half Simon King's age, but the absence of even the slightest hint of gray and the mod but dated hairstyle, when taken against the aging face, pinpointed Simon King as a man who aged without grace.

"How did it go this morning, Chip?"

Chip took a seat before the huge, neat desk. "Not well. I got appointed to a murder case."

King's smile faded away, replaced by a profusion of tight wrinkles. "You what?"

"Judge Pinter appointed me to represent a fellow by the name of Virgil Sampson. George Stringfellow had the case, but the Judge permitted him to withdraw. Mario Panzini was appointed as co-counsel."

The lesser King slapped his open palm on the desk. The gesture, lacking any force, came off as effeminate. "Damn Pinter!" King snapped.

"Should I have tried to avoid it?"

Simon shook his head. "You had no choice. If you don't know it already, I'm going to let you in on what we call some behind-the-scenes color. Pinter despises this firm. Despite our considerable influence and prestige, we've never managed to have much effect politically. Arthur and I are Republicans. In Custer County, that translates into political impotence. To make matters worse, Arthur has always insisted on campaigning with a vengeance against Roger Pinter, much beyond the traditional duties of the loyal opposition—even to the point of financially endowing certain dissenting elements among Pinter's own party who have mounted campaigns against him. Don't believe that old slogan about 'all being fair in love, war and politics.' Pinter would have welcomed our Republicanism with hearty goodwill. However, no politician takes kindly to the other side intervening in a primary."

"That seems sorta removed from my appointment today," Chip said.

Simon King rolled his eyes. "Christ! I wish they would include a course in practical politics in law studies. Pinter knows it screws us in several ways. First of all, it's time-consuming, for which you and Panzini will earn the whopping fee of 25 bucks an hour at max, but no more than $2,000. And Panzini will get most of it. Our anticipated fees from your work are more than that. You'll do the legwork, and our secretaries will do the paperwork. He'll prance into court and try the case and get the media attention. Then comes the appeal. That will be even more time-consuming for the secretaries. And if there is some screw-up, you'll get the blame."

Chip patted the thick files which filled his lap. "But Stringfellow has done most of the work."

Simon, his anger talked out, leaned back in his chair. "George is a good lawyer. That's one of the pluses to this new case of yours."

"I really liked him. What form of cancer does he have?"

"The killing kind."

Chip started to rise, feeling that the conference had ended.

"One more thing," Simon said. "I do have an assignment for you."

"Great," Chip said.

"Arthur's car is in the shop. They just called to say it's ready. Run down and get it, and gas it up. Bring it back here. The receptionist can tell you where the shop's at. It's in walking distance."

# THREE

Clarke Nelson, Custer County's prosecuting attorney, looked at that moment more like a South Seas tourist than the chief law enforcement officer of Custer County. Karen, summoned to his office, found him relaxing in his reclining desk chair, his feet propped up on his desk. He wore a bright yellow shirt open down to his chest, bright red and green pants, and canvas slip-ons. He puffed impatiently on a battered pipe. The radio forecast late afternoon thunderstorms, and he had promised himself at least 18 holes before they arrived.

"You look like an ad for 'Fruit of the Loom,'" Karen quipped.

Nelson smiled. "You're just jealous."

"What's up?" Karen asked, still greatly depressed from her brief encounter with Virgil Sampson. Since leaving the courtroom, she'd spent most of the time wondering if she had the stuff to be a prosecutor.

"We have a reported homicide," Nelson said, shifting to a sitting position in his chair. "I want you to handle it." Nelson was just beyond 50, but he looked younger by a good 10 years, an accomplishment he attributed to the exercise he got on the golf course. He'd been prosecutor for 15 years, and he had no greater ambition than to retire in the job. Fees he earned from civil cases—principally personal injury cases—augmented his less than adequate salary as a public servant. He brought such a forceful presence to the courtroom that other attorneys associated him with big personal injury cases just to have the advantage of his courtroom flair, none of which was apparent outside of the courtroom. It was as if he flipped some internal "on" switch when he found himself before a jury.

"The Sheriff just called," he went on to explain. "They have a body over in the Locust Drive area, an elderly woman. She's rather messy, I understand. I'm assigning you to the case."

Karen hadn't handled a homicide case from its inception. "What do I do?"

Nelson dropped his feet to the floor. "Go to the scene. Supervise the investigation. I hope you have some idea what you'll need when a homicide case gets to court. I've already called Dan Hemmings, and he'll be there shortly. When he arrives, follow him around as if you were an unweaned puppy. Learn from him. He's just about the best. He knows there's more to a court case than an arrest."

Nelson read Karen's distaste for the assignment in her face. "It's what you get paid for," he said.

"You and I both," countered Karen. "I'd think you'd come along on my first one." She enjoyed digging Nelson about the way he hoisted work off on his assistants. The amount of time he spent on a golf course was public knowledge, but the voters consistently returned him to office. This time, though, she was only half-kidding.

Nelson, sensing there was more to her comment than her usual ribbing, didn't even smile. "I've paid my dues. I've seen more than my share of blood and guts. You kids need a little exposure. If you ever get the killer to trial, you'll prepare and argue your case with a little more gusto. I don't hold my assistants' hands—particularly not yours, since my wife thinks I hired you because of your legs anyway."

By then a smile had appeared on his face. Karen's, too. "Okay, but I'm not ashamed of the fact that I have a weak stomach."

"It'll toughen up. One of these days I'd like to see one of you fill my shoes."

"The ones with those little metal spikes on the soles?" Karen quipped.

"Hit the road. A deputy's waiting to drive you over."

"And Hemmings will be there?" Karen asked.

"Shortly."

Dan Hemmings, a plainclothes investigator for the state police, was Nelson's fair-haired boy—the only cop Nelson trusted to handle murder investigations.

Karen turned to leave.

"Don't puke all over that pretty white dress," Nelson called after her.

Karen's first two years as an attorney had been frustrating, almost disenchanting. She'd spent fruitless months trying to organize a shelter for battered wives. Everybody had said it was needed, but no one, including the county governing body, considered it important enough to fund. Her court time had been consumed by divorce work and the defense of people who, for a variety of reasons (most of them indefensible), never paid their bills. Many of them were just "deadbeats," as the people in southern West Virginia so liked to say, but a good many faced mammoth medical bills. Karen cared not a whit for the deadbeats, but she agonized for those families forced to the brink of bankruptcy and beyond because of the evil costs of medical care. Unfortunately, the courts don't concern themselves with a person's ability to pay—only with their legal obligation to pay. In debt collection cases, unlike criminal cases, justice was seldom tempered by mercy.

Karen managed to retain her liberal philosophy, but her work with Legal Aid had moderated that philosophy by forcing her to face the fact that in most instances the people and the system were equally corrupt, each feeding off the other's blind greed.

When federal support for Legal Aid dwindled under the oppressive heel of the Reagan conservatism, Karen planned to return to DC, perhaps to go to work for a congressman . . . a senator if she was really lucky.

But Clarke Nelson had called her. He asked if she'd like to try a "different side of the law." The salary was a little better than she had earned at Legal Aid, and, unlike Legal Aid, she could accept civil cases on the side. Twice, in fact, Nelson had asked her to assist him with personal injury cases in other counties.

Chauffeured by a talkative but boring young deputy, Karen arrived at Gracie Mack's home just before noon. Police cruisers clogged the narrow, pothole-marked street. An ambulance was backed up to the front steps. Curiosity seekers crowded around a rope which cordoned off the crime scene.

Karen started up the front steps. Another deputy, this

one very young also and very baby-faced, stopped her at the top. "I don't think you wanna go in there," he said.

Already a faint hint of the horror drifted to her nose. "You're right. I don't," she said, "but it's my job."

"Don't say I didn't warn you, ma'am."

The odor, as if stirred by her defiance, rushed out of the house at her. Karen had never smelled anything so darkly revolting, and she swallowed hard, fighting her gag reflex. How many times had she read about such things? About bodies found . . . about the rank odor of decomposing human flesh. Karen as a teenager had consumed mysteries and police novels, and she remembered reading that the odor was unique, that it defied description and imagination. Once experienced, it would never be forgotten. She'd expected it to smell like a dead animal, more particularly like a dead rat. Dead rats, she decided, smelled better.

The deputy, having made his gallant gesture for the month, shrugged, shook his head and stepped aside for Karen. And she looked at him with mild surprise. Were they going to let her go in alone? She looked back for the deputy who had delivered her to the scene. He stood with the ambulance crew, laughing and joking.

The hell with them, she thought.

Karen braced herself and entered the house. The thickness of the stench dimmed the sunlight spilling into the room. It was as if she stepped into a stifling bank of corrupt mist. Karen covered her mouth and nose—a vain gesture—and then scanned the living room in which she stood. She noticed small particles of debris . . . of—

Oh, God! Of what?

Not blood. Surely not flesh!

But it was—flesh and bone and blood. Its pattern spread from a short hallway at the end of which a lump—"the lump"—lay under a sheet. Stains of something unwholesome seeped through the sheet.

"We were waiting on you," a voice said.

And Karen yelped and jumped.

"I'm sorry," said another deputy, this one a little older, a little more experienced-looking than the others she had seen. He must have come from one of the bedrooms.

Or he could have been there when she stepped into the room. If so, she hadn't noticed him, but then she wouldn't have. "Jesus! You frightened me!"

31

"Sorry," he repeated, not really seeming bothered by it.

She slowly moved toward the hallway, toward the kitchen, toward the lump under the sheet. "Christ! How long has she been dead?"

"Sometime after Saturday night," the deputy said, walking behind her. "A neighbor saw her on Saturday evening."

"But the smell—"

The cop shrugged. "It's been hot."

"Oh!" The dead woman lay at Karen's feet. Swallowing, Karen said, "Lift the sheet."

The deputy's look—one of sincere concern, perhaps as much for himself as her—made her want to tell him to forget it, to leave the body covered. "Are you sure?" he said. "There's really no reason for you—"

"Lift it." Already Karen wanted to vomit. She knew she was going to vomit. Others already had—men more accustomed to such horrors than she. The odor of their vomit mingled cloyingly with the aroma of death—a well-matched pair.

The deputy offered her a pearly white handkerchief. "It helps a little."

Karen accepted it. Then, with it covering her nose and mouth, she looked around for the bathroom. She was a woman, and, because of that, she didn't want to throw up in front of the officer. She found what appeared to be the bathroom door just as the deputy flipped back the sheet.

Karen looked down at poor Gracie Mack and never even thought about the bathroom thereafter.

How bleak the still sunny day had turned!

In the law office, surrounded by bound volumes of legal genius, in the courtroom amid the formalized pomp of procedure and officious decorum, death assumed a mannered, almost dignified sterility. The base horror of its violent manifestations was subrogated to great thoughts and precedented philosophy. Judges and lawyers, policemen, even witnesses, yielding to the momentum of the occasion, discussed death with a proper detachment which colored it with an unwarranted dignity. The thing that she had looked upon in that kitchen possessed not a shred of dignity.

Karen had to remind herself that the hunk of stinking,

maggot-ridden meat had once been a person—a living and breathing woman, a mother, a grandmother.

Now dead—probably through no fault of her own.

Karen had to remind herself of that also—that Gracie Mack couldn't help how she looked now, couldn't help the fact that she had become so . . . so revolting. Someone had done that to her. Someone—another human being—had killed her. If only he could see her now.

She stood in the backyard, sucking in warm and humid air, trying to find her composure, her own dignity. The remnants of the acid vomit burned the back of her throat and the interior of her nose. Sweat stained her dress. Any glamour that her profession seemed to have retained was no more. She'd left the last of it back in the house, spewed on the floor near the dead woman, mixed with the blood and flesh of Gracie Mack.

"You okay?" a voice asked.

This time the voice did not startle her. Maybe it was because she recognized the drawl of the Virginia Tidewater? Or maybe it was because she was numb . . . just a little beyond being startled by someone coming up behind her? She turned to greet Cpl. Dan Hemmings. He was an imposing figure of a man, dressed this day in faded jeans and a pale yellow knit shirt. He seemed to tower over her, and his face reminded her of a teddy bear. Others would have likened it more to the angry visage of a grizzly, depending upon the business he had with them.

"I will be," Karen answered.

"Don't feel too bad," he said, the softness in his voice surprising even Karen. "A lot of those guys in there did the same as you—or came so close to it that they can still taste it."

Karen sniffed back an accumulation of mucus which filled her irritated nose. "I've never seen anything like that."

"I've seen a lot. She's one of the worst. She's right at the height of her post-mortem bloat."

"Oh, God!" Karen said, wondering if she had anything else in her stomach to throw up.

"Sorry," Hemmings said.

"Can you tell what killed her?"

Hemmings arched his wide shoulders. "A cannon? Naw, just kidding. I'd say it was at least a .357 magnum—maybe even a .44 magnum, but you don't see many of them around, especially not in the hands of the lowlife. Whatever it was, her head just exploded. That was the skin of her face sagging beneath her chin."

Karen felt as if she'd turned green.

"Sometimes," Hemmings said, "it helps to talk about it."

"Just save me the clinical details. I'll wait for the autopsy results."

Hemmings kicked at a dried chunk of dog feces which lay in the grass at the toe of his booted foot. "It looks like robbery, pure and simple. 'Course, looks can be deceiving. They're moving the body now. I gave them the go-ahead. Hope that was okay?"

Karen nodded that it was.

"If you feel like it," he continued, "we'll go back inside and look the place over."

The prospect of entering that house again, even with the body gone, prompted Karen to retch again. She did have more in her stomach. Dark visions infested her psyche, images she never thought herself capable of producing. She associated the interior of the house with Hell itself, with belly-wrenching evil. No nightmare she had ever suffered equaled the effect created by Gracie Mack and her house.

"It was just so . . . so inhuman," Karen said when she regained her breath.

Hemmings self-consciously patted her shoulder. He couldn't show emotion easily, and for him that alone was a grand gesture. "You don't have to go to the movies to find monsters. We got plenty of 'em passin' themselves off as people."

Karen spent a few more moments just breathing. Then she ambled to the alley which ran along the back of the property. She looked down and noticed a spider, the kind she had always called a "granddaddy long legs." It scurried across one of the tire tracks in the alley. "A person just can't prepare herself for something like that," she said as she watched the spider vanish into a clump of weedy grass.

"Someday, when your stomach's back on even keel, I'll tell you about my first time. It was a woman, too, but she'd been dead about a week—in the woods. The animals—"

"Stop!" Karen cried. "Why do you cops do that? Why do you insist on rehashing gory war stories?"

Hemmings studied her. "Most people who aren't cops get some kind of thrill out of hearing them. And I think it's a way for us to deal with our own—" He stopped, trying to think of the right word.

"Oh, forget it," Karen said.

"You're stallin', Karen. You might as well go on back in that house and get it over with. It ain't gonna get any easier."

She drew in even more air. She found the deputy's handkerchief still clutched in her hands. She used it to wipe the drops of perspiration from her face. "Let's go."

Even with the body absent, the odor continued to pervade the house, just as heavy and revolting as when Karen had first stepped inside. It would take days to dissipate, Hemmings told her, adding ominously, ". . . if it ever does." He started to tell her of one house which had to be torn down. Three bodies had lain inside for three days, he said. Then he stopped, seeing the cold stare she gave him.

Karen lingered over the pile of glass and photos which cluttered the floor at the base of the metal shelf. A framed portrait on top, a picture of a woman of about 30, had survived the fall. The glass, though, was flecked with the fleshy shrapnel which suffused the room.

She snatched her hand from it. "Who cleans up this mess?"

"Once we're through and release the house, the family can—"

She gasped. "Jesus! You don't mean this woman's family must clean up?"

Hemmings shrugged. "It's not really our job, Karen."

"By God, it is this time. I'm making it our job." Her face flushed with disbelieving indignation. She looked to a deputy who stood in the arch of the front door. "I want this place cleaned up for the family."

The deputy's eyes rolled northward. "Like the trooper there said, ma'am, it ain't our—"

"Damn it, man!" Karen screamed. "Did you hear me?"

The deputy, the older man who had startled Karen earlier, clenched his jaw. He wasn't accustomed to being yelled at, especially by a woman, even if she was supposed to be an assistant prosecutor. "I'll discuss it with the Sheriff."

"You just do that," Karen snapped, "but you, the Sheriff, or whoever, had better see that the worst of this is gone as soon as possible."

"Like I said, I'll mention it to the Sheriff."

Hemmings, trying to ease the burgeoning tension, said, "That's the woman's touch."

And Karen wheeled on Hemmings. It had been the wrong thing to say. "Damn you! It's the human touch! Don't pull that 'woman' shit on me. You'll treat me as an assistant prosecutor—"

"Whoa!" Hemmings declared. "Ease up. I didn't mean to imply—"

"You did!" Then Karen seemed to catch herself. "I'm sorry, Dan."

Hemmings nodded his acceptance of the apology. "We're all a little on edge."

A few minutes later, as they were finally leaving the house, Karen asked, "Didn't the neighbors hear anything?"

"I've talked to a couple of them," Hemmings said. "They all said they heard what sounded like gunshots. In this part of town, that's not all that unusual for a Saturday night. And people around here don't jump to call the law. I'm gonna spend the afternoon talking with some others."

"I'll tag along."

"No way! No offense intended, but people—especially these people—are more likely to give me answers if I'm alone. That way they can backtrack later on what they said—no witnesses to confirm my side of the story."

"That's silly."

"I know it is, Counselor, but right now we need some leads, not iron-clad court testimony. Grab some lunch or something."

Karen said, "You've got to be kidding."

# FOUR

Mario Panzini's one-man law office wasn't anything near as "uptown" as the King firm's suites, at least not judging by the reception area. A pretty, busty secretary greeted Chip with a smile which Chip interpreted as "inviting." He introduced himself and was trying to examine her finger for a wedding band when Panzini entered from a door just behind her desk.

Panzini had phoned Chip earlier and asked him to come by after lunch. "Mr. Roth, I assume," Panzini said, offering Chip his hand. "And this is Vickie."

Chip shook her hand, too, noting in the process that she wore no rings. Her smile broadened.

As for Panzini, the attorney looked as Italian as his name sounded—olive-skinned, short and compact, dark hair flecked with gray. He spoke, however, with an informal and ingratiating country drawl so blatant that it seemed an affectation. George Stringfellow had the same dialect, but Stringfellow's seemed so much more natural. Panzini ushered Chip back through the reception area and down a hallway.

"I'd have taken you through my private door," he explained, "but you gotta enter my office from the right angle to get the proper perspective."

With an exaggerated flourish, he flung open the door to his office. "You like?"

Panzini's inner sanctum resembled the interior of a New Orleans whorehouse. The furniture was off-white—French Provincial, Chip thought. A royal blue carpet covered the floor, while gaudy gold curtains, held back with royal blue ties, framed the floor-to-ceiling windows. The windows themselves were shrouded by sheers which softened the outside light entering the room.

"It's . . . uh . . . interesting."

"If you like it," Panzini pronounced, "you got no class."

Chip frowned.

"It impresses the clients, at least my clients," Panzini explained. "My folks won't win any awards for class, but they all pay, a lot of them in advance. And you know why?"

Chip tried not to say it, but he couldn't stop himself. "The office decor?"

Panzini laughed, from his belly to his forehead. "That's a part of it," he said when he had stopped laughing. "You gotta be garish, flashy. That's the secret, kid. Mark it down in your little black book. See, people don't care if you win or lose. They just want you to make a big fuckin' noise on their behalf. Shout at witnesses, berate and belittle the lawyers on the other side, fight with the judge almost—notice I say 'almost'—to the point that he busts you for contempt."

Chip grinned at the advice, and Panzini directed him to a chair. The lawyer hustled around behind his cluttered desk and pulled a cigarette from a gold case which rested on top of it. He offered one to Chip, who declined. Panzini then continued to develop his formula for success. "The judges and lawyers understand. You make 'em understand. You can get away with murder as long as they understand. Don't take yourself or your work too seriously. In the end, nothing matters but the bottom line of your bank account."

Mario Panzini seemed a dynamo of verbal energy. Chip listened. He had no choice. Panzini's speech was like a bulldozer. "My old man, now he was a lawyer too . . . learned by the seat of his pants. He always said . . . you get a hundred bucks worth of advice for ten dollars from a fresh lawyer, and you get ten bucks of advice for a hundred from an old lawyer. Mark it down. It's another trick of the trade. The longer you practice, the more you charge. 'Course the King's a master of that, and he'll teach you that in no time."

Chip didn't agree with Mario Panzini. He had a little higher vision of the profession. He kept his peace, though, out of respect.

"Now take these appointed murder cases," he continued, pausing for a quick, deep breath. "I just love 'em. Pinter's a friend of mine, and he tosses more than my share my way. It's good and free publicity, with the emphasis on 'free.' I talked with old George today—shame about him. Anyway, this case'll be a snap. He's done all the work. All we gotta to do is march into court and try it . . . spend a few days playing the game."

"Then you don't think we need to ask for a continuance?"

"Hell, yes . . . we ask for a continuance! We cover our asses. That's rule number one. Write it down. This bastard Sampson's goin' down just as sure as hell. And he's gonna lose his appeal unless Rog fucks up too bad on rulings. Just like old lawyers, Sampson will lose his appeal."

Panzini snickered at the old joke, then rambled onward. "After that, the bastard will turn on us—sue you and me for ineffective assistance of counsel. Just mark my words. That's why we ask for the continuance until the next term—because it's expected of us. Pinter, of course, should deny the motion, but I've practiced in front of Rog for years. If we sound sincere enough, we'll get it. Rog hates gettin' reversed. Either way, the scab's not on our ass."

Chip, deep down, knew better than to ask, but he did it anyway—marched right in ahead of the angels. He didn't care a whole lot for this lawyer with whom he was suddenly associated and didn't mind the role of devil's advocate. "If it's all so preordained, why bother? Why ask for a postponement? Let's try the thing and get it off our backs."

The other lawyer, almost viciously, stubbed out his cigarette. "I know you got taught some mighty fine and fancy ideals in that school, but you're gonna find out that most of it was a crock of bullshit. The last thing a defendant wants is a speedy trial. The longer you delay, the better chance your client's got—especially if he's guilty. Now you got them files?"

Chip irreverently handed the files to Panzini.

The lawyer measured their weight in his hands. "Christ! Ol' George put in some time on this s.o.b. The first thing we wanna do is to petition the Judge for some extra expense money. Most of the time Rog's pretty stingy with the State's money, but this might be a different story. Given the weight of these files, I'll wager Stringfellow used up most or all the expense money. We'll argue there's another line of defense to be pursued, and we need some extra funds. We might not get it, but it might get us the continuance. You know . . . kind of a trade-off."

39

Panzini could read the doubt in Chip's eyes. "I know what you're thinking. I came out of school thinkin' just like you're thinkin'. I almost starved before I wised up. Now I sure as shit am not gonna sit here and try to justify myself to some virgin just out of law school. I don't mean to sound too goddamn blunt, but you don't matter a hell of a lot. We're gonna do the best we can for this Sampson creep. That means filin' every motion that's expected of us, arguing like hell for those motions, and creating a record which will show that we did our legal best."

Panzini took a pause to light another cigarette, then went right on talking. "Now, the best thing to come along in criminal law in the last century is the memory typewriter. My secretary out there types on a few buttons and presto! Out pops all the standard, ass-protectin' motions, and Sampson's got the best defense possible. When we get to trial, we do our part, and it's over. It's that simple."

"Can I ask a question, Mr. Panzini?"

"Call me Mario. And sure, ask away."

"Do you ever get a case that really matters to you? One that touches you."

"Sure. I go the extra mile in a personal injury case where I might get a third or better of any settlement. That touches me deeply. I'm still waiting for some guy to walk in here with his dick cut off in some mining accident—an accident that I can blame on one of those filthy rich coal companies. Sometimes I lose sleep worrying that the fellow, dick in hand, might call here and get a busy signal, then call your firm, or someone else."

Chip shook his head, even smiled a little, at Panzini's crude honesty.

Karen escaped the courthouse a little before five that afternoon. The last place she wanted to go was to her home. Once there, she would sit and dwell upon visions of Gracie Mack. Except for those times that she was on the phone during the afternoon, Karen had wiled away the time creating scenarios of just how Gracie Mack had died. Had she had time to think during those final moments of her life? If so, what had she thought about it? Had the bastard tortured her with the prospect of death? Or had he at least been merciful and quick?

Karen's own vanity—which she readily confessed to her-

40

self if no one else—played a major role in the discomfort she felt. The idea of dying like that was bad enough, but if she were to be found that way . . . so ugly.

It made Karen chill.

She prayed that she died peacefully, cleanly, dressed well (even if it was a nightgown), with her house in order and with nothing to leave a bitter memory in those who cared for her. And she hoped death waited until she was at least a hundred.

Karen paid no attention to the young man she passed in the courthouse hallway. He was exiting the Clerk's office. She sensed someone was walking behind her, but her mind was as far away as infinity. Outside, in the heavy, humid air of the late afternoon, Karen finally turned to see who was behind her. He was nice-looking, smiling, and familiar—very familiar. And he said to her, "Afternoon, Miss Kinder."

Perplexed—because he acted like he knew her, Karen stopped to study his face. She remembered. "Oh, you're Mr. Roth! You got appointed to the Sampson case this morning."

"I'm afraid so. I don't mean to be forward, but shouldn't we have at least passed each other in law school?"

"I'm an endangered species," Karen said. "I didn't graduate from West Virginia. I went to Antioch in DC."

Chip lifted his eyebrows. "I'm familiar with Antioch. I'm surprised to find one of its graduates down here. I'm even more surprised that you're on the prosecutor's side of the aisle."

Karen giggled. "So are they. I started off with Legal Aid. Thanks to the Republicans, I had to look for something else."

Chip Roth swallowed his fear. "How about a drink?"

Karen measured the man's face. He seemed about her age, and she wondered why he was just graduating from law school. Perhaps he'd been in the service. She was notorious for forming rapid first impressions, in this instance a favorable one. "You wouldn't be trying to brown nose a prosecutor?"

"Heaven forbid!" he answered.

He had an angular face with a strong nose and dark blue eyes. His dark hair was already lightly streaked with hints of becoming gray. The shadow of a heavy beard heightened his masculinity. He was a good-looking man who would become even more handsome as he aged.

And she decided. "I could use a drink today."

"Me, too." Then Chip Roth seemed indecisive.

"Did you have something to do first?" Karen asked.

"Oh, no! I was on my way home. I used to live in Wharton, grew up here, but I've been gone for awhile. To be honest, I haven't the foggiest notion of where to go for a drink."

"How about the Black Stallion? It's a small bar and restaurant—"

"I know it," Chip said. "I'd forgotten about it. Want to use my car. It's—"

Karen waved off that offer. "I'll take mine. I'll meet you there. I need to make a quick stop at the post office."

She recognized her streak of independence. It sometimes put off potential suitors, but she needed to maintain an equal footing, especially with a fellow lawyer whom she would face in court very, very soon.

The clerk in the Big A supermarket eyed the government check with immediate suspicion. It had been issued to a Gracie Mack who, according to the young boy displaying it in grimy hands, had endorsed the check on the back and sent him to cash it. She took the blue-green voucher and examined it. The endorsement appeared a little . . . well, kidlike, she thought. And the boy acted nervous, shifting his weight from foot to foot, glancing around as if to see he wasn't being watched.

"Sorry, young man. We just don't make a habit of cashing these kinds of checks."

The boy made a face. "My mom gets hers cashed here all the time. And my granny told me to get it cashed or else."

"Tell you what," the clerk said. "Have your granny come in with proper identification and then we'll see. And you tell your granny that the procedure is for her protection."

She handed the check back to the boy. He darted from the store. The clerk pondered the matter for a moment, then reached for the phone and dialed the number of the Wharton city police.

The Black Stallion's bowels were dark and air-conditioner crisp, a tranquil escape from the muggies which foreshadowed the predicted thunderstorms. Karen and Chip took a table in the rear of the restaurant. A waitress approached the table. It was early, and the place was almost empty. "Would you like a drink or a menu?"

"A drink for now," Chip said. He looked to Karen. "Maybe we'll have dinner later."

"Maybe," Karen said.

Chip ordered a bourbon and water, Karen a glass of white wine. As the waitress left, Karen slipped into a relaxed, thankful slump. Chip Roth had saved her from going home, from an evening of remembered despair. He'd caught her at a vulnerable moment.

"So you're a King hireling," Karen noted.

"Yeah. Chief errand boy."

"I confess I can't remember your nickname. I remember the King mentioning it, but—"

"It's Chip."

"And I'm Karen."

"I couldn't believe it," Chip said. "He makes fun of my nickname, and he's called 'the King.' "

"I bet he secretly loves it," Karen said. "He behaves like a monarch. He expects to be treated like one. I just loved to pull those stodgy tail feathers of his when I was at Legal Aid—not that I got the chance too often. And Clarke Nelson, when I went with the prosecutor's office, warned me about the King firm. Maybe I'm talking out of school, but his precise words were, 'no favors for the King's firm.' There's no love lost, and I get the feeling it goes beyond mere politics."

"I hate to hear that," Chip said. "It'll make plea bargaining a little difficult."

"If not impossible. Don't even think about it in the Sampson case."

Chip drank deeply of his bourbon, then said, "I saw him giving you the evil eye this morning."

Karen stared down into her wine. "That's what it felt like . . . an evil eye. He was raping me with his eyes right in the courtroom. He gives me goosebumps."

They talked shop for the better part of an hour. Neither had eaten any lunch that day, and the alcohol quickly suffused them with the conviviality of old friends, perhaps lovers. Outside they could hear . . . and feel . . . deep rumbles of thunder.

"This is relaxing," Karen said. "I needed this. I really did."

"Rough day, huh?"

"Just about the worst I've ever had."

"Sampson?" Chip asked.

"That was just the start. I saw my first murder victim to-day."

Chip's face turned serious. "Today? Here in Wharton?"

Karen nodded. "In the Locust Drive section."

"Naturally," Chip observed.

Karen bristled a little. "Do I detect a note of snobbery?"

"Oh, no! Like I said, I grew up here. Most of the trouble happens over in Locust Drive. Was it another beer joint brawl?"

Karen shook her head. "Not even close. An armed robbery. He . . . or they . . . went into an old woman's house and blew her head off, then ransacked the house. It was gross . . . very, very gross."

Chip asked her name. He didn't know Gracie Mack. "Any suspects?" he then asked.

"Not that I know of."

"When did it happen?"

"Sometime late Saturday night. The body was ripe."

"And they sent you to the scene?"

Chip knew instantly that he'd said the wrong thing. Karen, her face already colored by the alcohol, reddened even more. Even in the darkened musk of the bar, Chip saw her anger. "Damn! What is it with you guys? Just because I'm a woman. I bet you'd have puked all over yourself, too."

"I would have," Chip said. "I apologize."

"Accepted."

"I'm famished," Chip said. "How about a steak?"

Karen grimaced. "I think I'll settle for a vegetable plate tonight."

The city police took the call from the clerk at the grocery store. Recognizing the name of a murder victim, they relayed the tip to the state police detachment. The trooper on duty finally got hold of Dan Hemmings. Two hours after the boy's attempt to cash Gracie Mack's social security check, his description clicked onto the regional teletype. He was listed as a "juvenile, possibly armed and considered to be dangerous. Wanted for suspicion of murder and armed robbery, and attempted forgery and uttering."

# FIVE

Having nothing else to do that night, Virgil Sampson cruised up and down the main street of Wharton. He sat on the passenger side of a vehicle owned and operated by Maury Austin. The remains of a six pack of Falls City beer rested between Virgil's feet. He balanced the last can on his knee.

Maury Austin had better things to do than burn both his gas and his rubber on Virgil. After all, Virgil had shared only one beer with him. He'd hogged the rest.

But Virgil wanted to cruise.

If you hung around with Virgil, you did what Virgil wanted to do. So Maury cruised, thirsty and unhappy, but compelled to provide limousine service to his buddy.

"I'd like to fuck," Virgil announced.

Maury sighed inwardly. "We can stop at the Country Palace. I bet Mollie Sue's there. She's always there. She'll boff both of us."

"Naw. I know her pussy better'n I know my own hand. I want somethin' strange, goddammit."

"There'll be others there. Let's stop. I'm dry, and there ain't no more beer."

Virgil just ignored the plea. He leaned his head back on the greasy, ragged headrest of the 1973 Torino. "Man, I seen a piece o'ass today that made me drool. And get this! The bitch's a lawyer. Hell! She's a prosecutor, and she's gonna try to send me up for that killin'. Don't that beat all."

Maury fidgeted in his seat. Sometimes—most of the time, in fact—Virgil made him nervous, especially when he talked about the killing.

"Yep," Virgil went on. "I had to go to court this morning. She was there. Damn, she's something! A tight little piece . . . you can tell. Nice tits, little but yummy. Great

45

legs. And the prettiest blonde hair I ever did see. I bet it's real, too. They gave me two lawyers today, two new ones—a punk kid and a fuckin' wop."

"Good-lookin', huh?" Maury said, just to say something.

"You can say that again. Them little titties sit right up here." Virgil motioned under his chin. "She had on a white dress, and you could see her bra and panties right through it. I bet she's a real cocktease."

"Shit, Virg! You're just adreamin'. You ain't gonna get within a mile of her."

Sampson snickered. "We'll see."

The blue Torino slowed for a stoplight. The streets were still damp from the brief rainstorm that had passed through an hour or so before, and the car's slick tires slid a bit before they grabbed. Two girls, both of them plump, stood at the corner. They turned their heads at the sound of the tires.

"Lookee there, Maury. How about them two?"

"They're pigs."

Virgil just grinned, then opened the door.


"We're both smashed," Chip observed, a long time after they had both finished their dinners.

Karen giggled. "I don't care. I feel good."

Chip abandoned himself to her misty blue eyes. How lovely she was—this assistant State's attorney whose blonde hair, in the light cast by the table candle, cast a golden halo. In his mood, one of alcoholic fantasy, she merged with his vision of an angel. "I'd be pleased to take you home," he said. Even he wasn't certain what he'd meant by "taking her home."

Another titter from Karen. "I'm not ready to go home, not just yet. Tell me, Chip Roth . . . why did you decide to be a lawyer?"

Chip leaned back in the chair and tugged at the already loose tie. A juke whined out a beer-drinking, tear-encouraging country ballard. Chip's voice, when he spoke, carried above the song. "I seek to help the helpless, to befriend the friendless, defend the defenseless."

A couple of the other patrons turned at the sound of his voice, and Karen said to him, "Just what I thought."

"Whadaya mean?"

"You and I, Chip, are children of television, products of the boob tube."

"Whadaya mean?"

"We became what we became because of television. I bet you just loved to watch those old reruns of *Perry Mason.*"

*"The Paper Chase,"* Chip said, as if that somehow added a little more class to his motivation.

Karen's eyes sparkled. "No wonder you went to work for the King!"

"Whadaya mean?"

"Arthur King is the personi . . . personif—" Karen smacked her lips together, urging them to cooperate with the signals sent by her fuzzy brain. She decided to surrender. "Hell! He's just like John Houseman."

"The King?"

Karen nodded.

"You're smashed," Chip said.

"Agreed. But I'm also right. Cops become cops because of *Hill Street Blues, The Blue Knight,* and maybe even *Car 54, Where Are You?,* given a few of 'em I've seen. Doctors become doctors because of *Dr. Kildare* and *Marcus Welby.*"

"So why do criminals become criminals?"

*"Bonnie And Clyde . . .* or maybe they're just television critics."

"What if we were influenced by television? Where's the harm?"

Karen stared forlornly into the dregs of her latest glass of wine. "Because it's not real life. Take death. Television makes it so acceptable, so sanitized. You don't smell death watching a television."

"You see the actors smelling it," Chip said.

"Shit, Chip!"

"You're just bothered by what you saw today."

"You're damned right I am!" Karen, who had momentarily lost her passion for the argument, stumbled upon it once again. "If you were honest, you'd admit it isn't what you thought it would be like."

Chip laughed. "Jeez! It's only been one day for me. Now, I admit I didn't think I would be fetching the King's car."

"You Jewish?" she asked suddenly.

"Nope. Somehow we just ended up with a last name that sounds Jewish."

The waitress came around to the table and asked if they wanted another round. "Not for me," Karen said.

"Sure?" Chip said.

"I'm sure."

The waitress seemed to nod her head in agreement and spent a few moments totaling the tab. She dropped it on the table in front of Chip. Chip reached for it. "It's on me."

But Karen snapped it away from him. "No way. It might be considered an attempt to unduly influence a prosecutor. We'll go halfsies."

"Suit yourself," Chip said.

Karen fished around in her purse and withdrew a twenty which she handed to Chip. "You settle up. I'll call us a taxi."

"A taxi?"

"You sure as hell aren't in any condition to drive, and neither am I."

"But what about our cars?"

"I'm gonna get mine in the morning. I'd suggest you do the same thing."

"But I gotta be to work early tomorrow. God knows how many errands await my personal attention."

Karen went to find a phone, while Chip sorted out the bill. She returned to say that their taxi would be outside in a few minutes. "They had one in the area," she added.

They were silent for a moment, having arrived at that particular moment in the evening when interesting possibilities and questions come to mind. Karen ruptured the subtle tension to say, "I wouldn't put up with that, running errands."

"Beats the hell outa looking at dead people," Chip quipped, wishing immediately that he hadn't. Its mention doused her mood with bitter, dark brew.

"Let's wait outside," she said softly. "I need some fresh air."

The rain had come and gone, leaving a damp mist in the air which couldn't be seen, but which enveloped them just as soon as they exited the Black Stallion. Above them the heavens were thick with stars. The restaurant, sitting all alone in the rolling countryside, seemed on that night to be at stage center for a chorus of frogs and crickets and other music makers of the night. Chip slipped an arm around Karen. She tensed, but did not pull away from him. "It's lovely here," she said. "It's one of the reasons I decided to stay rather than go back to DC. It's an ugly town."

She shivered, and Chip felt it. "It really got to you today, didn't it?"

48

"Bad," she admitted. "It makes me wonder if I want to be a prosecutor."

Car lights engulfed them. A vehicle entered the parking lot of the Black Stallion. Karen now withdrew from Chip's touch. "There's our taxi."

Chip gaped. "It's a police car!"

"A sheriff's car," Karen said. She started toward it.

Chip hesitated.

"Come on," she urged, her mood now a little better. "I've got influence."

"What you have," Chip said, reluctantly joining her, "is balls—and I must be drunk to say something like that to you."

Mickie Sampson was frightened. He lay in his small, cot-like bed, his room dark. From all the way across the hall, he heard his mother snoring.

It had been on the eleven o'clock news—the story about the old woman Virgil had killed. He had watched it with his mother on the old black-and-white in the front room. He hoped she couldn't tell he was shaking.

"Can you believe that?" she had said. "Folks is just pure evil these days. Purely evil."

But Mickie hadn't been listening to her. He was thinking about the government check he'd tried to cash, now stashed in his bedroom under his pillow.

As he lay in the dark, staring at the faint rectangular block of light which was his only window, Mickie wondered when they would come for him. If he made it until morning, he'd get rid of the check . . . but how?

Mickie feared throwing it in the trash can. He had to be careful.

Had that store woman watched the news?

Would she remember the name?

Remember him?

If only he had listened to Virgil . . .

Virgil had known.

Mickie turned and cried into his pillow . . . for himself and for the old woman. "I'm sorry," he mumbled, hoping God and the old woman could hear him, but not his mother.

# SIX

Dan Hemmings started knocking on doors in Locust Drive just after sunrise. He carried with him the description of the young boy who had tried to cash the victim's social security check. For what it was worth he also carried an artist's conception of the boy.

Hemmings had been a cop for 20 years. Only twice had he seen an artist's conception which even half-resembled the suspect once he'd been caught. Maybe it was the artists he had to use. After all, Custer County and southern West Virginia weren't really hangouts for artistic types. Nonetheless, his detachment commander thought it sounded professional, having a police artist—in this instance, a long-haired freak who had wandered into the detachment a year or so back to volunteer his services. The kid drew well enough, but Hemmings found him revolting . . . figured he sold dope on the side. Hemmings found most of today's kids revolting.

The store clerk said that the kid had looked about 15, maybe a little younger. That report, too, revolted Hemmings—the notion of a juvenile killer. A person was just as dead, whether he was killed by a senior citizen or a toddler—dead is dead. Courts, though, had a thing about juveniles, and Hemmings detested trying to convict one of them of anything.

The Locust Drive residents who answered their door (many did not) were at first belligerent over such an early morning intrusion. Many of the men, probably unemployed and without purpose in life, had been sleeping. Hemmings was glad he hauled their asses out of bed. As soon as Hemmings flashed his badge, their irritation usually waned. None, however, tried to be too helpful. Locust

Drive residents were that way. They didn't appreciate cops. Hemmings didn't care for many of them, either. So it didn't bother him at all, disturbing them so early in the morning.

Chip surprised himself that morning. He awoke to the electronic whistling of his alarm clock without much of a hangover. On the other hand, he was without a car. The taxi out to the Black Stallion set him back a ten spot, which brought the previous evening's total to almost $30, or a fourth of his total cash on hand—with two weeks to go until his first payday.

Good going, he told himself.

Chip, as he drove his 1976 Toyota back into town and to work, couldn't help wondering if he somehow had offended Karen the night before. She had kept silent during the ride back into Wharton. He and the deputy had joked a little, but the cop hadn't seemed too pleased to be escorting two drunk lawyers to their residences. And it was a little difficult trying to manage a romantic parting with a deputy in attendance.

The bourbon shaded his memory just a little. Karen seemed a little sensitive, and perhaps he had said something he shouldn't have. If so, he couldn't remember what it was. He truly liked Karen, but he knew so little about her, other than that she was beautiful, smart, nice—

Chip didn't want to screw this one up. He wasn't comfortable with women, yet he always managed to fall head over heals in love with women, generally on the first date. He managed to hide it from them, but it played hell with his own sanity. The shrinks had a word for it—some kind of insecurity complex or something. When they didn't feel the same way about him (and more often than not that was the case), then he pined for days, sometimes weeks. The misery lasted until the next one came along.

Not that there had been all that many. In fact, it had been so long since the last that he'd gotten over her without a successor to ease the discomfort. Now that he was an attorney, he wanted to handle his love life with a little more self-respect. He'd take it soft and easy with Karen Kinder.

But God! Was she nice!

Chip met Simon King as he entered the building.

51

"Good morning, Chip."

Chip greeted his employer, addressing him as "Mr. King."

"Call me Simon. Call my brother 'Mr. King.' Did you meet Panzini yesterday?"

They entered the elevator.

"What a character!" Chip said as the door closed on them. No one else occupied the elevator.

"A word of warning, Chip. Panzini's a bit of a rogue. To Mario, ethics are obstacles to be sidestepped or overcome."

"I gather he's an opportunist."

They exited the elevator. The stodgy receptionist surprised Chip with the enthusiasm of her greeting, no doubt caused by the presence of Simon King.

The two lawyers walked on down the hallway toward their respective offices. "You flatter him by calling him an opportunist. The word I used was more to the point." Simon paused at the door to his own office. "Watch Panzini and be sure to always cover yourself. One of these days he's going to fall into the pit. I'd hate to have a member of this firm involved with him. Second, don't put any more time in on this case than you must. It won't even come close to paying your salary."

"What do I do today?" Chip figured he might as well ask if Simon was all that concerned about his time.

"Believe it or not," Simon said, glancing at his wristwatch, "you have a 9:30 appointment. A Mrs. Martha Testa wishes to file for divorce."

Chip grinned . . . a case at last.

"You know our fee scale?" Simon asked.

"Yes, sir. I studied it yesterday."

"Fine. Before you do a thing for Mrs. Testa, get half of the fee up front—in cash."

Chip had hoped that Simon King would have been more interested in giving technical guidance on the case. Simon's only concern, it seemed, was the fee. At least Mario Panzini wasn't a hypocrite.

Simon went on to explain: "Mrs. Testa files for a divorce on the average of four times a year, seasonally you might say. She'll know what information you need. A secretary will help you with the proper form. However, if her past record is any indication, she'll call in here to drop it before you even get around to dictating it."

The light in Chip's eyes dimmed.

Nelson's usually benign face telegraphed a quiet but intense displeasure. "You were at the Black Stallion with that new kid Arthur King hired."

Karen, stunned by his mood, gaped. "Yes. How did you—"

"I know most things. The Sheriff wasn't at all pleased that one of his deputies was asked to chauffeur two tipsy lawyers home. They do have better things to do."

"Would you rather I drove home drunk?"

Nelson's eyes stabbed her. "You had other alternatives. You could have called a taxi. Or you could have used your common sense and boozed it up at home. Furthermore, I'm not crazy about a member of my staff socializing with a member of Arthur King's firm."

Karen's temper also surfaced. "Now just a minute, Clarke. What I do on my time—"

". . . is just as much my business as yours, dear heart. You're not in DC. Nor do you work for Legal Aid. And while we're hashing out a few things, I also heard about your tantrum yesterday over who was to clean up the Mack residence."

"It wasn't a tantrum! Let's stick to your first complaint. I don't see how having dinner and drinks with Chip Roth compromises this office. If he was with any other law firm, you probably wouldn't say a word."

Never before had Nelson so blatantly chastized her. Normally, his criticism was satiric, biting, but never so confrontational.

"Okay," Nelson said. "I'm not going to tell you who you can see and who you can't, but I'm giving you ample warning. If you foul up the Sampson case because of this kid, you're out!"

Karen wanted to respond, but Nelson's intercom cut her short. She stewed as the secretary announced the arrival of Hemmings. Karen, having a moment to consider, said nothing after Nelson had hung up the phone. The two lawyers waited in a chilly silence until the state police corporal arrived.

"We've got a break in the Mack case," Hemmings announced as he entered Nelson's office.

Karen forgot her anger. "What is it?"

"Some kid—a juvenile, goddammit—tried to cash her social security check at one of the local supermarkets last evening. The clerk didn't fall for it, and she called the city police right after the kid left. We came out of it with a description." Hemmings handed Nelson a copy of the description and the artist's conception.

"A juvenile," Nelson moaned, just as discouraged as Hemmings. He passed the papers to Karen.

"Ain't it great?" Hemmings said to Nelson.

But Karen was frowning. "I don't think a kid could have done something like that."

Nelson smacked his lips at her naiveté. "Some of the most heartless, cold-blooded killers I've seen have been kids—young kids. You ever watch a group of kids torture a cat? A juvenile without conscience, without any sense of guilt, is 10 times worse than the worst adult. Even the best of kids have so little damned conception of the value of life."

Hemmings briefed them on his morning's activities. "I covered the whole neighborhood. One lady says she thinks she saw a kid and an older fellow lurking about the neighborhood at dusk, but she couldn't or wouldn't say whether he fit the description of the boy that we have."

"At least we have a place to start," Nelson noted.

"Well," Hemmings said, "we busted on fingerprints. There were a lot of smears, some clear prints belonging to the old lady, but we got nothing to help. I'm personally gonna deliver the slug we got to the CID. And maybe by then we'll have the autopsy results."

"Christ, Dan! Who needs the autopsy results?" Nelson pointed to the description of the boy which Karen still held. "Just be certain you get this on the teletype."

"Did it last night," Hemmings said.

The trooper turned to leave. "Hang in there," Nelson said to his back as he vanished from the office, then to Karen, "Are you ready for trial in the Sampson case?"

"Yes." Karen remained cool, still smarting from Nelson's tongue lashing. "I just hope Pinter doesn't continue the case."

"Don't hold your breath. The old sot's too afraid of getting reversed. With a new defense team, he'll tread lightly."

Karen visualized Virgil Sampson's face. "That guy gave me the creeps in court yesterday. I'm glad I'm prosecuting him. I won't let anything mess it up."

Nelson refused to grab her bait. In fact, he caught her by surprise. "We'll get together in a few days and you can go over the case with me so I'll be prepared. I want Virgil Sampson. He's dangerous."

Karen's hope—that she alone would try Virgil Sampson—vanished. The other assistants in the office had warned her, told her that Nelson would take over the trial, but she had hoped. She left his office wondering if he was punishing her for last night's transgression. If so, Clarke Nelson had something to learn.

Mickie never read the newspaper, not until that morning. He knew there would be something about the old woman's killing, and he wanted to read it—as best he could. Mickie had quit school the year before. By law, he was still supposed to be attending, but the local board of education seldom pursued truants, especially ones with such a lack of academic promise.

So Mickie slowly, and with difficulty, mouthed his way through the short article and the obituary which started on page one and then concluded on the second page. The article contained more words than the blurb on the television but little more information. Mickie, fresh as he was, expected to read his name in the paper. He was relieved when he did not.

Afterward, ambling down an alley in downtown Wharton, Mickie casually withdrew the stiff check from his hip pocket and dropped it into a trash can behind some alley tenements. He threw the newspaper in on top of it.

Mickie hadn't killed the old woman. In his mind, the worst he did was burglary. He'd never been in any real trouble. Once the city cops had arrested him for sniffing glue, another time for swiping hubcaps. They were all the time hassling him. Still, Mickie figured, if he got caught, and even if they got him for robbery, he'd get probation. All the kids did.

Virgil faced the murder rap, but, if it didn't worry Virgil any, then Mickie had decided—just at that moment—not to let it worry him. He hadn't slept at all the night before. That check under his pillow had been like a loud noise. And every time he closed his eyes he saw the old woman's face—damn her! Tonight, if she came back to haunt him, he'd just ignore her. Or maybe pretend to shoot her—

But she looked like his granny.

Still, Virgil had to kill her. Like Virgil said afterward, she'd seen them both—which kind of made it all her fault. His uncle was a pro. Virgil knew things Mickie didn't, like about the check. He should have listened to Virgil about the check. Feeling a little better about things, Mickie stuffed his hands in his pockets and shuffled away from the trash can with only a little remorse over the few hundred dollars he'd just thrown away.

Mickie hadn't peered into the gloomy shadow thrown by a decrepit set of steps which led up to the apartments. Rheumy eyes, belonging to a wino called Thunderbird, had noticed the bluish-green piece of paper flutter into the can.

As soon as Mickie was out of sight, Thunderbird slipped from beneath the steps and hobbled to the trash can. That piece of paper—longer than it was wide and of such a color—looked like—

By Jesus! It was! A check! A government check!

Thunderbird, enraptured with visions of a better brand of wine than his namesake, snatched the check from the smelly garbage and brushed a bit of mushy tomato from it. Thunderbird ignored the newspaper which covered it. Sometimes newspapers were useful to him but not for their content. Thus, the name of Gracie Mack, typed in computer print on the face, meant nothing to him. The amount did mean something—one hell of a good time. And he could even afford a cheap motel room for this drunk.

Thunderbird glanced around to be certain no one was watching and then stuffed his find inside the ragged old sportscoat he lived in. He headed for the grocery store. Maybe they'd cash the check if he bought a few things—no harm in trying. Besides, his shakes were coming back. Thunderbird needed a drink.

Two hours later, with the tremors tearing him apart, Thunderbird sat in the dismal office of the Custer County lockup. A big man who called himself a state police investigator hammered him with questions. Thunderbird knew most of the cops, at least the ones who wore uniforms. The city cops he knew by name. This bruiser, though, was giving old Thunderbird a rough time.

"I done tol' de city cops," Thunderbird whined at his interrogator. "I found it."

"Yeah," Hemmings drawled. "In a trash can. I've heard that crock of shit a thousand times."

Thunderbird, no matter how bad the shakes became, was no stoolie. He lived on the streets, and, even in a small place like Wharton, that meant conforming to certain rules. He hadn't known the kid who tossed the check into the trash can. He'd seen him before, hanging around on the streets. Thunderbird had seen almost everyone in Wharton twice. When a fellow spends as much time on the streets as Thunderbird, he develops a wide range of acquaintances. Not many friends, but a hell of a lot of people he recognized.

"So you just thought you'd go cash it?" Hemmings said.

"A man's gotta eat."

"Or drink."

"I don't know what got into me," the wino said.

Hemmings leaned down until the odor of the wino became unbearable. "Now you hear this, you old sot. That check belongs to a woman who was murdered a few days ago. Now, if you don't want to be booked as an accessory to that murder, you'd better start spitting out some information."

Thunderbird, red-faced from alcohol, went white. "Man! I ain't killed nobody. Never."

"What's that got to do with anything?" Hemmings eased away from Thunderbird, away from his stench. "Just tell me. How many times you pulled a few days for something you didn't do?"

Thunderbird didn't have to think very far back. "S'okay. By rights, I ain't no stoolie. You're making me talk."

"Have it your way," Hemmings said. "Just talk."

"I was behind them old apartments in the middle of town, the ones near that grocery where they picked me up. Anyways, this kid walks by and just tosses the check in a trash can, pretty as you please."

Hemmings hitched up his pants. "That's more like it. Is this the kid?" He handed the wino the artist's rendering.

Thunderbird, his hands trembling as they were, didn't

take the drawing. He just opened his eyes wide and stared at it for a long time. "Sorta bears a resemblance. I didn't get much of a look at his face."

Hemmings withdrew the drawing. "Then you and I are gonna drive around town for awhile. Maybe we'll see this kid, and you can finger him for me."

Thunderbird shook his head. "Now I don't know about that, sir. I gotta live in them streets. Some of them guys see me passing the time of day with the likes of you, well, it wouldn't do much for my reputation."

"On your feet!" Hemmings commanded.

"Hey," Thunderbird protested. "You ain't being right about this."

Hemmings shoved the frail man out the door. "Tough shit."

# SEVEN

"You got me in trouble," Karen said to Chip when he phoned her late that afternoon.

"How?"

"Nelson doesn't think it seemly, you and I going to dinner. And the Sheriff resented his deputy hauling us home last night."

"If it had just been you, that deputy wouldn't have minded a bit," Chip said. "As for Nelson, he just doesn't like defense attorneys."

"Especially ones who work for the King's firm," Karen added.

Chip couldn't divine Karen's attitude about the problem. "So what do we do?"

Karen, silent only for a moment, said, "Let's go out to the mall tomorrow night. We can grab some supper at the pizza parlor. Then you can come with me while I go shopping."

She couldn't see the broad smile that crossed Chip's face. "What about your boss?" Chip asked, keeping his satisfaction to himself for the moment.

"The devil with him. He doesn't run my life."

Chip's smile flagged just a little. "Are you just doing this to defy him?"

"Sure," she admitted. "That's part of it. If I didn't like you, though, I wouldn't do it."

"You're sure?"

"Pick me up right after work at my place, say around 5:30." She gave him the address.

Chip, after hanging up, almost danced a jig around his small office. At least something had worked out right. Mrs. Testa, the seasonal divorce client, hadn't even shown up for her appointment. After lunch, he'd been dispatched—by the receptionist, no less—to pick up a package at the post office. It was a personal item for Mrs. Arthur King.

Four years in college, three years in law school.

For what?

When he had returned, Simon had assigned him to research cases on workmen's compensation. As dry as the material was, at least it was lawyer's work.

A knock sounded on his door. "Come in."

Isaac Clausen, not a lot older than Chip and the newest partner in the firm, stepped into his office. "I haven't had a chance to welcome you aboard," he said to Chip, offering Chip his hand.

"Glad to be here." Chip wondered if he really was. He grasped the hand of Isaac Clausen and liked him at once. Chip judged people by their handshakes. Clausen's was dry and firm and cordial. The man was of average height, slight build, with thinning, straw-colored hair, and a pleasant, open face.

"Just wanted you to know I do my own errands," Clausen said. And that, Chip thought, cements the friendship. Still, he was uncertain how to respond.

Clausen sensed his predicament. "I started here just like you, Chip. I ran the same gauntlet. I don't know whether it's intentional or not, but I stuck it out. Most of them haven't. It takes awhile to build your credibility with this firm. If you tough it out . . . put up with the bullshit and Arthur King's pomposity, you'll find it a fine and comfortable place to work."

Clausen, after his speech, sat down.

"I was beginning to wonder," Chip admitted.

"I know. If I can do anything for you, if you just need someone to talk to, come over to my office."

"Thanks."

"I heard Pinter nailed you yesterday."

"You mean the murder case?"

Clausen nodded. "And he saddled you with Mario. You sure picked a bad day to join up, which, by the way, brings me to one of my main reasons for visiting you."

"What?"

"The County Bar association meets the first Monday of next month for its bimonthly dinner meeting. As an officer of the association, it's my duty and pleasure to inform you of your obligatory initiation."

"You're kidding."

"I do not jest. Each new member of the bar must deliver a brief address on a topic selected by an officer, in this instance myself."

"You mean a speech?" Chip asked.

"Certainly. It's a tradition. Limit your remarks to seven minutes. You're a local boy, right?"

Chip, already shaken by the prospect of addressing the bar of Custer County, nodded.

"Excellent. Your topic is to be growing up in Wharton."

Chip's face registered his disbelief.

"You didn't know?" Clausen asked.

"No! Not at all."

"I'm amazed. To enlighten you, we like for your address to be as humorous as possible. Some of the veteran members of the bar may heckle you, especially since a cocktail hour precedes the dinner. Don't look so worried. It's clean fun, and we haven't lost a lawyer yet. Nothing is sacred—save of course the reputation of the senior member of this firm and the dignity of Judge Pinter. One of the new attorneys hired by this firm, some years ago, decided to present a speech on Arthur King. The topic he'd been given was 'the strangest person I've ever known.'"

Chip covered his eyes with his hand. "Oh, no!"

"Oh, yes! I, of course, wasn't here then, but the story was passed on to me by a credible source. Arthur remained calm throughout the speech. The bar itself went wild. They loved it—one of the King's court spearing the regent himself. Arthur even applauded at its conclusion, or so I'm told. The young man thought he'd really pulled a coup until he came to work the next day."

"He was fired," Chip said.

"Actually he found the few personal effects in his desk placed in a paper bag and sitting in the front hall."

"What happened to him?"

"He stayed here. Several other members of the bar truly enjoyed his presentation, and he joined a smaller firm. Now he's our prosecutor."

"Clarke Nelson?"

Clausen nodded.

And Chip now understood.

To Hemmings, cases came in two varieties. First, there were those he called the "coffin" cases, the ones with the lids spiked down tight right off the bat. Most of his cases were coffin cases—murders, robberies and assaults in which witnesses or victims fingered the perpetrator immediately. A cop's duty in such a case was to mop up, to write the police reports for the grand jury and the prosecutor, to show up in court on time and make sure witnesses did the same.

The second type of case—Hemmings's favorite—was the "mystery," though, God knows, they often frustrated him. Solving such cases wasn't anything glamorous. Breaks came not like the flash of a camera's strobe, but rather from plodding and laborious routine. Sooner or later the pieces came together. Once Hemmings settled upon a "prime" suspect, he knew he'd be able to close the case before long.

A few unsolved mysteries blemished Hemmings's 20-year career. Each one vexed him like his old knee injury, received when he played football one season for Virginia Beach High School. And each one of his unsolved cases fell into that rather exotic classification of crime known among the brotherhood as "thrill killings"—no motive (other than madness), no prior connection between killer and victim, no way to home in on that "prime" suspect. Such cases were usually solved by sheer luck. Sometimes the killers are caught in the act, and the m.o. fits killings in other jurisdictions, thus allowing for all cases with the same characteristics to be closed. Hemmings knew there was a good margin of error in closing cases like that, but the FBI (God bless 'em) never went behind the Uniform Crime Report statistics.

The Mack case wasn't a thrill killing—a mystery for sure (at least for the moment), but the motive had been robbery. Items had been stolen, and they would provide the string which would grow into rope to hogtie the killer(s). The first strands had been woven together with the check, the boy, the wino and the grocery store.

That check, weighing so little, would bring—by its weight—the case crashing down upon the person or persons who killed the Mack woman. A phantom kid tries to cash her stolen check. A store clerk can recognize the kid.

A wino sees the kid throw the check away. Dan Hemmings was overwhelmingly grateful for the stupidity of most criminals.

Hemmings taxied the wino up and down the main street of Wharton for over an hour. The investigator had gotten nothing out of it but a noseful of bad smell and a nauseated stomach. Several times during that hour Hemmings pulled a small can of aerosol air freshener from the cruiser glove box to spray the air-conditioned interior of the car. He could have cared less about Thunderbird's feelings. If it mattered at all to Thunderbird, he never showed it.

Finally, no longer able to stand the rancid aroma, Hemmings took Thunderbird back to the jail and booked him as a material witness. A first-year lawyer could have had the old man out in a snap of the fingers, but there weren't any first-year lawyers where Thunderbird found himself. Hemmings went to the prosecutor's office to check in with Nelson.

The Custer County prosecutor demanded that his office be kept current on all homicide investigations. Sometimes Hemmings found it a nuisance, but at least Nelson cared. Hemmings had worked in counties where prosecutors walked into a murder case on the day of trial to ask the investigator about the case.

Hemmings had been instructed to report to Karen Kinder. "Got another break," he said as he entered her office.

"You got the boy?"

"Don't you wish. We found the check. A town drunk saw the boy toss it in a trash can. The wino tried to cash it. We got him in custody."

Karen was impressed. "Did you charge him with attempted uttering?"

"Hell, no! Nelson ain't gonna fool with prosecuting no drunk. He's being held as a material witness."

The look on Karen's face changed, degenerated. "You didn't get authority from the Judge to do that."

"Are you gonna tell on me?" Hemmings said, amused by her concern.

Karen just shook her head. "I won't stand for that kind of thing, Dan. If you want to hold him, then I suggest you get a warrant charging him with a crime."

"At which point," Hemmings snapped, "he gets a free lawyer and is released on his own recognizance!"

"Because he has rights!" Karen countered.

Hemmings found Karen a fine example of female flesh, but had little faith in her as prosecutor—just like he had little faith in female cops or female lawyers. So he wearily, but patiently, ran his hand through his short-cropped hair. "Let's do this my way this time."

"That man's being detained illegally."

"Hell, lady. We're doin' him a favor not charging him with the felony. Besides, he could use a day or two to dry out. Give me a break."

Karen couldn't withhold a smile. "So you're doing him a favor?"

"I know what I'm doin', Karen."

Hemmings had adopted that stern tone of superiority which came so easily to men armed with guns. Karen had met few police officers who either didn't come to their job with that attitude or developed it quickly once they became accustomed to the trappings of the position.

"I know what you're doing, too," Karen said. "You're breaking the law you swore to uphold. You know that we have to get consent from a judge to hold someone as a material witness. You're making decisions which should be made by this office."

Hemmings rose from his chair. "Let's talk to Nelson about this."

"He's on the golf course. Sit back down."

That sounded like an order to Hemmings. "Now, look—"

"Sit down, Corporal."

Hemmings glared for a moment, then sat down.

Karen, holding a pen in her hand, pointed it at the trooper. "Now let's get one thing straight between you and me—man-to-man, as you macho guys like to say. I've got this case, and you're not going to scamper to Nelson every time we disagree. It's my case, and I'm the one that's got to parade into court and make it stick. And I'd appreciate it if you'd treat me as your equal rather than your kid sister."

Hemmings just rolled his eyes. "Shit. It doesn't make a damn to me. You say the word, and I'll charge the wino with being an accessory to murder, if that'll make you happy."

"Why hold him at all?" Karen asked.

"He says he found the check, Karen, and I'd bet that he's bein' straight on that. On the other hand, maybe—just maybe—he's involved with the murder. Maybe he and this mysterious kid pulled it off together. Now I doubt that. I sincerely doubt it, but it's possible."

Karen had never thought of that. She dropped her eyes a little, and Hemmings said, "Now if you want, I'll go right now and get a warrant for him for uttering a forged check."

She thought for a moment, and then an image intruded into her mind's process, coming as a glitch which caused the thought process to crash, to abort. She saw the remnants of Gracie Mack's face. "I guess it'll keep until tomorrow," she then said. "I just don't like police tricks that smack of . . . of—" She wanted to be cautious in her choice of words. ". . . of highhandedness. It's a matter of principle."

Hemmings again rose to leave. "I don't get involved in fancy discussions about principles. I'll leave that to you lawyers and the judges. I try to catch criminals, and I try to give you the evidence to nail them. You can talk all you want about the law and about rights, but I can tell you one thing—I get by with a hell of a lot. The law isn't anything more than what the judge says it is, the judge you or I happen to be in front of at that moment. I'll take my chances, and I'll do things my way as often as I can get away with it."

And with that he left.

Karen stared into the void he left behind. Dan Hemmings didn't give a damn about principles. He'd just said that. And poor Gracie Mack—what did she have to do with principles? Karen had let Hemmings get away with jailing the alcoholic when she knew it was wrong. Was it happening to her, too, she wondered. One bad case—one butchered face—and she, too, was allowing her convictions to weaken, to slide.

Late that evening, beyond that day itself and into the next, the promised thunderstorms—near death without the sustenance of solar heating—made another brief and impotent appearance. They rumbled and grumbled. Lightning flashed brightly on the northwestern horizon. And just a few drops of rain fell on Custer County.

They splattered big and wet on the windshield of Maury Austin's Torino. Once again he was hauling Virgil Sampson around Custer County. Virgil's kid nephew was with them.

The drops increased as they passed an old junkyard. Virgil told Maury to stop the car.

"What for?" Maury asked, hoping it didn't rain too hard, wanting in fact to get home. Only one of his wipers worked, and he himself was bone-tired.

"Let's get us some car parts," Virgil explained. "Maybe we can find something to fix that wiper with."

"I don't know what's wrong with it," Maury countered.

"Hell, we'll just see what we can find then."

"Come on," pleaded Maury.

"Ain't nobody around," Virgil said. "I know a guy who'll buy anything we get. I need some walkin' around money."

"Ah, let's go home, Virgil," Maury said, "before this rain gets too bad."

Virgil put his arm around Mickie, who sat in the middle between the driver and his uncle. "How about you, kid? You wanna get some old car parts? Maybe hubcaps. They sell good."

"I'm with you," Mickie said.

Virgil reached across Mickie and squeezed hard on Maury's leg. "I said stop the fucking car."

# EIGHT

Pine Ridge Mall was Custer County's pride. When plans for its construction were first released, cynics pooh-poohed the idea, saying that a county with 60,000 people couldn't support a big-city mall.

Mall developers, though, had done their homework. Custer County sat on the fringe of the southern West Virginia coalfields. The mall, the marketing specialists decided, would draw not just from Custer County but from an eight-county area. Smartly placed political contributions uncovered future highway developments, thereby endowing the Pine Ridge project with bright, profit-making promise.

Six years later, Pine Ridge Mall opened amid much celebration, and the marketing specialists converted all but the most persistent cynics. The large hub stores boomed. Smaller stores, often strapped to meet the high mall rent, struggled, but, as soon as one folded, another was ready to take its place.

Pine Ridge Mall became the social center of Custer County. People went to the mall just for the experience. Friends and acquaintances gathered on the mall benches, beneath and around lush indoor gardens, to gossip and chew the proverbial fat. In the summer months, many a healthy male spent the better part of a Saturday afternoon watching women—young and old—jiggle and bounce their way up and down the mall in short shorts and T-shirts, their multiformed breasts often unhindered beneath the thin material. Wives and girl friends, probably well aware of the voyeuristic intent of their men, used the time to shop. The men paid the price for their voyeurism when the charge account tabs arrived the next month. It was quid pro quo. People wondered what they had done before the mall came to Custer County. Television seemed mundane by comparison.

Karen, a big-city girl, thought herself fortunate to have settled in so backward an area with such a progressive retail outlet. Clothes were her vice.

Chip had found her apartment without trouble, and they had enjoyed a drink before going to the mall in Chip's Toyota. They arrived just ahead of the evening crowd, and Karen led him straight to the pizza restaurant. Chip, as he followed her, gawked at the mall's spacious interior.

"I can't believe you haven't been here," Karen said as they entered the restaurant.

"They built it while I was in school. My mother left after Dad's death. I just never came back to Wharton. This place is bigger than most of the malls in Pittsburgh."

"And quite a few in DC," Karen added.

They held off the shoptalk until after they had ordered a single medium pizza and a pitcher of draft beer. "How's the murder case going?" Chip then asked.

"To me, slow. Dan Hemmings, the state police investigator, says he has leads."

"I still can't figure out how a Legal Aid lawyer ends up trying to send people to jail. That seems totally out of character for you."

"Financial considerations mitigate political philosophies," she said.

"Meaning you sold out."

Karen chuckled. "That's precisely what my roommate Myra said."

"I didn't know you had a roommate."

"I don't—not any more. She liked to smoke dope, and every now and then, when she felt particularly charitable to the male of the species, she'd screw one of them in the center of our living room floor—not caring who was there. She's an instructor of English at Custer College. We decided it wise to part company when I became an assistant prosecutor. We're still friends, but she tries not to smoke dope around me anymore."

"I heard a fascinating and enlightening story about your boss the other day," Chip told her.

The waitress delivered the beer, and Chip waited for her to leave. Then he told Karen about the speech Nelson had

68

given at the bar meeting. Karen was stunned. "I've never heard that. No wonder he despises Arthur King."

"Did you go through the initiation?"

Karen nodded. "Did I ever! I was asked to address the subject of 'women in the law'—naturally. The joke was on me. No one told me to make my speech humorous. The omission was intentional. Was I fresh then! I carried the banner of women's lib a little higher than I do now. I was with Legal Aid and was untouchable by the powers that be here, so I figured I'd give their stodgy old asses hell."

Chip jokingly covered his ears. "I don't think I want to hear the rest."

"Sure you do. I got up at the meeting, cleared my throat, and looked over the solemn faces of the Custer County Bar. Not a woman among them. I pointed that out to them. I berated them and chided them, and delivered a hellfire and brimstone condemnation of the discrimination against women."

Karen paused.

"What happened?" Chip urged.

"God, it was terrible. Just after I finished with what was my opening salvo, the back door to the meeting room opened, and this tall, striking redhead strides into the room. She walks toward the front of the room, but takes a seat beside Clarke Nelson."

"Was she a lawyer?" Chip asked.

"Just wait a minute. Smoke filled the air—cigar smoke, no less. It obscured vision back into the room. I didn't know what to say. So I figured the hell with it, and I decided to press on. As I get all revved up again, this woman stands and cries out in a suspiciously falsetto voice, 'Give 'em hell, sweetie.' That brings the house down. I still hadn't really figured things out."

"Oh, God!" Chip wailed. "What's in store for me?"

"Oh, I'm not finished yet. While the woman is standing there, Clarke Nelson stands up and grabs her boob and squeezes it. It burst. It was a damned balloon, and the woman was one of the assistant prosecutors in drag. I was furious—worse, I was mortified. I snapped out a few words about their lousy, chauvinist sense of humor and stormed from the room. I stayed miffed until the next dinner meeting."

"I'm surprised you even went."

"I didn't want them to think they'd bested me. Anyway, I saw how badly they mistreated a young male lawyer, and I found myself laughing at him. It's a tradition, and it breaks the ice."

Chip didn't like it. "It sounds childishly cruel to me."

"It serves a good purpose," she responded. "It reminds us freshmen lawyers not to take ourselves too seriously."

The waitress brought their pizza. Just before they started dividing it, Chip said, "It's hard to take yourself very seriously when your sole function is to be a Boy Friday."

Virgil Sampson spent a lot of time at the mall. Like many male Custer Countians, he liked the scenery. On that evening, he and Mickie sat on a bench ogling the passing women. Virgil, however, wasn't subtle. When a woman passed who struck his fancy (Virgil wasn't choosy), he whistled, and sometimes even let out catcalls. The presence of a companion with the woman didn't dampen Virgil's enthusiasm. Sometimes the guys got upset. Virgil cooled them down in a hurry. So far, in all his time of girl watching, not a single man had taken him up on his offer to go outside.

On this evening, Virgil and Mickie sat on a bench in front of the entrance to the bookstore. The parade of women had not been especially impressive that night, and Virgil was just about ready to suggest to Mickie that they find something better to do when his eyes snapped to attention.

"Lookee there!"

"What?" Mickie said.

"There's that woman lawyer." Virgil pointed her out to Mickie.

The young boy stared for a moment, then announced rather proudly, "I know her, Virg!"

"You're shittin' me?"

"No, I'm not. She helped momma once when she was trying to get some money the gover'ment owed her. She's real nice."

Virgil leered. "Damn right she is."

"Naw, Virg. I mean nice-nice. She treated me good."

The woman had just exited the bookstore and appeared

70

to be waiting for someone else to come out. Soon, a young man joined her, carrying a bag in his hand.

"Goooddaaaamn!" growled Virgil.

"Whatsa' matter?"

"That's my fuckin' lawyer with her! That's that fuckin' kid I told you 'bout. Man! That ain't right!"

The harsh volume of his voice attracted stares from several other persons seated on nearby benches. Mickie was even afraid the two lawyers had heard. He studied them, and they walked away together, apparently having heard nothing.

"Come on!" Virgil said.

"What we gonna do?"

"Follow 'em."

Mickie didn't want to, but he knew he had no choice. The two attorneys walked across to an expensive women's dress shop and went inside. Mickie and Virgil took a seat on the bench facing its door. "Let's just sit here," Virgil said. "I wanna see if they recognize me."

Ten minutes later, Karen and Chip came out. The woman never even gave Virgil the first glance, but the guy looked Virgil right in the face without the slightest hint of recognition. "That bastard!" Virgil snarled. "Didn't even know me. And look at them two, thick as fuckin' flies. Come on!"

"Virgil." Mickie wanted to end it here. The woman lawyer had been really nice to him. She treated him like a person, not a kid, and he didn't want Virgil to hassle her.

"You can sit here if'n you want," Virgil said. Virgil left him, and Mickie, resigned to his fate, hurried to catch up with his uncle and join the pursuit.

Karen guided Chip into an exotic gift store, noted in Custer County for its esoteric collection of offerings. The section which attracted the most attention, both favorable and critical, boasted such items as battery-operated vibrators, flavored lubricants, love creams and adult board games.

The prosecutor's office had received several complaints from some of the local ministers, and Nelson had offered to investigate the situation. Following that investigation, Nelson left the shop with a jar of Strawberry Joy Jelly and two Playmate jigsaw puzzles. When the ministers called

71

back, Nelson had told them that he found the store's contents an outrage, but he added with appropriate solemnity, that the store violated no current statutes. The ministers, proud of their public-spirited prosecutor, thanked him anyway and bemoaned the decadence which had invaded Custer County.

Karen browsed through the store with Chip at her elbow. When they reached the collection of sexual aids, Karen lifted a box of body paints from a shelf and handed them to Chip. "Are you artistic?"

Chip, whose exposure to such items had been limited, studied the instructions on the box for just a moment, then blushed. "Oh, I see."

Karen snickered and put the box back on the shelf. She moved to a rack of risqué postcards, leaving Chip to ponder the display of items from which she had withdrawn the body paints. The malls in Pittsburgh had similar shops. Once Chip and a friend had even gone into an adult bookstore in Pittsburgh, which was within driving distance of West Virginia University. Seeing such items on display in Custer County, though, was something of a shock.

Karen had moved to the other side of the display rack, and neither she nor Chip noticed the tall, bulky figure that had moved beside Chip. A hand, its nails dirty and long, lifted a long vibrator from the rack. Chip noticed the hand, but he didn't want to sneak a peak at the man.

Act sophisticated, he told himself.

But then Karen gasped. Chip glanced over the top of the rack at her. She was white-faced, her head just visible above the display rack. Her hand covered her mouth, and she appeared frightened. Chip looked around, and he caught sight of the back of a man leaving the store.

He hustled around to her. "What happened?"

Other people in the store were looking.

"Didn't you see him?" she asked.

"See who?"

"Sampson."

"Who?"

"Damn it! Your client! Virgil Sampson! He was standing right beside you."

Chip shrugged. "I probably wouldn't even have known him."

Karen shivered. "He recognized me. He had a . . . a vi-

72

brator, and he was sort of . . . kind of brandishing it at me like—" She trembled even more. "God, he gives me chills! I looked right into those eyes."

"Are you certain it was him?"

"Jesus, Chip! I'd know him anywhere."

"Don't overreact."

"Overreact! That bastard threw me a kiss! Let's get out of here."

"You shoulda gone in there with me," Virgil told Mickie as they left the mall.

"But she knows me!"

"She knows me, too! That was the fun of it. You shoulda seen her face when she saw me. I bet I scared the piss outa her."

"Did that other lawyer see you?"

Virgil shook his head. "The bastard! I was right beside him. He didn't even recognize me. I could smell that sickly sweet perfume he has on, man's perfume. Probably half faggot."

They reached the main highway back to Wharton, and Virgil stuck out his thumb at a passing car. It whizzed by, and Virgil shot the bird at the driver, hoping he had glanced into his rearview mirror.

"I wonder where she lives," Virgil then said, waiting for the next car.

Mickie knew his uncle, knew what the sound in that voice meant, the look in his eyes. "I wouldn't mess with her."

Virgil ruffled his nephew's hair. "Who knows, kid? She gets to know me good enough, she just might toss the case for me."

73

# NINE

Mickie spent most of the next day with his uncle. The prime topic of conversation was Karen Kinder, whom Virgil had started calling "the blonde fox." The conversation was lopsided. Once or twice, Mickie had tried to dissuade his uncle from expressing any active interest in the female lawyer. Virgil finally ended Mickie's interruptions by cuffing him on the ear.

About three that afternoon, a sunny Thursday afternoon, Virgil, accompanied by his cowed nephew, located Maury Austin in one of Wharton's downtown beer palaces. He persuaded Maury to lend him and Mickie the Torino. Maury's common sense had screamed at him to refuse. Self-preservation, also a part of his common sense, caused him to say "yes." Virgil would have taken the car anyway—after knocking Maury around a little

At 4 p.m., the Torino, occupied by Virgil and Mickie, pulled into the parking lot of the Custer County Courthouse. Mickie kept an eye on the parking lot, while his uncle swilled three cans of Falls City beer and fooled around with a cheap eight-track tape deck which Maury had installed under the dash.

"Wish we had some friggin' tapes," Virgil said, sifting through the jammed glove box in search of one. "Fuckin' Maury probably stole the tape player and forgot the tapes."

Karen Kinder walked out of the courthouse. Mickie, knowing that Virgil was paying no attention, thought about keeping quiet, but he was too young to die. "There she is," he said without enthusiasm.

Virgil whistled softly as the woman, dressed in a yellow, white and green dress, strode purposefully across the park-

74

ing lot and got into a bright red Ford Mustang. "She drives a Ford, too," Virgil said. "Damn! She makes my tongue hard. Did you see them legs?"

Virgil fired up the noisy Torino and pulled out into traffic one car behind the Mustang.

"What if she ain't goin' home?" Mickie asked.

"Then we'll find out where she is going. Maybe to that young punk lawyer's place to fuck him."

After several turns leading into a residential area, the Mustang pulled into a parking slot in front of an apartment complex. Virgil pulled over to the curb about 50 yards from the yellow brick apartments. Virgil squinted into the afternoon sun as Karen Kinder exited the car, pulled a set of keys from her purse, and let herself into an apartment.

"See. She don't live too far from where she works," Virgil noted.

They maintained a surveillance until just before dark, at which time Mickie announced that he had to go to the bathroom. Virgil himself had finished his last beer. He had left the car once to relieve himself in a stand of trees and undergrowth adjacent to the street. Virgil wasn't concerned about Mickie's pressing problem, but he was thirsty. So they left.

On Friday afternoon, as Karen pulled into the parking place in front of her apartment, she noticed the blue Torino parked just down the street. She couldn't have identified it as a blue Torino, just a blue car with a bad case of leprosy. She didn't see the single individual occupying the car. He had slipped down out of sight. Still, it seemed out of place in the neighborhood.

It was Friday night, however, and she dismissed it from her mind. She had a date with Chip that night, and she had a great deal to do before he arrived.

Two hours later, as Chip pulled into the street where she lived, he, too, noticed the car, and he noticed that it was an old Torino eaten up with rust. Chip thought it not at all strange, but then his mind was on Karen.

Thirty minutes after that, as Karen and Chip left her apartment to go to the movies, the sun still hung well above the western horizon, and its rays shone almost directly into the interior of the blue car sitting just down the street from her apartment. Karen's eyes caught a movement inside. She thought someone had just ducked down. She stopped to peer at the car.

"What is it?" Chip asked.

"That car," Karen said. "Someone's in it."

Chip could see only the glare of the westering sun. "How the hell can you tell?"

"That car was parked on the street when I came home," she told him.

"Looks like a rolling piece of junk." Chip then opened the door for Karen.

She took one last look at the Torino. "I wonder who it belongs to."

"Maybe it's just broken down. It looks like a prime candidate for the junkyard."

Karen shrugged it off and got inside Chip's car. He backed the Toyota out and headed away from the other car. Karen turned to look back. "Chip! I saw someone! He ducked down out of sight when I turned. This time I'm certain."

"Maybe he's working on something under the dash?"

"Go around the block!"

"But we're going to be late."

"I don't care, Chip. Go around the block!"

"If you insist. I think you're getting paranoid."

Chip made the circle. Just as soon as they turned back on to Karen's block, she cried, "I told you so. It's gone."

The Torino was nowhere to be seen.

Karen's voice grew strident. "It was there when I got home. Someone's following me."

"You're jumping to conclusions," Chip said.

Karen didn't respond. Throughout the 10-minute drive to the theater, she said nothing at all. She was just a little piqued at Chip. She was also worried. She thought about Virgil Sampson—about his dark, depraved eyes which had undressed and abused her twice already, and which offered the promise of much worse.

# PART TWO

"No person . . . shall be compelled in any criminal case to be a witness against himself . . ."
   —Amendment V,
   Constitution of the United States of America

# ONE

Dan Hemmings loved his garden, small though it was. He had trouble finding the time to keep the small 8 x 18 plot fertilized, debugged, and weed-free, but the solitudinous nature of his gardening freed him from the dismal preoccupation of his job.

On this Saturday morning the ground was dry. The recent rains, though accompanied by a lot of lightning and noise, had produced little actual moisture and had barely succeeded in dampening the top inch of soil. The heat of the day sucked that small amount of water right back up.

He loved the clear breathless mornings of late spring. The world was so quiet. Most of civilization still slept. The streets were without cars, the lawns and sidewalks without children. Dan knew from experience that the immediate post-dawn hours were the quietest of the day. Criminals liked to sleep late. For the past two Saturdays, first a pesky but useless rain and then work had prevented him from setting out his tomato transplants. If not planted soon, they would hardly have time to produce before the first frost.

The sun was a little higher when he came to the last row. Just as he started to set out the first plant in that row, his wife swung open the screen door. Hemmings knew all too well the look on her face.

"Goddamn," he growled, totally exasperated. "I told you to tell anyone who called that I wasn't home."

"I did. You'd better take this one."

She'd been married to a cop long enough to know which calls justified a disregard for his orders.

Dan muttered a few choice words, then went to answer the phone. A dispatcher told him that the clerk from the supermarket had called. The boy who had attempted to cash Gracie Mack's check was back in the store.

"Detain him!" Hemmings said, stunned that the city police had even needed to call him.

But the dispatcher paused with maddening uncertainty. "Our officers weren't sure if there were outstanding warrants."

"Jesus, woman! He's a murder suspect. For God's sake, detain him!"

"We didn't mean to—"

The investigator sighed. "Look, just tell your boys to hold him until I get there, and get to it—before he slips through our fingers."

"Yes, sir."

Hemmings slammed down the telephone.

"You have to leave?" his wife asked.

"I guess so." He considered trying to get the last half dozen tomato plants into the ground before he left, but decided against it. The Wharton city cops quaked with the insecurity of the poorly trained when asked to do real police work. If he wasn't on the scene in a hurry, they might let the kid go.

"Would you get those transplants out of the sun?" he asked of his wife.

Mickie exited the store just as the city police cruiser wheeled into the parking lot. The boy carried a can of snuff in the paper bag and broke into a trot as soon as he saw the cops. He almost eluded them, too, as they started inside the store to verify the identification and check with the clerk. One of the officers, though, saw the boy running while looking back over his shoulder at the police.

Mickie was apprehended just at the edge of a large field. "I didn't steal nothing," he cried as an officer snagged him by the arm.

"Just move over to the cruiser, son."

Mickie tried to jerk away, but the officer sensed the preflight tension and tightened his grip. "Don't give us a hassle, kid. Make it easy on yourself."

"I ain't done nothin', man! You can't grab me like this." Mickie tried to display the bag of snuff. "I paid for this stuff. I got a receipt."

The cop didn't seem to care.

Hemmings arrived at the parking lot about 15 minutes later. Two uniformed state troopers pulled in right after him. They relieved the city of Mickie Sampson and escorted him inside the supermarket. The clerk stood just inside the door.

"Is this him?" Hemmings asked.

The clerk nodded.

Mickie started to cry.

Clarke Nelson met Hemmings at the courthouse. The boy sat in the prosecutor's conference room, while Nelson and Hemmings discussed the matter just beyond his hearing.

"We can't question the kid without his parents and a lawyer present," Nelson told the investigator.

"He just lives with his mother," Hemmings explained. "I gather his father skipped out years ago."

"Then we need her and a lawyer."

Hemmings's patience long since had expired. "Christ! I despise dealing with these goddamn juveniles. Why don't they just turn the world over to them?"

"Do we have a choice," Nelson quipped. Nelson had learned long ago that the best way to handle frustrated cops was simply to ignore their frustration. "What's his name, Dan?"

"Sampson . . . Michael David Sampson. They call him 'Mickie.' "

"Sampson!" The name jolted Nelson. "Any kin to Virgil Sampson?"

Hemmings nodded. "A nephew."

"And we try his uncle in a few weeks for murder," Nelson observed, his mind racing.

Hemmings said, "Maybe it runs in the family."

Nelson's gaze fixed on some distant object down the hallway, but his thoughts drifted much farther away. "I wonder if his uncle has anything to do with this. That kid's been crying ever since I arrived. He just doesn't seem the type for this, not alone anyway."

"The thought crossed my mind. If I could just talk to him—"

"Not until he has a lawyer. Charge him with trying to pass the check today. We'll get an attorney for him first thing Monday morning."

81

Hemmings mumbled, "Shit." And Nelson headed for the golf course.

Karen and Chip spent Saturday in Roanoke, Virginia. Karen hadn't forgotten about the blue Torino, but the 90 miles which separated her from Custer County—not to mention the thrill of shopping—lessened its threat.

For Chip, the trip was a mental discomfort. On Friday before he had picked up Karen, he'd stopped at the local bank and managed to borrow $500. The bank, noting that he was the newest member of the King firm, processed his application immediately. Now, if he could pay it back as effortlessly . . .

On the way back, they stopped at a rustic but expensive restaurant between Roanoke and Custer County. It was just before midnight when Chip's Toyota turned the corner onto Karen's street.

"My God!" she cried as the Toyota's headlights illuminated the same blue Torino.

Chip's face also registered concern. "I'll check it out this time."

"Be careful. I've got a bad feeling."

He pulled the Toyota right in behind the Torino. Karen studied the license plate, memorizing the number. Chip opened the door and stepped out. The Torino's engine roared, and Chip heard it slammed into gear. Spinning and squealing tires fired gravel and dust into Chip's astonished face. They pinged off the finish of his Toyota.

"Hey, you bastard!" Chip screamed, covering his face against the barrage of projectiles.

The car, its tires still screaming, vanished around the corner. Karen jumped from the car. "I told you," she cried.

The gravels had peppered Chip's face. One jagged rock had produced a small nick on his chin from which a small drop of blood had appeared. Gritty dust burned his eyes. "The bastard's crazy, whoever he is. Did you see that?"

Karen hadn't even thought about the possible injury to Chip until she saw, glistening in the lights of his Toyota, the blood on his chin. "Oh! Are you okay?" Karen wiped away the blood with her finger, lovingly caressing his skin in the process.

"Son of a bitch," Chip grumbled.

Karen tapped her forehead. "I got his license number. Let's find out who the bastard is."

Inside her apartment, she dialed the number of the Sheriff's department. After she identified herself, the dispatcher promptly punched the number into the teletype. Moments later, he announced, "Got it."

Karen had a pencil and some paper ready to jot down the information.

"It's registered to a Maurice Austin, Rt. 4, Box 295-AA, Wharton, WV. It should be displayed upon a 1973 Ford Torino two-door. I also checked NCIC, and he's got no wants or warrants."

Karen thanked the dispatcher and handed the paper to Chip as she hung up the phone. "The name doesn't mean a thing to me," she said.

"Maybe he's just an admirer," Chip suggested.

Karen associated the vehicle with Virgil Sampson. She didn't care who it was registered to. Sampson had something to do with it. The suspicion made the goose bumps appear once again. Chip enfolded her in his arms; it was their first true embrace. More from habit than anything else, Karen started to pull away just as she had that night at the Black Stallion. She caught herself and made up for it by pressing her body tightly against his. And she kissed him. Together they slipped down to the couch.

"I'm falling in love," Chip whispered.

Karen brushed her fingers across the small wound on his face. "If we were smart, we'd drop this whole thing before it gets out of hand."

He kissed her this time. His hands danced across her breasts; his fingers paused over her nipples, taut with desire, which pressed against the thin cotton of the blouse she wore. "I want you," he said.

She snuggled against him, so very comfortable beneath his weight. "I thought you said you were shy."

"I am."

His lips dropped to her neck. His teeth teased the soft, warm skin. He followed the path of open flesh to her chest where he awkwardly tried to undo the top button. At that point, Karen eased away from his touch, her face now clouded with some unspoken worry. "We'd better think about this, Chip."

He sat up. "What do you mean?"

83

Karen straightened her mussed hair and also sat up. "You and I both spent a long time becoming lawyers. Our relationship will affect our careers. How can we do this and be . . . be adversaries in a courtroom? It frightens me."

Chip lowered his head. "You're worrying about Nelson."

"I am not . . . not like you mean."

"I don't understand, Karen. I honestly don't." Chip rose to his feet and walked over to the living room window where he parted the curtains and peered outside . . . just in case.

No Torino.

He turned back to Karen. "I'm not just wanting to hop your bones. I feel something for you. The sex can wait, but I get the impression that your doubts go beyond the sex."

"I feel something for you, too. And you're right. I'm not sure that 'doubt' is the right word. Let's just say I'm concerned."

"You care for me; I care for you. It's simple."

That made Karen laugh a little, not viciously or satirically, and she said, "Since when was anything ever simple." She fell against him and put her arm around his neck.

# TWO

Virgil Sampson entered the beer joint where he was to meet Maury Austin to return the car. He found Austin drunk, almost unconscious, with his head laying on the long bar. Sampson lifted his head from the counter.

"They got Mickie," Maury Austin moaned.

Virgil wasn't certain he understood the muted, slurred words. "What'd you say?"

"Mickie! They got 'im."

Virgil gaped. "Who got 'im?"

"De law."

Virgil, his face colorless, plopped on the stool beside Austin. "What for?"

Austin managed to shake his head. "Don't know. His momma, she called . . . called fer ya. You s'posed to call her."

Virgil slammed his hand on the bar. The beer joint's owner—a wizened old woman with no posture or teeth—rushed over to the disturbance. "None of that, Virgil. I won't have that in my place."

"Fuck you!" shouted Virgil.

"You get outa my place, Virgil Sampson! Go on . . . you get!"

Again Virgil pounded the bar, this time with such force that the bottles sitting beneath it rattled—hard enough, Maury Austin thought, in spite of his alcoholic haze, to crush every bone in Virgil's grimy hand.

"You don't give me no orders!" Virgil snarled at the pitiful little woman. A veteran of such confrontations, the woman bristled, her yellowish-gray face flushing deep with anger. "I'm gonna call the law."

Virgil was over the bar in an instant, reaching the pay

phone on the wall before the old woman could even move.
"I need this," he said. His voice possessed such cold menace that the old woman backed away. She had known more
than her share of degenerate men . . . married three of
them, in fact. She'd taken beatings before, but she avoided
them whenever possible.

Virgil lifted the receiver and withdrew a dime from his
pocket. He jammed it into the coin slot. "What's the number at the Sheriff's department?"

The old woman, taken aback that Virgil Sampson was
calling the cops, reeled it right off. She knew it by heart.

"You all got Mickie Sampson in jail," Virgil demanded
of the sleepy voice that answered the phone.

"Nope."

"I hear otherwise."

"What's it to ya, anyway?" cracked the dispatcher, who
knew a smartass when he heard one. "Who is this?"

"I got a right to know if you're holdin' Mickie Sampson.
This here's Maury Austin, a friend of the family."

The dispatcher was silent for a moment. "Give me your
name again," he then said.

"Maury Austin, goddammit."

"I see," the dispatcher said. Virgil could hear papers
shuffling on the other end of the line. And Maury Austin,
the real Maury Austin swaying on the barstool, buried his
head in his hands, muttering slurred curse words.

"The Sampson kid's not here," the dispatcher said.
"He's being held at the juvenile detention center."

"What's his bail?"

"None set. Won't be until he goes before Circuit Court
on Monday morning."

"Hey, you cain't hold nobody without bail," Virgil cried.

"You a lawyer, Mr. Austin?"

"Look, copper. I know more'n you know, and—"

The dispatcher grew weary. "Look, buddy. Why don't
you just come down here to the jail and tell me what you
know."

"Fuck ya mother!" Virgil said, then slammed down the
phone.

"Damnation, Virg!" Austin whimpered. "You talked
shit to 'em, and you used my name."

"Nothin' they can do," Virgil said.

"Then why'n the hell didn't you use your name?"

Virgil, by then beside Austin, latched onto the back of Maury's long hair and gave it a vicious tug. Maury, his balance impaired by drink, sprawled down on the dirty floor. "You don't like it," Virgil said, "then you do somethin' about it."

Karen sat on her sofa, Chip in the chair across from her. "I just need some time to think things over," Karen told him.

Chip wanted her. He ached to make love to her, but he said, "If you think it will help."

The phone rang. Karen, startled by the lateness of the call, glanced at a clock on the living room wall. It was nearly one a.m. "Who the devil—"

"Want me to get it?" Chip asked, since he was closest to the phone.

"I'd better." Karen answered the phone. Her voice was wary.

"You called in that license check a little earlier." Karen sighed her relief. It was the jail dispatcher.

"Yes. Yes, I did."

"Well, a few moments ago, the owner of that car—at least I think it was the owner—called in here."

Karen nodded, anticipating his words. "—to report his car stolen."

"No, ma'am. He was a real smart mouth. He called asking about the Sampson kid they arrested today."

The name startled her, just as it had startled Clarke Nelson earlier that day. "What Sampson kid?" she asked.

Chip, still sitting in the chair, tensed as he monitored the conversation.

"I thought you knew about it," the dispatcher told Karen. "They arrested Mickie Sampson. He's the one that tried to pass that check taken from that woman who got the cap popped on her last weekend."

"The cap popped on her?" Karen detested police lingo.

"Yeah. The woman who got shot."

"Gracie Mack," Karen said.

"Look," said the dispatcher. "Maybe I shouldn't have called. I just figured that you knew, you being an assistant prosecutor and all."

"No! No!" Karen said. "It's my case. I've been out of

87

town all day. You say you got this call from Maurice Austin."

"Well, he called himself Maury Austin, but I figure it's the same jerk."

"So what did he want?" Karen asked, growing impatient with the progress of the conversation.

"First, he wanted to know if the kid was in jail. Then he wanted to know about bail. He got right nasty when I told him that bail hadn't been set."

"Mickie Sampson?" Karen mused aloud. The name struck some nerve deep in her head, something beyond the fact that Virgil's last name was also Sampson. The associations were colliding in her brain . . . Gracie Mack, Mickie Sampson . . . Mickie Sampson, Virgil Sampson . . . Gracie Mack, Virgil Sampson. She couldn't create the proper flow chart for her thoughts. The Torino kept fouling things up, a Torino owned by an Austin man who had just called the jail about Mickie Sampson who had Gracie Mack's check.

"You there, Miss Kinder?"

"Uhh . . . yes! Thanks. Thanks for calling."

"No trouble. Just wanted to let you know."

Chip, who had been fidgeting, asked as soon as she hung up the phone, "What about Sampson?"

Karen didn't answer. Instead she hurried to the living room window and peered out into the dark night. She expected to see the blue Torino.

"Karen! Who was that? What's happening?"

Karen continued to gaze outside. Down the street, a night mist lightly fuzzed the street lamp. It cast a dull shroud over the shadowy landscape. Nothing moved, not even the leaves on the trees.

"Karen!"

"They arrested a kid by the name of Mickie Sampson today. He was the one who tried to cash that check taken from the residence of Gracie Mack."

"My client? He's not Mickie. He's—"

"No, not Virgil! This is a juvenile. Maybe he's not even related. I know that name from someplace."

"Is that all?"

"No, a person by the name of Maury Austin—get that . . . Maury Austin!—just phoned the jail about the Sampson kid. The dispatcher said he was a real jerk."

Chip, too, made the associations.

"Maybe you'd better leave," Karen told him.

"Maybe I better stay."

She marched on him. "Don't you see! What if Virgil Sampson had something to do with the Mack killing? He saw you and me together at the mall. Ever since then, I've been trailed by that damned blue car! It's owned by somebody very much concerned with the Sampson kid."

Chip threw up his hands. "Who says the kid in jail is even related to my client?"

"It's too much of a coincidence," Karen said.

"Stranger things have happened."

She walked away from him. "Just go, Chip. We'll talk about it later."

"What if I withdrew from the Sampson case?"

She wheeled. "Then another case would come along."

"So it's over. Is that it?"

"God, Chip! Don't push so damned hard. Just give me some time to think. Please, that's all I ask."

"I still plan to withdraw from the Sampson case," he said as he headed for the door.

Karen sighed. "Pinter won't let you."

After Chip had left, Karen wanted to cry. She was scared, and she didn't know of what. Her heart urged her to cry out after Chip, to call him back, but for so many years the desires of her heart had been suppressed by the demands of her intellect and ambition. Now her insides raged with a battle between the two . . . heart and mind. When she heard his car start, she released her tears.

# THREE

Even the wispiest of clouds abandoned Custer County on Sunday. A gentle but hot breeze kept the atmosphere barely alive. Chip, in his stuffy apartment, sweltered so that to escape it he spent the balance of the day driving about the countryside, refreshing his memory about his native county. He drove by the farmhouse in which his grandparents on his mother's side had lived—the farmhouse where he had spent most of his summers. During those hot summer days, he had worked the huge fields of tomatoes and corn with his grandfather and spent the dark nights listening to every creak of the huge house. There was no dark any blacker than country dark.

From there, he drove to the cemetery where his father was buried. He hadn't been to the grave since the funeral. Funny, he thought (feeling very guilty), it should have been the first place he visited when he returned a week ago. Standing over the grave, the sun thumping him with its heat, Chip said aloud, "I'm sorry." His dad would understand.

Back on the road, Chip noticed the heavy traffic. Hot though it was, many Custer Countians relished the heat. Coming out of a cold and damp spring, they would proclaim the day beautiful.

Not Chip.

His mood was storm-dark, his thoughts colored gunmetal gray by the towering thunderheads of his misfortune. He recognized his self-pity and damned it, thereby hoping to lessen it. The admission helped not in the slightest. It was love sickness. Chip knew the symptoms all too well. He parked awhile at the city swimming pool, listening to the jubilant cries of children, envying the oily, glistening bodies of lovers, wishing that he and Karen lay slick and thick among them.

. . . love sickness . . .

Chip agonized through an almost sleepless night, his body depressed by the heat and his mind obsessed by—

. . . love sickness . . .

Chip had no immunity to the disease at all. And having it once did not thereafter instill any immunity, at least not for him. He could see Karen's point, and that made it all the worse. He had worried at the question all day. Could he truly give Virgil Sampson a 100 percent defense if she were on the other side? Could he forget that Virgil Sampson—an evil man, according to all—seemed (from admittedly circumstantial evidence) to be harassing this woman for whom he cared so much? Which made him then question whether Virgil Sampson deserved a 100 percent defense? Chip, thereby, intuited the answer to his first question. Worse, it confirmed what Karen had been saying. He damned Virgil Sampson.

He failed to notice that the moonlight, earlier so silver and bright in the sky, gradually ceased to filter through his curtained windows. His mind was occupied by other matters. Nor could he notice that the temperature outside began to drop as a strong breeze gusted away the smothering heat. His apartment, with its three small windows, imprisoned the heat, guarding it from the surging storm winds.

Outside his apartment, while he fretted away the long dark hours, a frontal boundary, herding thick clouds, pushed in from the northwest. At the insidious moment the clouds swallowed the moon, Chip was pondering the thought of marriage. Together they could start a law firm . . . Roth and Roth, Attorneys At Law, partners in life.

For the first time in many hours, he laughed.

His mind probed other less ridiculous alternatives. Maybe Clarke Nelson needed another assistant? What if he pulled the same trick Nelson had pulled, satirizing the King? They'd probably tar and feather him for his efforts.

Just before dawn, as a northwest wind whipped the thin curtains on his bedroom window, Chip eased into a brief and troubled sleep. The sharp, catastrophic crack of a nearby lightning strike jerked him awake an hour or so later. As he drove to work, he noted that the weather had fallen in sync with his mood. The sky was thickly overcast, puffy gray, ready to unleash a deluge. Maybe an omen, he worried.

Two cars behind Chip's Toyota, Hemmings piloted his unmarked, personal cruiser toward the courthouse. He, too, had spent an unsettling Sunday, his own well-being haunted by an altogether different tribe of demons. He'd managed to finish setting out his tomatoes and had reserved the balance of the day to gnaw at the Sampson matter. It tortured him—having the kid in custody, yet unable to even talk to him. He hoped the Judge would appoint a "reasonable" lawyer, one who could see the benefits of co-operation.

Hemmings noticed the Toyota pull off into a lot just ahead of him. He didn't know Chip Roth, and of course he did not suspect the common concern which ruined both of their sabbaths. Hemmings drove by, on toward the courthouse, lost in thought over Gracie Mack and offended that the damned system cared so little for her plight.

As he entered the courthouse lot, the clouds relaxed. Dense rain cascaded upon Wharton. The gods of weather, it seemed, had been toying with Custer County for a week, creating dodges of towering clouds from the unnatural humidity, only then to taunt with brief showers, teasing gusts of cool wind and impotent rumblings of thunder. On this day, the gods reached down to flood the county, and Hemmings, now cussing the extremes of the weather as well as the extremes of the system, dashed for a door. Once inside, he shook like a hulking dog and headed straight for Nelson's office.

The prosecutor and Karen Kinder awaited his arrival. "You're soaked," Nelson said.

"Shit! It came down all at once."

"At least it waited until Monday," Nelson said, his ode underscored by a clap of thunder.

"You okay this morning?" Hemmings said to Karen.

Nelson answered for her. "She's not too well." Then the prosecutor told the investigator about the blue Torino, about the phone call to the jail, about Karen's confrontation at the mall, even about Chip Roth. As he spoke, Karen felt as much a part of the investigation as did Gracie Mack . . . well, almost.

"I'll bet you even money that Virgil Sampson pulled the trigger on the Mack woman," Nelson concluded.

"He scares me," Karen admitted, feeling very badly because she felt so woman-like.

"You'd better watch yourself," Hemmings cautioned.

She had expected something more. "Gee, thanks!"

"Let's go see who Pinter appoints to the kid," Nelson said.

"You shoulda let me talk to him yesterday," Hemmings replied. "I think we lost our chance."

Judge Roger Pinter stared down from the bench at Michael David Sampson. "Are the young man's parents to be present?"

Nelson rose from his chair at the counsel table. "Your Honor, he lives with his mother. His father apparently left the home many years ago. His mother was advised of this proceeding, and she advised, in turn, that she could not be present."

Pinter, feigning the wisdom of the ages, just shook his head. "Can your mother afford to hire an attorney, young man?" the Judge asked.

The boy dared not look up at the imposing figure of the Judge. He shook his head and mumbled, "No. I ain't sure she would if she could."

Pinter leaned back in his chair and scanned the courtroom. More than half a dozen attorneys waited to make motions to the Court, and each one tried to erect a shield of invisibility or in the alternative a subtle facial plea for mercy. One of those attorneys was Isaac Clausen, and upon him the Judge's eyes stopped.

"Mr. Clausen." Pinter's eyes sparkled. "This young man needs your assistance. With your experience—"

Clausen stood. "Your Honor, with all due respect, I believe I may have a valid conflict. Mr. Ethan Roth, the newest member of our firm, was recently appointed to represent a Sampson. Perhaps the Court would inquire if this young man is related to an adult defendant by the name of Virgil Sampson?"

Pinter lurched forward. "This is a forgery case. Mr. Roth was appointed to a murder case. I see no conflict . . . no conflict whatsoever."

Nelson moved quickly toward the bench. "Your Honor,

Mr. Clausen has a point." The prosecutor spoke across the bench in a low voice. "This case might very well involve Virgil Sampson, Judge. If that occurs, and mind you that we can't be certain, then the conflict would become unacceptable."

Pinter cast a suspicious glance at Nelson, but he knew of Nelson's enmity toward the King's firm. For that reason alone, Roger Pinter yielded the point. "Very well, Mr. Clausen. You dodged the bullet this time."

Clausen, having earned hard stares from the rest of the lawyer corps, sat back down. Pinter again surveyed the attorneys, and this time settled upon Frank Keeling, an attorney who had practiced law for a great many years, but who confined himself to real estate, wills, estates and divorces. Poor Frank Keeling scrupulously avoided criminal work . . . until that morning. "Mr. Keeling, please step forward."

Keeling, of average height with a bulging belly and a ruddy red face, rose to his feet. His face hinted at dismay. He ambled forward to stand beside his client.

Pinter looked over the top of the bench at Mickie Sampson. "Frankly, Mr. Keeling, I normally set bail in cases such as this. However, the juvenile statutes demand that I give some attention to the welfare of the child. I'm appalled that his mother cares so little as to not appear for this hearing. I'm going to take the matter of bail under advisement until a juvenile worker can investigate the young man's home circumstances."

Keeling nodded his understanding. Pinter then spoke to the boy himself. "Lad, do you understand all this?"

"I . . . I think so." Mickie kept his eyes to the floor.

"The man beside you is Frank Keeling. He's your lawyer. You must trust him and help him. And Mr. Keeling—"

"Yes, Your Honor."

"You, of course, know that you have a right to a probable cause hearing in magistrate court within seven days of the young man's arrest."

Frank Keeling hadn't handled a criminal case in two years. Never had he represented a juvenile charged with a felony. Nonetheless, he nodded his head. "I do, Your Honor, and I hereby request such a proceeding."

"So be it," Pinter said. "I hereby remand Michael Sampson to the custody of the Juvenile Detention facility pending a preliminary hearing."

Mickie, for the very first time, lifted his eyes to the Judge. Tear tracks streaked his face. "You mean I gotta go back to the jail?"

Keeling, putting aside for the moment the misfortunes of his own fate, placed a gentle hand on the boy's shoulder. " 'Fraid so, son. You'll be treated fine."

Nelson sidled over to Keeling. "Frank, I need to see you for a second."

While the prosecutor escorted Keeling into the conference rooms, Hemmings kept the deputy from leaving with Mickie. Nelson, closing the door to the room, said to Keeling, "We need to interview your client."

"I bet you do," Keeling countered. "Tell me, what's so special about this case? I'm a piss-poor criminal lawyer, but I've got a pretty fair sixth sense. It's warning me that I'm in a lot deeper than it seems."

Nelson peered out the window. The rain had let up a bit, but it still fell hard and steady. Below the window, streams of water washed down the street. "That check the boy tried to cash belonged to the woman who was murdered last weekend . . . the Mack woman. The kid might be involved."

Keeling rapped his fist on the scarred surface of the conference table. "Shit! That's outa my league. You should have told Pinter."

"You'd better get accustomed to the idea, Frank. You might well be defending that kid on a murder charge—as an adult, I might add."

"Not me!" retorted Keeling. "I'll just come straight out and tell the Court I'm not competent. It would be the gospel truth."

Nelson abandoned the window and sat down at the table. "What about it, Frank? Can we talk to your client?"

Keeling walked to the window, stayed only for an instant, then began to pace the small room. "Hell, Clarke. You're putting me in a bitch of a position. I don't know what to do."

No wonder the young man's name had seemed so familiar to Karen. Until she saw him in court that morning, she just couldn't put the name and face together. She had represented Mickie Sampson's mother in an action against the State. Mrs. Sampson had been denied unemployment benefits about a year ago, and she had come to Legal Aid for representation. It had been a drawn-out matter, which Karen had lost.

Mickie Sampson had accompanied his mother to Karen's office several times and had even been present for a hearing before an administrative law judge. The kid had made an impression on Karen. He had been mannerly, well-behaved, and, during the long hearing, he and Karen had spent time talking during an extended recess.

As she waited for Nelson and Keeling to finish their conference, Karen watched the boy surreptitiously. The Judge, for the moment, had retired to chambers. The boy, now handcuffed by the deputy, sat on a bench facing Karen. When Karen had first entered the courtroom, Mickie Sampson saw her, and Karen knew that he remembered her. Not once, though, had the boy looked at her. Karen, as hard as she tried, could not envision that . . . that child gunning down anyone. She even remembered their conversation. He'd told her that he wanted to work on cars when he finished high school, either that or join the Marines.

Typical boyhood dreams.

And not once throughout the Sampson case—the Virgil Sampson case—had she put together his name with the name of Mickie's mother—not until she saw him just a few minutes earlier. She wanted to go to him, talk to him, find out why in the hell—

But she was a prosecutor . . .

Nelson decided to try to soft-soap Frank Keeling. "If it's any help, Frank, I don't believe your client was the trigger man. He doesn't seem the type, and we just can't see him able to even use a weapon like the one that killed Gracie Mack. Now, I'm not making any promises right now, but it might be to his advantage to talk to us."

Frank had made up his mind. "Not right now, Clarke. Give me a little time to think about it."

Nelson popped his knuckles. "And while you're thinking about it, we have some cold-blooded monster prowling the streets."

Frank Keeling just smiled. "Don't pull that shit on me, Clarke. I've got to cover myself. I'll get back to you today."

* * *

Karen read the disappointment on Nelson's face as he and Keeling exited the rooms behind the bench. "Take him back," Nelson snarled to the deputy as he walked by.

Hemmings cursed under his breath.

The deputy led Mickie right in front of Karen. The boy's head was locked down and away.

"Hi, Mickie," Karen said.

The boy stopped, his face still turned away. "Hi, Miss Kinder."

The deputy, too, paused, waiting to see if he was to take the boy away. Nelson motioned for him to go ahead, and he nudged the boy toward the door. When Mickie Sampson reached it, he made a half-turn to look back at Karen, who smiled at him.

"You know him?" Nelson asked.

"I represented his mother when I was at Legal Aid. He impressed me then as polite and rather serious. He's not a killer, Clarke."

"If not," Hemmings said, "then I bet he's an accomplice. I guess the lawyer won't let us question him?"

"Shit!" Nelson said. "I was worried that Pinter would appoint some lawyer who would be too smart to let us interview the kid. Instead, he appointed one that's so damned dumb he's afraid to let us see his client. He's gonna let me know today, which means that he's gonna call some other lawyer for advice."

"Which doesn't make him as dumb as you say," Karen chided.

The three of them left the courtroom and walked back to the prosecutor's office. "Listen," Nelson said as they walked, "if Panzini and your boyfriend move to postpone the case on Virgil Sampson, we're gonna fight it tooth and nail."

"My boyfriend?" Karen snapped.

Hemmings sidetracked the confrontation by asking, "Why don't you let me pick up Virgil Sampson for questioning?"

The three of them settled down in Nelson's office. "No friggin' way," declared Nelson. "We got nothing on him."

"Maybe it would stop him from harassing Karen," Hemmings suggested. "I could at least warn him away."

"I don't think Karen's in any real danger," Nelson said, adding, ". . . if she's careful."

Karen, still smarting from the quip about her "boyfriend," said, "Just how am I supposed to be careful? Do I go in hiding or something? Am I supposed to make my life uncomfortable until we lock up that creep?"

Nelson smiled. "Where's that devout liberalism, Karen? You wouldn't want us to pick up Sampson for something he hasn't even done yet, would you? Hell, according to Hemmings here, you crawled his frame for tossing some wino in the can for the night."

"I'm just—" She stopped herself before she said "scared." ". . . forget it."

For the first time, Karen felt trapped by her ideology.

# FOUR

"This research needs to be completed today," Simon told Chip as he handed him a list of issues involved in the settlement of an estate. "The fellow died without a will, and it will be a bitch to settle."

Chip accepted the documents, thankful at least that it wasn't the King's laundry list. "I'll get on it right now."

Simon fished around on his desk for something. He finally lifted a small note from a corner of the desk pad. "And here's a message from Panzini. He wants you to meet him at his office at 11 a.m."

Puzzled, Chip accepted the note. "Did he call you?"

"He spoke with the receptionist. She gave the message to me."

Why had the receptionist delivered his phone messages to Simon King? The implication reaffirmed Chip's opinion of his position with the law firm. He struggled silently to control his resentment.

"A word of caution," Simon said, apparently oblivious to Chip's seething anger. "We can't have you frittering away time on this Sampson matter. I want to be apprised regularly of the time you commit to that case. Just put it in a memorandum."

The hell with you, Chip thought. "It's a murder case, Simon. It's going to take some time. I've got to protect myself and this firm from—"

"Let us worry about the firm, Chip. I've practiced law long enough to know you can provide that s.o.b. with a credible defense with a minimum of time and effort."

Chip started to argue, but he realized it was a vain gesture. "Is it okay if I meet with Mario today?"

"As long as that research is finished by today."

Chip finished half of the research well before 11 a.m., fuming all the while over his conference with Simon. Given his mood, he almost pranced into Simon's office to tell him to shove the job. Prudence—or perhaps simple fear—forestalled his resignation.

The rain had lessened to a drizzle by late morning, so Chip, protected by an umbrella, walked to Panzini's office. Chip wanted the time to think, to clear his head. As dissatisfied as he was over his job, even that was overshadowed by the dilemma with Karen. He was within 100 feet or so of Panzini's office when the clouds unleashed another deluge. He dashed for the office door.

Sunshine awaited him inside. Panzini's secretary came from behind her desk to take his dripping umbrella and his sportscoat, which had been soaked in spite of the umbrella. "Just have a seat, Mr. Roth. Mr. Panzini's on the phone."

As she moved about the office, Chip seized the chance to admire her form. She had caught his attention on his previous visit, but on this day she looked so much better. She was almost—but not quite—pudgy. She boasted a mammoth pair of breasts which, when she sat back down, brushed her desk top. The proper word, Chip decided, was Rabelaisian, almost a caricature of the mistress-secretary. He thought of Dolly Parton in *Nine to Five.* Yet, she exuded an aura which denied one's primal assumption—that she was simply a sexual convenience or decoration for her employer. Already, she had spent enough time in the sun to own a dark tan, which—when combined with her dark brown hair and deep chocolate eyes—offered a breathtaking vision . . .

. . . darkly sensual . . .

"You have a lovely tan," Chip remarked.

"Thank you. I went to the beach for a week just before Memorial Day. The weather cooperated."

Chip suspected that she had a dark complexion anyway. In an ethnic sense, she bore a resemblance to Mario Panzini. "Are you related to Mr. Panzini?" Chip asked.

She laughed. "Everyone thinks that. We're both of Italian descent, but we're not related. My name's Vickie Carmichael."

"That's not Italian."

"Oh, my mother was Italian, born and bred. Daddy met her when he was in the service."

"And you're not married?"

"Not anymore."

The answer startled Chip. Never would he have imagined her as "once married." She didn't have that married look . . . that wifely look.

"Are you?" she asked, her dark eyes gleaming.

"Never."

He thought of Karen, feeling guilty for flirting. Worse, he was comparing this woman to Karen. A great gap separated their personalities. Karen exuded a classy kind of reserve, a coolness which—Chip suspected (perhaps hoped) —camouflaged a heated passion. Vickie, quite the contrary, radiated the innocent but burgeoning sensuality of a love child, thus the surprise that she was a divorcee.

What have I got to lose, Chip thought. "How about dinner tonight? Maybe we can go to the movies if there's anything worth seeing."

Her long-lashed eyelids fluttered at him as she pondered his proposal. Just as she seemed ready to answer, Mario Panzini exited his office. "Mornin', Chip. Glad you could make it."

Chip and Vickie exchanged looks, a gesture not lost upon Panzini. "I was telling Vickie here that you're just about the most eligible young bachelor in town, at least in legal circles. Wasn't I, Vickie?"

Vickie blushed through her tan. "Mr. Panzini!"

"I give you fair warning, Chip," said Panzini. "She's a good secretary, and I don't want her getting married and leaving me."

Chip thought Panzini was joking, but he wasn't certain. He saw no humor on Panzini's face. And Vickie's pinkish hue had turned red. "Mr. Panzini! You oughta know better'n anyone else that I'm not anxious to marry again."

Finally Panzini grinned. "Come on back, Chip."

This time Chip was spared the trip down the formal hall and was led instead through the door in Vickie's office. "She's a good girl," Panzini said, taking his seat behind the desk and motioning for Chip to sit. "She married a drunken sadist when she was 17 . . . a real lowlife turd. He whipped up on her about once a week. She came to me for a divorce. About that same time I needed a good secretary. She couldn't type 'shit,' but I sent her to school at

101

night and struggled along with her. She ain't turned out bad. Her momma comes from Italy."

"I asked her if she was related to you," Chip said.

"Whatsa matter, Chip? All us dagos look alike?"

"Oh, no! I didn't mean—"

Belly laughing, Panzini waved off Chip's concern. "Forget it. I'm proud to be Italian. Just don't mess over my girl out there."

The warning, coming in the middle of the laughing, caught Chip unaware. "Sir?"

"Don't hurt her," Panzini said, the good humor gone.

Chip didn't quite know what to say. "Look, we're not getting married or anything. I did ask her out, and she didn't have a chance to answer before you came out. Besides, she told you she isn't interested in marriage."

"Bullshit!" Panzini said. "The poor thing's lonely as hell. She'll marry the first bastard who asks her—at least the first one with a little promise, like yourself."

"But he's got to ask you for her hand first," Chip quipped.

Panzini eyed Chip for a few long, silent moments. Then he started chuckling again. "I like you, Chip. I ain't asking what your intentions are. You're a healthy kid; so was I many years ago. I know what your intentions are, and I can't blame you. She's a good-lookin' little thing. Just don't mistreat her. Not that I think you would, mind you, but I don't know you too well. And I can tell she's rather taken with you."

"Let's discuss the Sampson case."

"Now don't get steamed, kid. I like you. Like I said, I'm just concerned."

Chip felt like a farmhand asking the cattle baron father for his daughter's hand. But he wasn't asking for her hand. He doubted the wisdom of seeing the girl at all . . .

. . . but she's so damned sexy . . .

And she hadn't even said "yes" yet.

Panzini flipped open the Sampson file. "I've looked over Stringfellow's work. We got no defense at all. None whatsoever. Sampson claims it was self-defense. The rest of the world, including the half-dozen eyewitnesses, call it murder. There's only one legal issue in the case—will we get first degree or second degree? If the bastard walks away with anything less than a life sentence, we'll have done

102

him a big favor. Just between you and me, Chip, they oughta send him up for the rest of eternity. I gotta walk these streets, and I'd rather not have that scum walkin' behind me."

Thinking of Karen, Chip silently agreed.

Panzini lit a cigarette and started to offer one to Chip, then said, "I forgot. You don't smoke. I got a call from our client this morning. That's why I called you. He wants this case put off as long as possible."

"I'm not surprised," Chip said.

"There's more. He's not at all happy with you, kid. He says you're playing footsie with the prosecutor's office."

Chip catapulted from the chair. "That bastard. Karen Kinder and I had dinner together at the mall last week, and he saw us together. He made some obscene gesture at her."

"Sit down, kid."

"I'd rather stand."

"Whatever," Panzini shrugged. "I told you Sampson's a royal pain in the ass. By him seeing you and that female prosecutor together, he's already got the start of a case against us for ineffective assistance of counsel."

"Why, for God's sake? For all he knew we were just talking business."

"Were you?"

"Of course not!"

"If you ever get called to a witness stand, are you gonna lie and say it was a business meeting?"

"Absolutely not!"

Panzini flipped a long ash off his cigarette. "So you've compromised us already."

Chip resumed his seat and leaned toward Panzini's desk, oblivious to the curling plumes of smoke which floated into his face. "I'd be more than happy to withdraw."

Panzini chuckled. "Kid, it don't make a popcorn fart to me. Pinter, though, ain't gonna allow you to withdraw. Now he might file an ethics complaint. He'd love to embarrass the King."

"He's small-minded," Chip snapped.

Panzini flicked the still smoking cigarette into an overflowing ashtray. "He's the Judge, kid; he's entitled."

Virgil, sitting on a wet bench in a small park across from the courthouse, stared at the barred windows on the basement floor. He had come to see if Karen Kinder went out for lunch. Instead, he'd found himself entranced by the bars of the Custer County lockup.

The way Virgil figured, he had a good chance to walk away from the beer joint killing. He had a trick up his sleeve called Maury Austin. Maury had a fairly clean record—just a couple of busts for being drunk. Austin had been there that night, but he hadn't seen anything. Virgil planned to correct Maury's memory. Virgil was going to tell Maury what he saw, and then Maury was going to testify.

Or Virgil could run. The arrest of the kid made that alternative all too plausible. If the kid talked, then Virgil faced a second murder rap and might very well get slapped with a bail he couldn't post . . . which would mean then that he couldn't run.

The kid was the key. Virgil, for the moment not thinking about Karen Kinder, considered instead how he could get to the kid. Life was getting too complicated for Virgil. As the old song went, Virgil had mountains to climb.

# FIVE

Art Louck heard the muffled sobs coming from the small room which housed Mickie Sampson. It wasn't uncommon. A lot of kids cried when they were placed in the detention center. Louck, a social worker for the center, understood the tears. The sound made by the lock when it clicked shut transformed many a case-hardened delinquent into a teary-eyed, snotty-nosed kid. And the Sampson kid hadn't seemed all that case-hardened. Louck had interviewed Mickie when he was first committed, a routine designed to detect evidence of violent personalities, self-destructive personalities, and kids who were addicted to drugs and/or alcohol.

Louck unlocked the door and peeked inside. "You doing okay, Mickie?"

"I don't wanna spend the rest of my life in here," Mickie said through his tears.

That forced Louck to suppress a smile. The kid was just charged with attempting to pass a forged check, which—with his age and lack of a criminal record—would probably warrant minimally supervised probation. "I doubt you're ready for the big house just yet."

The worker sat down beside Mickie on the narrow bed. The kid was small for his age, but intellectually well developed. He lacked education, of course, but he had smarts, a quality which only rarely found its way into the detention center. "You feel as bad now as you ever will. Things will only get better if you do what's right."

"You just don't know," Mickie said, the words gurgling out.

"I shouldn't really say this, but I don't think you'll stay here for very long, not for what you did." Louck had a

105

policy. He assumed that every kid coming into the center was just as guilty as the petition said he was. If a few of them did suffer from the proverbial bum rap, then they too would probably benefit some from the counseling. Louck wasn't bound by the presumptive constraints of the judicial system. "When you do get out, remember how badly you felt in here. Maybe you won't ever be back again."

"I bet I never get out of here," Mickie said.

"Ah, come on. You need to keep things in the proper perspective."

Mickie gazed up at Louck. "Tell me something. Will they—" The boy halted in mid-sentence.

"Will they what?"

"If I was with somebody," Mickie said, his words issuing forth with a pained and wretched slackness of pace, "who did something real bad . . . just about the worst thing a person can do, would they get me for just being with him . . . even if I honest-to-God didn't know that was what he was gonna do?"

Louck tensed. "What are you talking about? I don't understand."

Again the boy began to cry, this time with such uncontrolled fury that Louck took him in his arms.

Nelson, Hemmings, and Karen were rehashing the Mack case when a secretary, via the intercom, told Nelson that Frank Keeling wanted to talk to him. Nelson didn't answer at once. "I'm taking bets he won't let us talk to the kid."

"I'm with you," Hemmings said.

Karen made it unanimous.

Nelson pushed the button and answered the phone. "What took you so long to get back, Frank?"

"Research," Keeling said.

"I hope you discovered that it's to your client's advantage to cooperate."

"No can do," Keeling said.

Nelson nodded knowingly. "You're not doing that kid any favors, Frank."

"Maybe, but for right now he's off limits. Get it?"

Nelson got it all right, and his voice assumed a sharp edge. "Damn it, Frank! Don't you see—"

"The decision's final."

"Who did you call for your research?" Nelson snapped—and was at once sorry for his words. He heard the hissing intake of air on the other end of the line.

"Look, Nelson. I don't—"

"Christ, Frank! I know you don't practice much criminal law, and I didn't mean to throw insults. Just get a second opinion. Hell, maybe even a third—"

The phone clicked in Nelson's ear. He stared at the now useless instrument. "The bastard hung up on me."

Karen giggled. "I don't blame him."

Louck made the boy look up at him. Art Louck recognized pure panic in the wet, swollen eyes.

"I didn't kill her!" Mickie wailed. "I didn't know he was gonna kill her. I swear to God I didn't."

Louck's bearded face paled. His knees trembled. With stuttering trepidation, he asked, "Ki . . . kill who?"

The words spoken, the confession issued, Mickie managed to control his crying. He used his shirtsleeve to wipe the dampness from his cheeks and nose.

Louck wasn't certain he heard the boy right, not through the tears. "Tell me again, Mickie. What you just said."

"That old woman," Mickie said softly. "He killed her."

Louck was without words. He remembered reading about the murder of an old woman. He had skimmed the news story. He finally was able to ask, "You mean the woman on Locust Drive?"

Mickie nodded.

"Jesus!"

At the sound of his voice, the bitter feeling it betrayed, Mickie began to bawl again, and Louck didn't try to stop him. His own thoughts were preoccupied by his duty—whatever it was. He wasn't sure. The boy hadn't mentioned the other person's name. Perhaps he should find out.

He took a firm grip on the boy's arms. "Who killed her, Mickie?"

"My uncle."

"What's his name?"

"He'll kill me!" the boy cried. "Oh, God! He truly will!"

"They'll lock him up, Mickie. You'll be safe here."

Mickie violently shook his head. "He always gets out. Then he'll get me, no matter where I am."

"Not this time, Mickie. What's his name?"

Mickie knew he'd said too much already. It really didn't make any difference what he said now. "Virgil," he said, as if Louck should have known who Virgil was.

Hemmings, wanting so badly to talk to Mickie Sampson, accepted Keeling's answer less pleasantly than the two attorneys. "He's a good cop," Nelson said right after Hemmings had left, cursing and condemning a system which he felt stymied him at every turn.

"If you say so," Karen said.

"Stay in this job long enough, and you'll understand his feelings."

"No way."

"You'll see. Hemmings has broken some damn tough cases. He frets over cases. He can be soft as a baby's behind or tough as an alligator's hide. As much as he bitches about the system, he seldom botches a case. He's like a good musician. He knows how to ad lib a coverup for his errors."

"I know I'm too hard on cops," Karen admitted, "but why can't they just take the system as it is and live with it?"

"Like you're living with Virgil Sampson? It's the same thing, you know."

"I don't always like the system," Karen emphasized, "but I do accept it."

"Which system are we talking about?"

"The judicial system, of course."

"Which judicial system?"

"Okay," Karen sighed. "What's your point?"

"We've got as many different systems as we have judges. In this county, we have four courts—three magistrate courts and a circuit court. Each one interprets the same law a different way. What may be today's law is tomorrow's mistake. Neither the cops nor the judges will even know it until the copying machines do their jobs and the post office delivers us the latest rendition of the word from on high."

"The law adapts—" Karen started to say.

"Bullshit! It flip-flops. I've heard all that garbage about

a living, breathing constitution. It's pretty hard to swallow in the face of dead, unbreathing corpses like Gracie Mack. You saw her, Karen! By the time that case gets to court, no one will remember her as a person with feelings and hopes and a lot of her life to still live—no one but the cops who saw her and you . . . and, of course, the scum who killed her who, by then, will be blaming her—Gracie Mack!—for his predicament."

The intensity of Nelson's diatribe intimidated Karen a little. He was suddenly before a jury, lost to the bloodlust that came over him when he was after a verdict. Nelson caught himself. "Hell, Karen. I have a lot of respect for this so-called system, but I've seen a lot of evil walk scot-free from a courtroom. We just need to adjust the balance a little."

The intercom eased the tension. Nelson was informed that a juvenile detention center social worker wanted to speak to him. "Take a message," Nelson said.

The secretary said, "He insists."

Nelson cursed and jabbed at the flashing button on the phone. "Nelson here."

The male voice on the other end was agitated, short of breath. "Sir, this is Art Louck. I'm a social worker for the detention center."

"Slow down," Nelson commanded. "What's up?"

"That Sampson kid—you know who I mean?"

Nelson bolted upright, staring hard at Karen. "Of course."

"He just told me he was involved in the murder of that woman last weekend."

"He what?"

"He said he was there when the old woman was killed. He told me who actually did the murder."

Nelson, still staring at Karen, said, "Why were you questioning him?"

"I wasn't!" Louck retorted. He expected the prosecutor to be pleased and was offended by the somewhat accusatory tone. "He just blurted it out. It's eating at him."

"Who did he say killed her?"

"His uncle. A man named Virgil Sampson."

Nelson pounded the desk with his fist. "Bingo!"

* * *

Mickie, now alone in his cell, wondered how long he had to live. Not long, he figured.

But he felt good, better than he had since—

Her face again invaded his mind. This time, though, it was a whole face, a smiling face. That nightmare at least was gone. Others awaited him in the darkest hours of the nights to come.


"We can charge him!" exclaimed Karen upon hearing the news.

"Whoa! Not so fast. Let's think about it."

Karen couldn't believe her boss. He had just been handed Virgil Sampson to do with as he wished. "Think about it! That scum killed that woman. What's to think about?"

Nelson stunned her once more. He laughed. The cold-blooded bastard laughed! Karen trembled with indignation. "How can you—"

"Listen to yourself, Karen! Now you sound like a cop. 'Arrest him!' you cry. 'Arrest! Arrest!' Well," Nelson smiled. "The hell with the arrest. I want to convict him."

Karen didn't understand. "So what do we do?"

"Analyze the situation. We have a statement by a juvenile to a social worker assigned to the detention center. The juvenile incriminates himself and a second party. Now, what have we really got? Let's go one step at a time. First the juvenile . . ."

"I don't see a problem."

Nelson sighed. "You're assuming that the social worker won't be viewed by the law as a cop. Should he have advised the kid of his rights?"

"If it was a spontaneous exclamation, then it doesn't matter. The statement's admissible."

"In other words, you do think it might be possible that this social worker, working at a place which restricts freedom, might be just as hamstrung as a cop?"

Karen's confusion heightened. "But they aren't policemen! They don't have to advise defendants of their rights."

"I bet I could find a few cases in other jurisdictions that to one degree or another contradict that theory."

His point was slowly becoming clear to her. "Let's just argue that it was a spontaneous statement. That eliminates the issues of whether a social worker in that context is a cop."

"Okay, let's just do that for a moment," Nelson said. "Then where do we stand as it relates to Virgil Sampson? Will that oral admission be admitted against Virgil Sampson in the preliminary hearing?"

"It's enough to charge him," Karen said.

"The preliminary! Will we survive a preliminary hearing?"

"On the kid, yes."

"But," Nelson snapped, "not on Virgil Sampson—not unless the kid actually takes the stand and submits to cross examination. As it relates to Virgil Sampson, it's inadmissible hearsay, therefore useless to us in court."

"If we get a warrant for Virgil and arrest him," Karen suggested, "then maybe he'll talk."

Nelson cast up his hands. "Now that's really thinking like a cop. Arrest him without sufficient probable cause in the hopes it'll scare him into confessing. Virgil Sampson doesn't scare very easily."

Karen dropped her head. "You're right, damn it! Okay, how do we proceed?"

Nelson reclined in his chair. "Hemmings takes a written statement from the social worker. Based upon that, we secure an arrest warrant for the kid. Maybe we can wrangle a search warrant for the kid's home from someone. Maybe we'll luck up and find physical evidence to implicate his uncle. We call up Frank Keeling and scare the hell outa him. I'm not ruling out the chance that we can get that kid on the stand against Virgil Sampson as early as the preliminary hearing."

# SIX

Frank Keeling didn't enjoy being a lawyer. He didn't enjoy being a husband nor, for that matter, a father. He was a deacon in the Wharton Methodist Church. He detested the sham every Sunday morning. Sex and food and movies bestowed upon him no pleasure. His sprawling component stereo system was seldom played—by him. His son, obnoxious punk that he was, used it to play, quite appropriately, "punk rock" when Frank wasn't home. His daughter—who had married a crude beer truck driver just in time—was about to make him a grandfather. For that, Frank held out some hope. Perhaps he might enjoy being a grandfather . . . all the pleasures of kids without the bother.

Frank Keeling, short and ruddy and very bald, truly enjoyed just one thing. He loved bourbon . . . Ancient Ancient Age, in fact. He'd drunk plain old Ancient Age for a long time, up until its initials (AA) staring at him from the bottle reminded him of those damned meetings his wife had briefly insisted that he attend. He mixed his Triple A in a 1:1 ratio with water, using an empty bottle. He kept one such bottle of the special stock in the refrigerator at home and a second in the smaller fridge in his office.

When Frank didn't come to his office drunk, he came in reeking of the previous night's drink. Several times he'd struggled into court drunk, a circumstance not lost upon Judge Pinter. The Judge had ignored his transgression. Pinter could have done little else. He had assumed the bench several times in no better shape than Frank Keeling. Once they both had arrived in the courtroom drunk: The case was postponed.

Frank baffled the gurus of Alcoholics Anonymous. Martha Keeling made him attend the meetings for a short time. He admitted that he was an alcoholic, a drunk—seemed in fact, in his own low-key fashion, to relish and advertise his affliction. Frank didn't consider his condition a disease. To him, he drank out of personal choice. It was—the Wharton Methodist Church notwithstanding—his religion. He admitted that he couldn't turn his back on the bottle any more easily than a Baptist could disavow his God.

Frank Keeling didn't appreciate the world through sober eyes. Since the world didn't seem on the verge of any great change, he saw no incentive to drop the booze. The Keelings' firstborn had died at the innocent age of six—a victim of spinal meningitis. Frank had drunk himself comatose. From that time on, more than 20 years, he altered bitter reality with the demon spirit.

A pity and a waste, people lamented—for Frank was a good man who attended church, sometimes hung over but never drunk. He didn't abuse his wife or his children. He didn't mess around. He just drank a lot of Triple A.

Never did he pass out. Never did he become sick.

He practiced the simplest forms of law he could. He avoided controversy and complexity. He traded a good chunk of his earning potential for his peace of mind. The choice was a conscious one. In spite of his lack of ambition, he lived well.

Thus, when the Honorable Roger Pinter assigned him a juvenile case, Frank probed the past few months, trying to think of something he had done to offend the Judge. After all, they were bottle buddies. It left Frank to wonder.

From his front office came the staccato music of the IBM typewriter. Frank listened to its rhythmic song as he poured himself an afternoon bracer. Just as he took the first sip, he heard the phone ring. Something—intuition, maybe just the all-day anxiety—prompted him to grab a long and deep second sip. His secretary buzzed him. It was Clarke Nelson.

"You sitting down, Frank?" Nelson said.

"Cut the crappola, Clarke."

"Your boy just confessed to murder."

Chip searched the aging storefronts for the laundry, the name and address of which he had written down on a small slip of paper. He was on the right side of the street, but somehow the place eluded him. Exasperated and almost frantic, he checked his watch. The afternoon was running away. He still had to complete the research Simon had asked him to do.

And he had a 6:30 dinner date with Vickie Carmichael . . . if he could find the fucking laundry!

Finally, after several trips up and down the street, he saw it—or at least its entrance. The laundry was on the second floor above an old hardware store. The doorway, with its name, was offset deep in the shadows. Upstairs, amid the cloying odors of cleaning fluids, Chip found an old man, withered and bored, perusing a copy of *Hustler*. "I'm here to pick up Arthur King's laundry," Chip said, wishing that he didn't look so much like another lawyer. It was humiliating.

"Oh, yes!" The King's name doused the old man's voyeuristic interest in the magazine and sent him hobbling to a shelf bearing a small batch of cleaned shirts. He sorted through them for what seemed an eternity, handling each one of them carefully and several times as he looked for the King's name. Chip shifted his weight from foot to foot. He looked at his watch several times. "I'm kinda in a hurry," he finally said.

"I ain't makin' you stay," the old man said. "And I sure as shit can't give you them shirts until I find them, now can I?"

Chip sighed. About three minutes later, the old man lifted a packet of cleaned shirts from the shelf. "Here they are! Bet I picked 'em up five times. Been a snake they'd bit me," he said, still holding the shirts, wanting to say something and knowing that Chip had to listen until he got his hands on the shirts.

"The King's one of the few folks in town what still has his shirts dry cleaned. Yes, sir! An old-fashioned gentleman. You kin tell Mr. King we didn't put quite as much starch in 'em this trip, just like he asked."

Chip reached out for the shirts. "I'll tell him."

"You be sure." The old man kept the shirts in custody.

Chip's temper slipped. "Give me the shirts and put it on Mr. King's tab. I've told you I'm in a hurry!"

Chip was tossed the shirts, and he turned and almost ran from the laundry. The old man shouted something after him, but Chip didn't catch it—which was probably just as well.

Frank Keeling spilled the glass of diluted bourbon on his desk. The amber fluid doused divorce papers and letters certifying clear titles to various property transactions. "Damn you!" Keeling cried, ignoring the spilled bourbon. "You questioned him without—"

"Hold on, Frank! It's what we in the business of criminal law call a 'spontaneous exclamation,' not to mention a 'declaration against interest.' Do those words ring any rusty bells, Frank?"

"Screw you! I never claimed to be a criminal lawyer. To whom did my client make this spontaneous statement?"

"A social worker at the detention center."

"Sounds awful shaky to me. I think even a half-ass criminal lawyer like me can get that tossed out."

Nelson snickered. "You'll get your chance to try, Frank. Your boy's gonna be charged with first degree murder."

"How did you get that social worker to drag it out of him?"

"Easy, Frank," Nelson said. "I'm still willing to talk a deal, but you just may say something to queer even that."

Frank paused, then said, "On a murder charge? What kind of deal do you have in mind?"

Nelson cleared his throat. "The kid says someone else pulled the trigger on the woman, that he just went along for the ride. Between you and me, counselor, I tend to believe the kid. He says his uncle—a piece of pond scum called Virgil Sampson—shot the old woman. But he was in that house with Virgil Sampson, and they both went in with intent to commit a felony. Under the felony murder rule—"

"You're not over my head yet," Keeling said. "What's the deal?"

"I want the uncle. He comes up on another murder charge very soon. I'd be willing to discuss something less than first degree if your client will give us a written statement and agree to testify against Sampson at a preliminary hearing."

"You must think I'm crazy, Clarke."

"Take it or leave it."

"The hell with you!" Keeling said, injecting into his

voice as much indignation as he could. "I'm no Perry Mason, but I'm not about to let my client testify at this stage. No way!"

"The deal might not come around again."

"The way I see it, you gotta have the kid."

"Maybe we'll come up with some physical evidence based upon the information the kid's already provided. Maybe the kid will say something else he shouldn't. We just might be able to nail them both without any deals."

Nelson had a point. Keeling had enough sense to know that in most cases he was obligated to tell his client of any deals. The client, then, made the decision. However, he doubted that that would apply to a juvenile. Keeling mulled over the offer, then decided to make a counterproposal. "You need this kid so bad, Clarke, I'll recommend that he help you if you agree to try him as a juvenile, not an adult."

It was Nelson's turn to grow incensed. "Christ! If we did that, this kid wouldn't pull two years. We're talking about an armed robbery and a felony murder."

"I thought we were talking about nailing this kid's uncle," countered Keeling, who now tried to stop the bourbon from spreading over any more of the documents on the desk.

"See you in court," Nelson said.

The phone clicked in Keeling's ear.

Not bad, he thought. He felt like a lawyer. He also felt the chilly bourbon dripping on his lap. He buzzed his secretary, told her to bring some paper towels into his office, then went to mix himself another bourbon.

# SEVEN

Vickie pressed her warm, ample thigh against Chip's. The sensual pressure of her body caused him to respond. Her hand casually rested upon his. The Black Stallion—Chip had settled for a known quality—was again dimly lit and not very busy, but still Chip glanced around to see if there were people he knew in the night spot. He saw no one who looked familiar or who even seemed to be paying him any mind.

They both sipped cocktails. "I bet Mario's a real case to work for," Chip said, a little surprised at his quick erection. Vickie wore a thin summery dress, cut low enough to display her bulging and deeply tanned cleavage. He wondered just how much of her body was tanned.

"He treats me like a father," she answered.

"I noticed."

Vickie smiled. "What did he say to you?"

"Never mind."

The waitress—the same one that had waited on Karen and Chip before—came for their dinner order. If she recognized Chip, she didn't show it.

"Tell me what he said," Vickie persisted after the orders were placed.

"He thought I might take advantage of you."

Vickie shook her head. "He makes me so mad sometimes."

"He's just worried about you."

"I can take care of myself," Vickie sniffed.

"How long have you been with him?"

"Five years. Boy! Does he do the business! I couldn't believe it."

"I bet."

The caress of her thigh intensified. She was one of those rare women whose presence augured sensual delight. Chip remembered a girl whom he had met in college. She had a reputation for screwing just about anyone who asked. Once, at a college dance, Chip had asked her to slow dance with him. Her body had melted against his. She, too, had caused him to become aroused from nothing more than the pressure of her body. She had known it, and she exploited it, pressing the top of her thigh right against his erection. Strangely, the gesture hadn't seemed lewd or trashy. Her sensuality had seemed natural. Her body had been so in tune with Chip's that for once in his life Chip felt as if he could dance, which of course he could not.

When the music had ended, Chip had thanked her. She had paused for a moment, as if she wanted to dance again, but the band had launched into something frenetic. Chip had shrugged, and the girl vanished into the thickly crowded dance floor. Chip hadn't pursued her. It was one of those moments that one regretted for the rest of one's life.

Truth be known, Chip always found sex something of a clumsy and uncomfortable experience. The sensations were pleasant enough, but the act always seemed to spring from pressure and tension. The vibrations which preceded it, at least in Chip's experience, detracted from its pleasure.

Vickie, though, possessed that same lusty quality which Chip had found so special in that girl in college. She didn't make Chip feel guilty or calculating because he wanted to make love to her. Vickie wasn't gorgeous, but she defined the word "femininity."

He tried not to think of her as a "cure." So what if he had thought of Karen only once or twice during dinner?

Karen worked late at the courthouse that evening. Nelson had instructed her to be certain they got the Sampson kid bound over to trial at his preliminary hearing. The State's evidence consisted solely of the boy's admission to social worker Art Louck, so Karen immersed herself in the rules of evidence regarding spontaneous exclamations and the possibility that the magistrate court might rule that Louck should have advised the kid of his rights (as ludicrous as that seemed to Karen).

By all rights and by any standard, the statement should

118

be admissible. Magistrate courts—the state's lowest judicial level—were presided over by lay judges who were often swayed by the most erroneous arguments of law. Therefore, Karen prepared for any kind of fluke.

The county law library was well stocked, and her research ventured beyond the case law of her own state. A western state's Supreme Court had held that, while a store security guard is not officially a cop, he was still bound to read an alleged shoplifter the Miranda warnings—"their rights"—before questioning them or taking any statement. No such precedent existed in West Virginia.

What about a social worker employed by the Department of Welfare and working in a custodial capacity at a juvenile lockup? Could Frank Keeling argue that the statement was inadmissible because the social worker had not advised the kid of his rights? As soon as the worker recognized that the kid was on the verge of making some incriminating statement, should the worker have stopped Mickie Sampson and advised him of Miranda? Even more to the point, even if Louck had done so, would the statement—if it were viewed as anything other than a spontaneous admission—be admissible since the kid's lawyer was not present?

To Karen, the questions were absurd. First, the statement was spontaneous—not prompted by anything Louck had done and, therefore, should be admissible for that reason alone. Besides, Art Louck probably didn't even know the standard Miranda warnings. She couldn't find the slightest evidence that Art Louck had any obligations to play cop. Nor could she find any case which stated specifically that a person in Louck's capacity was excluded from the requirement. The question just hadn't come up in any of the jurisdictions she researched.

Karen slammed a huge law book closed. Keeling might convince a magistrate court judge of anything, but it wouldn't be because Karen hadn't done her homework. If the case got tossed out, the kid could always be indicted anyway. It would be humiliating, but . . .

Karen photocopied some of the more relevant West Virginia case law and left the courthouse. The sun had just set. The cold front which had moved through that day left a slight chill in the summer night, a welcome relief from the heat of the past few days. As she drove home, Karen kept her window down, allowing the cool rush of air to toss her hair and refresh her. The bright glare of oncoming headlights made her squint. Traffic seemed heavy.

She dismissed from her mind weighty legal issues only to find her thoughts homing in on Chip. She wanted to call him. Karen didn't really think she owed him an apology . . . just a call. She wanted to see him . . . wanted to be with him. Perhaps if they were more experienced attorneys, they both could better separate their official duties from their private affections.

Things were growing emotionally complex. With Chip's client likely to be charged at some point with the murder of Gracie Mack, Clarke Nelson's warning assumed an even greater presence. The beer joint killing, even for Karen, possessed a distant, unattached quality. Not so with Gracie Mack. Karen cared personally about Gracie Mack, just like Nelson had said. She'd seen Virgil Sampson's handiwork in that case.

Karen didn't commit her heart quickly or without deep thought. She hadn't loved often. When she had, it had been passionately but consistently disastrous. Somehow, she always fell for the wrong guys. She had a penchant for malcontents, rebels entranced or perhaps obsessed by a variety of causes. Such men made lousy lovers, but their passion for justice stroked some chord in Karen.

Chip, on the other hand, seemed different. He seemed . . . well, moderate. Yet beneath the staid patina Karen divined an independence of spirit which she found enchanting.

Karen, having first checked for the blue Torino, pulled her car into the parking space in front of her apartment and got out. Crickets serenaded the starbright sky. The moon had not yet ascended (Karen didn't even know if it was supposed to), and the lights on her apartment house cast only an insufficient glow into the street and bushy thicket on the other side.

Karen fumbled for her keys. Just as she found the door key, something—a noise perhaps, maybe just some unheard vibration or sensation—prompted Karen to glance over her shoulder. She stared across the street into the black shapes which huddled in the thick foliage.

Her eyes zeroed in on a form . . . a—

Karen gasped. The dark silhouette of a man stood with

legs apart, arms folded across his chest, his featureless face directed toward Karen. He took the first step toward her.

"Oh, no!" she cried, feeling the fear balloon in her gut.

She dashed toward her left, away from her own apartment door, toward the door of a neighbor whom she knew only slightly. She pounded on his door, not daring to look back. An outside light flashed on, startling her. A young man—she knew that his name was John—opened the door. He wore a thin, silken robe, and his face reflected obvious displeasure at the intrusion. When he saw that it was Karen, his glare softened.

"What's wrong?" he said, looking over her shoulder. "You're trembling."

"There's a man behind me." Karen turned to point to—

He was gone!

A woman came to the door behind John . . . not his wife, Karen thought, feeling her own humiliation. John wasn't married. "What is it?" the woman asked of John.

John, ignoring the woman's question, stared beyond Karen and into the dimly lit street. "I can't see anyone."

"There was a man lurking in the shadows," Karen said, feeling terribly foolish. "He started toward me."

The look on the woman's face said it all.

"I'm sorry I bothered you," Karen said.

"Don't be silly," John said. "I'll walk you to your door."

The woman, her face not at all friendly, said, "Be careful, John." Her tone suggested that she wasn't as concerned about his personal safety as his fidelity.

Once she was safely inside her apartment, Karen collapsed into a chair. Her stomach was turning and twisting, and her knees quivered. Someone had been there, and Karen knew who it was. Still she shamed herself. She was an adult, an assistant prosecuting attorney. Yet she behaved like an hysterical woman. After a few moments, still uneasy in spite of her self-condemnation, Karen rose from the chair and went through her apartment turning on all the lights. Then she went to the telephone.

# EIGHT

It had been Vickie's idea to go to his apartment rather than to the movies. Chip had not minded at all. His apartment was cramped, but he'd had the presence of mind to straighten up a bit before he left . . . wishful thinking at the time. They had been at his place for an hour, and already Chip was lost in the mammoth pillows of her breasts. Her huge dark nipples held him in an oral trance, and she seemed quite content to permit him to nurse.

They had bantered back and forth throughout the evening. As God is wont to do sometimes, he had endowed Vickie Carmichael with the essence of physical sensuality and denied the added boon of a sharp wit. She carried on a fine conversation until a discussion became cerebral, at which point she possessed enough common sense to change the subject or simply to listen.

Chip had been seduced . . . and he loved it, for he bore no guilt. With Vickie, sex was a natural extension of a fun evening.

"That feels good," she purred, massaging his body with her own, whipping him into a tormented state of desire which allowed Chip only to moan his response.

And then the phone rang.

"Let it go," she said, pressing his face into her breast.

Chip hadn't heard it. "What?"

Only then did he hear it.

"Shit! I better answer it."

"Spoil sport."

"Relax a minute." He hurried to the phone. As he left, Vickie's fingers replaced his lips on the hard nubbens of her nipples. Chip reached the phone on the fifth ring.

"Chip! Thank God! I thought you weren't home."

God! It was Karen! She rushed back into his life with all the sudden fury of a flash flood.

"Karen! What's wrong?" He heard the edge in her voice.

"A man was waiting for me outside my apartment tonight. I know it was Virgil Sampson . . . I just know it."

Vickie stepped into the living room, her body still nude, and in the dim light Chip marveled at her statuesque beauty. Karen's presence on the other end of the line, however, doused his lust. "Maybe it was just a prowler?" he suggested.

"It was Sampson! You don't know what's happened. Your client killed Gracie Mack."

Chip felt her words more than he heard them. The joining of the two names . . . Gracie Mack and Virgil Sampson . . . stunned him for a moment. In fact, for an instant, Gracie Mack's name produced no associations. When his memory got into step, the implications stunned Chip, so much so that he said at once, "I'll be right over. Are you at home?"

"Hurry," Karen urged.

"Who's Karen?" Vickie demanded to know just as soon as Chip said "goodbye."

"A friend . . . someone's been prowling around her house. I need to go there."

What else was there to say? Chip, in a way, was being punished too, for his body still ached with need. Vickie's imposing unclothed presence did nothing to lessen his dilemma. She threw up her hands in frustration. Her magnificent breasts rose up with the gesture and settled in a series of jiggly, disconcerting bounces. In the light of the living room, they seemed even more succulent . . . two white globes surrounded by the bronze of her tanned chest.

"I'm sorry," Chip said, really meaning it. "If you want to wait—"

"Hell, no! I just hope you have time to drop me off at my house."

Karen sat down to wait . . . to a brief wait, she presumed. She knew not about Vickie; that Chip had to drive four miles out of town to take her home before he could come. She considered watching television, something she rarely did, but she vetoed the idea. Its sound would camouflage any noise from outside. Instead, she listened to the silence, at least for what passed itself off as silence this side of death. On this night, even the quiet sounds of life's background seemed loud to her. She heard the whirring of the building's air conditioning, and she wondered if it was always so loud. She heard distant street sounds—an infrequent horn, a loud exhaust, even the squeal of tires.

From a blue Torino?

"Don't be silly," she whispered.

She wanted to hear the sound of Chip's Toyota—that high, lawnmower-like putter so characteristic of foreign cars. The Torino sounded different, more like the throaty roar of a car souped up for dirt track racing.

And she watched . . . mostly the doorknob. What if it turned ever so slightly? Like in the movies? She'd scream, by God . . . just like in the movies!

Once she thought she heard the high-pitched cry of a woman's passion, perhaps from John's apartment next door. Never had Karen listened so intently, and she hadn't thought the walls of her apartment building quite so thin. The thought of John and his woman making love just on the other side of the wall for a moment detracted Karen from her fear. It was only a brief lull. A light scraping sound from just outside her front door snatched her back to her terrified reality.

Her stare locked onto the doorknob.

Vickie rebounded quickly. Her hand probed gently between Chip's legs as he turned into the short driveway leading up to the small cottage. As they parted, she kissed him, her tongue pushing deep into his mouth. "I hope I didn't seem too mean," she whispered into his ear. "I do understand."

"You're very kind," Chip said, his choice of words sounding a little stiff. He wondered what she understood.

"Maybe we can get together again?"

Chip should have taken her to her door, but the fear in Karen's voice had seemed too genuine. He said instead, "I'll call you. I promise."

Damn! Where is he?

Karen wanted to pace, but she dared not move. The mere prospect of her silhouette in the window might draw him to the door, she worried. She caught herself biting her nails, a habit she had broken in high school.

Outside, deep in the bushes across from Karen's apartment, the murky shadow of the man stood perverted guard. His eyes didn't leave the bright front window of Karen's apartment. Maybe she called the police. The prospect worried him not at all. He could slip away easily, using the heavy undergrowth as cover.

And what if he was caught near here?

He hadn't done a thing wrong . . . not tonight . . . not yet.

Karen heard the Toyota's engine. "Thank God!" she gasped as the small tires crunched into the parking space. She rushed to the door and opened it.

"He was over there," Karen said before Chip was even out of his car. Karen pointed into the thick foliage across the street.

"And you recognized him?" Chip asked, standing by his car and peering at the heavy shadows.

"No, but it was him!"

Chip led her into the apartment and sat down with her on the couch. "Did you call the cops?"

"What for? He hadn't done anything."

"You called me instead." It flattered Chip.

Karen, who had changed into a night robe, smelled the alcohol on Chip's breath. Worse, she smelled a heady perfume, a feminine odor which spoke of kept secrets. "You want a Coke?" she asked.

"That'll be fine," he answered.

As Karen poured the Coke, she thought of what Bette Midler's character had said in *The Rose*—that she could smell another woman a mile away. It was true. Karen smelled another woman, and she didn't even have the right to get mad.

"I hope I didn't intrude on your evening," she said when she returned to the living room with his soft drink.

Chip stiffened, wondering how she knew. She read the confusion on his face. "She uses a rather potent perfume," Karen explained.

Chip twisted in his chair. "I got the impression you didn't want to see me anymore."

125

Karen sat in a chair opposite him. Her robe gaped open to reveal the gentle swells of her breasts. "I didn't say that, Chip. I said I needed some time to think. However, I'm not mad or anything. I don't really think you and I are that far along yet."

Damn me, she thought.

"I didn't mean it that way, Chip. I apologize. Just don't tell me who you were with."

"What's this about Sampson? The new development."

"You'll have to swear you won't tell anyone."

Chip frowned. "I don't know. I do represent him."

"Not on the Mack case . . . not yet anyway."

"Okay. Tell me."

And she did, all of it, to which he said, "And Nelson and you are going to charge Sampson based upon an oral admission by this kid?"

"God, no! We'd never get by the preliminary hearing, not without the kid's testimony."

"But you believe the kid?"

Karen nodded. "Absolutely."

Karen caught him staring at the gap in her robe. "Are you listening?"

Chip blushed. "Of course."

"Please try to withdraw from the Sampson case," she said.

"Judge Pinter wouldn't permit it. You said that the other night."

Karen ran a frustrated hand through her thick blonde hair. "Tell him the truth," she said.

"I can't."

Karen stood up. "Why? Because you want to represent him?"

"It beats picking up laundry. I've done some thinking too, Karen. We can't solve our problem by withdrawing from this case. You know that . . . you knew it the other night. Would you withdraw from prosecuting the case?"

Karen stared at him, unable to believe him. "Are you kidding? You didn't see that woman! I want you, Chip, but I also want to prosecute this case. I want to lock that bastard away until his . . . his thing shrivels up and falls off. I'm not sure I can do both, either intellectually or emotionally. He scares me, Chip. He's trying to intimidate me, and it makes me mad because he can!"

126

Chip stood up and took her in his arms. They slipped down on the couch and for a while they forgot about Virgil Sampson.

Virgil toyed with the knife in his jeans pocket. When the punk lawyer pulled in, the woman had pointed at him, as if she could see him. Virgil knew she couldn't, but he hoped the punk lawyer would come looking. The kid hadn't. Instead he had gone into her apartment. Virgil gave him credit for a little smarts.

After about an hour, Virgil decided the lawyer wasn't going to come out.

So Virgil slipped from the cover and moved quickly across the street. He drew the knife and moved behind the little foreign car.

Two quick jabs, and the air hissed from the car's rear tires.

# NINE

First thing Tuesday morning Mickie Sampson again stood before Judge Pinter's towering bench, this time to be arraigned on a juvenile warrant charging him with the murder of Gracie Mack. Frank Keeling stood by the small boy as Pinter, his glasses perched low on his red pointed nose, read the charge. As in the case of all juvenile matters, the courtroom had been cleared of all persons whose presence was not germane to the proceeding.

Karen sat at the State's table, her eyes affixed on the young boy. She saw his profile. His lower lip quivered as Pinter read that "He, Michael David Sampson alias Mickie Sampson, did willfully, intentionally, maliciously and feloniously shoot one Gracie Williams Mack—"

The boy didn't react to the legal jargon, not until the Judge spoke the words "shoot one Gracie Williams Mack," at which point Mickie cried out, "I didn't shoot her!"

Keeling put an arm around the boy. Pinter rapped his gavel.

"Virgil shot her! I didn't!"

The sharp crack of the gavel meant nothing to Mickie Sampson. The child—he was a child, Karen thought—was emotionally wrecked. He lacked the discretion or sophistication to realize that one contained one's emotions before the bar of justice. The boy couldn't understand why the Judge was saying that he'd shot the woman. He'd told them who shot the woman, at least he'd told the social worker. It must have seemed as if Doomsday was at hand. He sobbed violently, which prompted Pinter—not known for his patience—to declare a brief recess. "Bring your client under control," he growled to Keeling.

"He's just a kid," Keeling said.

Good for you, Karen thought.

Pinter, though, didn't care. "He's old enough to show the proper respect for this Court." With that admonishment, Pinter abandoned the bench and vanished into the sanctuary of his chambers. Keeling and Art Louck, accompanied by a deputy, took the boy to the rooms behind the bench.

Karen sat alone at the counsel table. Nelson had provided her with her script for the morning. As soon as the child was arraigned, then Karen was to move that he be held without bail and that the case be transferred to adult jurisdiction.

She massaged her weary eyes. Chip hadn't left her apartment until dawn. Within seconds, he had knocked on her door. She would never forget the look on his face . . . a sick, kind of pitiful look. "My tires have been cut," he said, as if announcing a death in the family.

"Sampson!" Karen had gasped.

Chip had not argued. He had cursed instead. And Karen had dressed quickly and drove him to his apartment. She hadn't heard from him since.

A dismal end to what had been a memorable night.

The first time they made love they both had been awkward and uncomfortable, more concerned with image than pleasure, but after that first time it mellowed and became good. She felt fulfilled as the sun came up, and she found herself feeling like sated women feel in romantic novels . . . warm and good and well-loved. She had been a little sore, too, something that romantic writers often failed to mention. It was a good soreness.

But now, hours later, she again found herself doubting their wisdom. While they had made love, someone—Virgil Sampson, they both knew—had slit Chip's tires. Her eyes itched from lack of sleep. Her hands trembled from all the strong coffee she dumped into her empty stomach. The conflicts and doubts had rushed back with the news of the savaged tires, and she saw a future of problems. The day was nice enough. Bright sunlight streamed into the dark courtroom, and the air was warm without being heavy. Things, they say, look better in the light of day. Karen found herself wishing that she was back in her darkened bedroom, nestled in Chip's love hold. She imagined the flat tautness of his belly, the suede-like texture of his—

The door to Pinter's chambers opened and the Judge

swished out. He motioned for the bailiff to retrieve Frank Keeling and his client. Karen shook off her fantasy and watched the court reporter load a stack of papers in her stenotype machine.

This time the boy listened without making a sound as Pinter again read the charge and concluded by saying that "by such act Michael David Sampson did maliciously and feloniously slay, kill and murder Gracie Mack."

Mickie flinched, but he didn't break.

Attaboy, Karen thought. Hang in there.

Pinter, having completed reading the formal charge, peered down at Karen. He said nothing, anticipating that the assistant prosecutor had a motion to make. Karen, uncomfortable with the predictable nature of her function, paused intentionally, trying to throw Pinter just a little off balance. She thought she saw the flicker of impatience.

"Does the State have anything to bring before the Court?" Pinter finally said.

Karen stood. "Yes, Your Honor. The State asks that the defendant be held without bail. Given the nature of the charge and the fact that this young man's safety might best be served by his continued detention, we feel such a request is very much justified. Also, we move that jurisdiction of this matter be transferred from the juvenile court to the circuit court and that he be tried as an adult."

Karen looked down at Mickie. Tear stains streaked his face, and his eyes twinkled with the moisture, but she saw more than the tears in his eyes. She saw the pain that comes from a betrayal. Even she had deserted him. Meanwhile, as Karen tried to reach to Mickie Sampson with her own eyes, to try to tell him that it was her job and that it was for his own good, Frank Keeling argued in favor of bail. He asked that the Judge schedule a transfer hearing on his juvenile status.

Just as Keeling concluded, Mickie looked away from Karen and lowered his head. Pinter, however, was ready to address the boy, and he wanted his attention. "Look up here, lad."

The boy ignored the command. Pinter's lips narrowed, his brow furrowed. "Young man! Look up here now!"

Slowly, with an air of silent defiance, Mickie obeyed.

Pinter cleared his throat. "I hereby direct that you be remanded to the juvenile detention center in lieu of $25,000 bail. Further, I shall schedule a hearing on the transfer motion the first of next week. If there's no other business—"

Keeling moved toward the bench. "Your Honor, I do have one other matter which I would like to bring before the Court in a bench conference."

Pinter motioned for Karen to join them. She and Keeling both stood on tiptoes to lean over the bench. The aroma of both stale and fresh drink assailed Karen's nose. She couldn't tell which one had been drinking the night before and which one had indulged so early in the morning.

"I ask to be relieved from this case," Keeling whispered. "As your Honor knows, I practice very little criminal law, and in all candor I don't feel competent to provide this young man with proper representation."

The Judge glanced to Karen. Her script offered nothing on the new development. She didn't know what stand to take. Quickly she decided, "The State objects. Mr. Keeling is a member of the bar and should bear the same responsibility as other attorneys in representation of indigent defendants."

Pinter, with mercy displayed in his bloodshot eyes, looked at Frank Keeling. "Motion overruled," he told the lawyer.

Keeling's face dropped. "In that case, Judge, with all due respect I want my motion put on record as well as your ruling on that motion. The record should reflect my opinion—for my own future protection."

Pinter's ruddy face flushed even more deeply. "No way," he said in a voice loud enough to be heard in the rear of the courtroom. "I'm not about to let you create that kind of a record."

He caught himself and softened his voice. "I simply won't permit it, Frank. Absolutely not."

Keeling looked as if he wanted to retort, but he kept his peace, clenching his lips, and muttered, "Yes, Your Honor."

Karen left the courtroom to find Clarke Nelson. He was in his office, and Karen told him about Keeling's motion. "I hope you opposed it," he said.

"I did," Karen said, relieved that she had made the right choice.

"Good! Let Keeling suffer."

"Frank wanted Pinter to vouch the record showing his motion to be relieved. The Judge refused to let him do it."

Nelson smiled and shook his head. "If we don't fuck up this case, Pinter will do it for us. By the way, Hemmings has gone to get a search warrant for the kid's house."

"On what grounds?" Karen asked. "We have no probable cause—"

"Maybe not," Nelson interrupted. "That's not the point. I could make a strong argument that it's proper to search the kid's house, but I've got bigger game on my mind."

"If you can get someone to issue the search warrant."

"No problem," Nelson said. "I sent him to Magistrate O'Donnell. He'll issue anything." He smiled at Karen, just like a sneaky cat. Nelson knew Karen's feelings toward the magistrate.

"If any evidence he seizes is tossed out against the kid," Nelson went on to explain, "it will still be admissible against Virgil Sampson, who has absolutely no right to privacy in the kid's residence."

"You mentioned that the other day. I had forgotten that."

"That's why you're the assistant," Nelson quipped.

After lunch, Karen crossed the street to the suite of offices which housed the county's magistrate courts. It was her afternoon to appear on behalf of the State in the glut of misdemeanor cases and felony preliminary hearings scheduled before Judge O'Donnell. As a Legal Aid lawyer, Karen had suffered through many uncomfortable days in O'Donnell's court, battling his plaintiff-oriented vision of justice, which often had pitted her against both the Court and the plaintiff. Karen, who tried to think well of most people, had come to detest the shriveled little man who lorded over his small and dismal court with the cavalier persuasion of a medieval inquisitor.

And Judge O'Donnell felt no great empathy for Karen, at least not until she had turned prosecutor. On her first appearance in his court as a prosecutor, O'Donnell had called her aside and told her that he was happy to see that she had become one of "the good guys."

On this day, she was scheduled to interview a series of complainants during misdemeanor pretrial hearings. Most of the cases involved domestic disputes and neighborhood squabbles. Based upon those interviews, Karen would decide which cases to bring up for trial and which would be dismissed. Most of the cases would never make it to a courtroom.

A multitude of litigants jammed the small lobby—wives who had filed complaints against husbands for assault, husbands appearing chauvinistically defiant or apologetically contrite, indignant merchants who had taken valueless checks from defendants who also were present . . . hopefully. Laced among the generally underdressed parties were a few suited men, obviously distressed at their company but anxious to play lawyer and defend themselves on the horrid offense of speeding. Even less common were a few uniformed officers who came to plead with Karen to prosecute their marginally prosecutable cases.

True justice at work.

Ten times more people paraded through the county's magistrate courts than through the circuit court. Many of them came away from the experience feeling sullied by the mere contact with it, and Karen cringed at the perception of justice which many citizens received in Judge O'Donnell's court. He mauled a system which most people considered quite hallow. Magistrate courts, Karen had decided long ago, were both the heart and the rectum of the judicial system, and O'Donnell's court possessed more qualities of the latter than the former.

Karen greeted O'Donnell's secretary and accepted from her a stack of files which constituted the afternoon's docket. She started with the top file—a complaint filed by a wife alleging that her husband had abused their child. She called out the woman's name. A frail and bedraggled girl, hardly more than a child herself, rose in answer to the name of Roslyn Smithers. A man also stood, and Karen knew he had to be the husband.

"If you're Mr. Smithers," Karen said, "then just have a seat. I just want to talk to your wife."

The man puffed up. "That ain't fair!"

Karen turned her back on his protest and guided Roslyn Smithers into the small office area which she used for the interviews. Another woman emerged from the crowd of people and started into the office with them. "Who are you?" Karen asked.

"Her sister."

Karen looked to Mrs. Smithers for confirmation. "Do you want her present?"

"Yes, ma'am," the woman-child said, casting a wary eye at her husband who prowled like a caged panther among the other people in the lobby.

Karen closed the door behind the two women, and all three of them sat down around the small desk. Karen scanned the woman's complaint. "According to your sworn statement, your husband smacked the child in the face."

"He truly did," the complainant vowed. "He hit her smack in the mouth."

"Was he disciplining the child?"

"It ain't his'n to hit," the woman said.

Karen arched her eyebrows. "Were you married before?"

Roslyn Smithers lowered her eyes. "No."

What now, Karen thought. "Who is her father?"

Ros Smithers glanced at her sister. "What was that guy's name? You 'member?"

Chip proofread a second draft of a divorce petition. The woman had walked in off the street, and she'd been sent to Chip. He had excused himself to go find Clausen who, it turned out, was to be in court most of the afternoon. Chip's secretary, whom he shared with Clausen, recognized his plight and provided him with a list of questions which he then asked of the woman. First, feeling much embarrassed, Chip had told the woman that half of the $400 fee would have to be paid in advance. The woman had withdrawn a clutch of money from her purse.

After she left, Chip had dictated the petition. It appeared a simple case: no children, no house to fight over, a simple divorce by mutual consent. And his petition was word for word a copy of the form used by Clausen. He had taken the first draft to Simon King for his approval.

"What about the fee?" Simon had asked, even before looking at the document.

"Half up front," Chip said.

"Good." Then Simon had read the petition. "This won't do," he had announced.

It's Clausen's standard form, Chip had wanted to scream, but he didn't.

"I don't like the form," Simon said. "Have my secretary

provide you with a copy of the one I use. Then have it re-typed."

"Yes, sir," Chip said. He started to leave, but Simon stopped him.

"Did you find out any personal information about this lady?" Simon asked.

"Enough for the divorce."

"No. I mean who she was before she married. Who she's related to. Who her husband's related to?"

"Was I supposed to?" Chip hadn't ever heard of such a thing. What difference could it make?

Simon made a face. "Chip, you must always find out who this firm is representing. This is a small town. What if her husband's the brother of the bank president? The bank has us on a sizable retainer. We need to know about such conflicts before we lose good clients—not afterward."

Chip's muscles flexed. His temper strained for its freedom, but he suppressed his frustration. "I won't forget next time."

"It only takes once, Chip. Get a hold of the woman and find out. Don't dare file this until you have the information and run it by me."

"It's an amicable dissolution of the marriage," Chip countered.

And Simon King smiled, the gesture inferring experienced patience rather than amusement. "That's what they all say. It's amazing how often these 'amicable' divorces become legal bloodbaths. You might suggest that the woman consider alimony—if we agree to represent her."

"She was insistent on that point. She wants nothing but out."

The smile on Simon King's face was gone, replaced with a livid expression of displeasure. "We aren't in this for our health. If these people develop a few differences, it'll mean a few more chargeable hours. One measure of your success with this firm is your ability to ring the cash register."

Chip, shocked, kept silent. His employer was suggesting that Chip promote litigation, that he attempt to encourage trouble between the two people.

And Simon wasn't finished yet with Chip. "Have you applied for membership in the Jaycees yet?"

"The Jaycees?"

"I specifically mentioned that to you during the interview."

Chip recalled it, but he feigned ignorance. "I was very nervous. If you did, it slipped my mind."

"There's no 'ifs' about it. You were made aware of our policy on that point. We expect you to become a member. It builds contacts with people in your peer group. It's good for the firm. We encourage you to join any respectable or fraternal organization, and we, of course, will pay the dues."

# TEN

The search of Mickie Sampson's home—proper or not—
produced two pairs of blood-stained blue jeans and some
jewelry which was left in the pockets of the larger pair of
the jeans. Mickie's mother, a gaunt, spindly woman who
worsened her appearance with thick makeup, attempted
to thwart the search. In fact, Hemmings threatened to arrest her for obstructing an officer before she settled down.
Once the search was complete, Hemmings confronted the
woman with the evidence. "Know anything about these?"

Her resistance turned to cavalier disinterest. "Not a
damn thing," she said.

"We found them in Mickie's room."

"Maybe he was doin' some painting?"

Hemmings tossed the pants at her. The woman squealed
and jumped out of their path. "That's not paint on there,"
Hemmings growled. "Paint don't smell like that."

"God knows what he's been into," Mary Sampson said,
shaken by the incident. "I ain't never been able to do
nothin' with that boy, not since my old man ran out on
me."

"Aren't you worried about him?" Hemmings asked.
"I'm told you haven't even been out to the detention center
to see him."

" 'Course I'm worried. I ain't got no way to get out there.
You all got him a lawyer, didn't ya?"

Hemmings nodded. "Of course. If you're interested, his
lawyer's name is Frank Keeling."

"I said I cared, didn't I?"

Fifteen minutes after Hemmings left her house, Mary
Sampson stood at the foot of the steps leading up to the

house of her mother-in-law. Virgil sat above her on the front porch, sucking on a can of beer and swatting at wasps which buzzed about the weathered wood of the house.

"What you got my boy into?" Mrs. Sampson demanded of her brother-in-law. Cautiously, she ascended the steps.

"Woman, what are you talkin' about?"

"The law just searched my place. Had a warrant'n everything. They found things, too."

Virgil choked a little on the beer. The afternoon had turned warm and so, too, had the beer. "What'd they find?"

"Some jewelry and two pairs of pants covered with blood."

"Maybe Mickie did kill that old woman." Virgil grinned down at Mary Sampson.

"You kilt her. You were with him!" Mary Sampson accused, now on the porch and shaking her finger in Virgil's face.

"Ain't nobody can prove that."

"My boy shouldn't have to take the rap by himself, Virgil Sampson! Now that ain't right."

Virgil continued to smile. "Whatsa matter, woman. You gonna lose part of your check or somethin' with that kid in the slammer."

"You're no good!"

"Shhh! Not so loud. Momma's asleep. No sense gettin' her all stirred up over this."

Mrs. Sampson's eyes narrowed. "You black-hearted—"

Virgil sprung to his feet and slammed the woman against a rough timber which supported the sagging porch. "You lookee here, bitch! You don't talk to me like that! Nobody does! You hear me? And you best tell that kid of your'n to keep his mouth shut. If he gets me messed up in this thing, he'll be wishin' he was in the pen already."

The woman knew Virgil Sampson. He was crazy evil, and she saw the evil sparkling in his dark eyes. When he got that look, an evil glow, Mary Sampson knew better than to push him. She just nodded back at him.

He let her go. "Now get the fuck outa here."

"I came to see your momma."

Virgil leaned toward her again. "You shit, too! You gonna git behind my back and fill momma's ears full of them crazy lies of your'n. You go! And you remember what I told you about that little bastard of your'n."

Mary Sampson scooted down the steps. Once she was out into the grassless, dusty yard, she called back to him. "You gonna get yours one day, Virgil Sampson. You cain't treat folks the way you do."

Virgil tossed the almost empty beer can at her and laughed as she stumbled out of its path.


On Friday night, Chip and Karen drove 30 miles to see a movie. The same film played in Wharton, but they dared not be conspicuous. The inconvenience of the drive was little compared to the mutual discomfort they felt in having to sneak about as if they were conducting some kind of illicit affair.

After the movie, Chip drove straight back to Karen's apartment. "Wouldn't it be nice to be able to stop at the Black Stallion for a drink?" he remarked as they pulled onto her street. This time both of them looked for the blue Torino . . . also for someone lurking in the shadows.

"Come in for awhile," Karen said.

"I'm not sure I can afford to buy two more tires," Chip said.

"If that's a joke, it isn't funny."

"It's not a joke."

But Chip went in with her. Just as they closed the apartment door, a figure stepped from the cover of the woods across the street. Neither saw him. With his hands in his pockets, a smile on his face, he walked off to find a telephone.

One drink later, Karen and Chip lay together in her bed, their nude bodies uncovered and highlighted by the silver moonlight which was diffused through the room by the sheers of the windows. "You're skin's so soft," Chip said, lightly caressing the modest but firm mounds of her breasts. Her small but hard nipples tickled the palm of his hand.

"Thank you." She twisted a little to press her body against his, and it seemed as if they had all the time in the world. Both wanted the ecstasy to last through the night. She grasped his penis. "You're so hard."

The phone sounded, emitting a shrill electronic whistle.

The sound shocked them both. Late night calls were never good news. "Christ! It's late," Chip said.

Karen snatched for the phone, trying to reach it before it cried out again. "Hello."

"Are you fuckin' him?" The voice on the other end was muffled but no less harsh.

"What?" Karen sat straight up in bed.

"If he ain't got that prick of his in you by now, he ain't much of a man."

Karen threw the phone across the room. Sick to her stomach, she tried to reach the bathroom.

Early the next morning, Karen and Chip sat in the spacious and opulent living room of a ranch-style home which belonged to Clarke Nelson. Karen, still on the brink of hysteria, had told Nelson of the phone call, discreetly choosing to leave out their circumstance when the phone rang. From the gleam in Nelson's eyes, he didn't have to be told.

"You both asked for it," Nelson said. He was dressed in a casual attire designed obviously for the golf course. He had a 10:30 starting time and checked his watch.

"Is that all you can say?" Chip asked, offended by his apparent lack of concern.

Nelson stared knives at the young lawyer. "If it is Sampson, and there's no evidence of it, then he's your client, counselor."

Karen hissed. "Damn it, Clarke. He's staking out my house! He's intimidating me! He's making obscene phone calls!"

Nelson had been a prosecutor too long to be much moved by such things. "Prove it, Karen. Prove it's Sampson. When you can do that, then come to me."

"I'm not some creep off the street!"

—which made Nelson chuckle. "No, but the same rules apply to you that apply to some 'creep off the street.' "

Chip said, "Can't you at least put a guard on her house?"

Nelson threw up his hands. "Christ! Television is going to be the downfall of our country. We don't even have enough cops to guard the jail." Nelson glanced at his watch. "Look, Karen, I understand how you feel, but you're a lawyer—just like your friend here—and you know what we can do and what we can't do. Until he does something we can prove, we can't even go to the Judge on this."

"I understand how people feel now," Karen said.

"It's a cold and heartless fact. We punish people after the fact. Besides, I warned you—"

"Don't hand me that, Clarke. That's the last thing I want to hear."

Nelson's voice softened. "I'll get a hold of Hemmings. Maybe we can scare Sampson off your case, but if you two keep seeing each other—"

"Now just hold on—" Chip started to say.

"We tried to be discreet," Karen explained, motioning for Chip to ease up.

"There's no such thing in a small town," Nelson answered.

Chip stood up to leave. "I intend to keep on seeing Karen as long as she wants to see me."

Nelson nodded. "And if Karen keeps seeing you, then she'll have to suffer the consequences."

"I think you're glad he's hassling her," Chip charged.

"You go to hell," Nelson snapped.

Chip whirled for the door. "I'm leaving, Karen."

Nelson, however, called to him. "Wait a minute." He rubbed his hand through his hair in a gesture of frustration. "Sit back down. I'm sorry I lost my cool."

Chip glared at the prosecutor.

"Stay," Karen said.

Chip did.

"I was young once, too," Nelson said. "My courtship was no less troublesome. Hell, her old man despised me . . . still does, in fact. You two are a little different though. Soon you're gonna lock horns in a major murder case, a case with some rather extraordinary circumstances since this Sampson fellow may well end up charged with another murder. It's going to generate a lot of attention and a lot of pressure. And your client, Mr. Roth, knows you're . . . er, romantically involved with the prosecuting attorney."

"I don't think it will affect my courtroom ability," Chip retorted.

Nelson smiled. "Don't get hot again, but you really haven't had enough experience to know. Besides, you've got to consider the appearance as well as the reality. Par-

141

don my crudity, but if you were coming up on a murder rap and your lawyer was screwing the lawyer on the other side, how would you feel?"

"He might be right," Karen said.

Chip again rose to leave.

"Can't you two just cool it until after this trial? Hell, if you got it that bad, go down to Virginia or some place for the weekends. Just cover your trails."

"We'll discuss it," Chip said coldly.

"Okay," Nelson said, frowning as he saw that he wouldn't make the 10:30 starting time. "I'll get Hemmings to shake Sampson down a little. And Karen, haven't you got somebody you can stay with until he gets off your case?"

Karen looked at Chip, who smiled. Karen then smiled.

Nelson read their minds. "Oh, shit!"

And, although not one of the three wanted to, they all started to laugh.

# ELEVEN

On June 20, 1863, Virginia, suffering in the throes of the Civil War turmoil, gave birth to the state of West Virginia. The new state's conception came earlier during the war fever. During its germination, it was nurtured not so much by its mother state as by Lincoln's federal government which saw the movement for the separation of western Virginia as a chance to weaken Virginia, the confederate state which provided the staging area for assaults upon the North.

After West Virginia's secession and formation as a new state, its birthday became a state holiday. Few states in the Union so glorify the dates of their conception, but then few states in the Union seceded from the secessionists.

But the Civil War was long ago, and Judge Roger Pinter's memory not very good. Besides, he'd always thought West Virginia something of a traitor anyway. If the jurist, a hundred years after the fact, had been forced to pick sides, he would have preferred the South. Not that he chose to schedule Mickie Sampson's transfer hearing on a state holiday because of his basic empathy for an ancient cause—he just forgot that June 20th was a holiday. When reminded of it by both his court reporter and his secretary, he was too stubborn and too proud to admit that he had erred.

A few legal purists wondered if any minute technical point was in danger of violation because of the holiday scheduling, but no one really dug too much at the point. Only a very few people were inconvenienced.

Seated in the courtroom waiting for Pinter to emerge for Mickie's transfer hearing, Karen made acquaintance with her own emerging cynicism. She cared not a whit that it

143

was West Virginia Day. To her, a native of the federal precinct of DC, the celebration seemed feeble anyway.

Her mood was gray and dismal. The ritual had grown so damnably predictable. As soon as the Judge emerged from his chambers, Karen would move for Mickie Sampson, who sat alone some 10 feet from her, to be tried as an adult. It meant the boy's life. In Juvenile Court, the worst he might suffer would be incarceration in some youth facility until he reached 18, perhaps 21 in his case. As an adult defendant, which he was almost certain to become in just a few short minutes, he might be sentenced to serve the rest of his natural life in the penitentiary, starting off, of course, in youth facilities to be transferred later to the prison. The young boy, arriving at the prison at the age of 18, would make a welcome contribution to the prison's sex life.

The Judge, Karen forecast, would listen attentively, as evidenced by his pursed lips and furrowed brow, to both sides of the argument. Thereafter, he would appear pensive and much burdened by the weight of his job, thoughtful for a right and proper time. Then, solemnly, he would—without a doubt—transfer Mickie Sampson to the general jurisdiction of the Circuit Court.

A foregone conclusion.

It was theater, pure and simple. Karen suddenly found it hypocritical and depressing, especially the Judge's efforts to appear as though the decision was difficult and troubled him. Juveniles facing murder charges were always transferred.

Not that the crime did not revolt Karen. She still snapped awake in the middle of the night, her dreams haunted by an image of the much-dead Gracie Mack. She had lived through Gracie Mack's death every night since she had viewed her body, each time a different variation upon the same theme and each time with Virgil Sampson leering both at her and his victim with all the soulful evil he could manage.

But neither she nor anyone else believed that Mickie Sampson pulled the trigger. Or that little Mickie Sampson even suspected that his uncle had killing on his mind. Certainly the young mind of Mickie Sampson possessed some criminal intent when he entered the woman's residence in the company of his uncle, but no one really cared about that. No one gave a shit about rehabilitating the boy or really even punishing him. The rites they were about to celebrate were something else. It was a way to get Virgil Sampson. The boy was a step toward that goal. Given the "rolling stone-like" quality of the judicial system, Mickie Sampson was about to suffer the wrath of the State's indignation, a simple proxy for his uncle. For now, the boy's head—served upon the public platter—would do just fine.

Karen's representation of Mary Sampson was hardly more than a blurred recollection. Strange, but Karen couldn't even reconstruct the woman's appearance. Yet she could vividly remember the boy who came with his mother to her office. Mickie, even then, had made an impression, a good impression. Karen recalled marveling at the boy's good behavior, something of a surprise given his background. Karen could remember it as if it had happened yesterday . . . or could she? Perhaps it was only an illusion, a trick played upon her by her mind. Why could she not summon forth a mental image of his mother?

"All rise!" cried the bailiff with his high and pitiful nasal whine. While the small courtroom population stood, the officer droned out the archaic opening of court. Karen used those brief moments of withered pomp to frame her argument—not that what she said mattered at all. Pinter sat down with a whoosh into the great chair behind the bench and moved at once to the matter at hand.

"Be seated. Miss Kinder, you may renew your motion," Pinter said.

As the others in the courtroom sat down, Karen—still on her feet, said, "Your Honor, we have filed the necessary written motions. We ask—"

Karen directed her eyes to the boy, who studied intently the scarred tabletop of the defense table. ". . . that Michael David Sampson be transferred to adult jurisdiction. The gravity of this alleged offense supports such an action, and the State believes the interest of the people of this State would be best served by such an action."

With that said, Karen sat down. Pinter was caught off guard, perhaps even napping and at the very least daydreaming. He'd anticipated a longer argument by the State.

"Uh, yes! Uh, thank you, Miss Kinder." His eyes flashed perturbed confusion at Karen. "Mr. Keeling?"

The defense lawyer, no less stunned by the brief argument, shuffled through his papers, stalling to arrange his thoughts, and then stood. "We strenuously object . . ."

Keeling's pro forma arguments floated over Karen's head. As she had resumed her seat, Mickie had looked over at her. His eyes bore no malice. Karen was taken back. Even at his age, he should have felt some resentment. Perhaps he didn't realize the full consequences of the morning's hearing. The boy grinned at her . . . sort of, and Karen discreetly returned his smile. For an instant, the image of his mother—vague and inconstant—fluttered around Karen's head, but it drifted away from her.

Damn! It worried at her.

Frank Keeling sat down.

The Judge looked to Karen. "The State's response, Miss Kinder?" Pinter leaned back, expecting a lengthy rebuttal.

Karen hadn't heard a word of Keeling's argument. It had been longer than hers, she thought. She had come to court with a developed list of arguments in support of the State's motion. Why the hell bother, she decided. Karen didn't even bother to rise. "No response, Your Honor. The State believes its motion speaks for itself given the alleged offense and submits to the Court."

The handful of other attorneys that holiday morning emitted a dull rumble of astonishment. Pinter catapulted up in his chair. "The bench appreciates your brevity." The stinging sarcasm of his voice was lost upon no one.

He tapped his pencil upon the surface of the bench. His face twisted itself into an expression which he believed projected an image of deep judicial concern.

Theater, Karen thought.

She had heard they had schools for judges where they taught proper demeanor upon the bench—the fine art of appearing painfully wise . . . "Pansophy I" maybe? Or "advanced acumen?" If Pinter had ever attended such schools, he must have graduated at the very top of the class.

With a decisive flourish, the intense judicial expression softened. Karen suppressed a smile at the irreverent notion that he had developed the gesture seated on the toilet, following the completion of a satisfying bowel movement.

Judge Pinter unveiled his decision. "The State's motion

is granted." It surprised no one. The true drama had been Pinter's effort to create drama. "If there's no other business—"

Keeling jumped up. "One more thing, sir. The defense asks that we be granted both medical and psychiatric evaluations."

Again Pinter turned to Karen. "Does the State wish to be heard?"

Karen, who could feel Pinter's continued anger, slowly stood. "The State would ask of the defense if the purpose of the exam is to prepare a psychiatric defense or merely to determine the defendant's competency to stand trial?"

"The latter," Keeling said.

"Then the State has no objection."

"So be it," Pinter said. "Miss Kinder, I'd like to see you in chambers."

The sharp rap of the gavel closed the session.

Most professional people work in offices. Judges insist upon "chambers," most of which are decorated with ponderous and overstuffed chairs, a large and uncluttered desk, thick and rich carpeting, and a dimness which casts the pallor of gloom over their interiors. The intention is to create the impression of cerebral cells in which weighty questions receive monastic attention. Judge Pinter's retreat defined the national stereotype. The room projected so much solemn dignity that it dwarfed its inhabitant.

He ignored Karen as he stripped away the black robe to reveal a wrinkled, worn white shirt and a red tie with globular stains near the beltline. The belt itself was cinched tightly around the thin waist, gathering the too-large pants into bunched pleats around the waist. Clothes may or may not make the man, but robes create judges. Or so thought Karen, who viewed Pinter without the cloak of his power and decided he resembled a failed Fuller Brush salesman.

"Sit, Miss Kinder."

She eased herself down into one of the large chairs, being careful to pull her dress down as she did so. Some men prompted that reaction.

Pinter, for once uninterested in Karen's legs, paced the dim confines of his inner sanctum. "I frown upon an attor-

ney taking one of my rulings for granted. You have a function to perform, Miss Kinder—a role to fulfill."

. . . theater, Karen mused for the third or fourth time.

The Judge, still pacing, continued his lecture. "In the future, I shall expect—no, I demand—that you argue your
motions fervently. Everyone in that courtroom homed in
on the obvious facts that you anticipated my ruling. We
have an image to project."

"I admit I anticipated your ruling," Karen replied. "It
was the proper ruling."

Pinter halted beside her chair, glowering down upon her
with his sternest judicial expression—probably from "Advanced Judicial Severity," Karen said . . . only to herself.
She found herself face-to-face with the revolting stains
upon his tie. "And what would you have told Mr. Nelson
had I overruled your motion?" Pinter asked.

"Did you even consider that?"

"Now see here—"

But Karen, uplifted by her own indignation, mounted
her feet. She didn't have to talk to stains. The Judge's
freshly scented alcoholic breath washed over her. "With
all due respect," she said in a clipped, not-too-respectful
voice, "we waste too much time playing games—keeping
up a facade. You knew how you were going to rule last
week, probably when that child was first charged with
murder."

"Be seated, Miss Kinder."

"I'd rather not." Karen, at that moment, couldn't even
construe Roger Pinter as a judge. "I see no sense in theat-
rics. I knew how you would rule. Frank Keeling knew how
you would rule. So, too, did you. I'm not saying you were
wrong. It was the only decision."

"I should hold you in contempt," Pinter growled.

"I'm not being contemptuous, just honest, but, if you do
intend to sanction me, then I ask that you have your reporter make a record for the appeal."

Pinter's eyes narrowed to threatening slits. He seemed
on the verge of summoning his reporter. Instead, he
walked behind his desk as if seeking its buffer. "Young
lady, you've committed a grievous sin. You appear before
me regularly. You would have done well to remain on my
good side."

"May I go, Your Honor?"

"When I'm finished!" He was almost yelling by now. "You young upstarts come out of law school thinking you're gonna whip us dinosaurs into line. Well, I tell you this, girlie! The worst man in my class knew more than the best of you young hotshots. You have no respect!" He was shaking his finger at her, and his ruddy face was puffed with anger. Then, he caught himself. "Go! Get out!"

Karen started to walk out the door leading through the office of Pinter's secretary and straight to a courthouse corridor. At the last moment, she thought of the passel of lawyers who would be waiting outside to see if she had been reduced to tears by Pinter. So she whirled and exited through the narrow corridor which led into the courtroom. She pranced into the courtroom with an unworried smile and a victorious bearing. The lawyers pretended to be uninterested.

# TWELVE

Governments always seem more generous with their employees than private enterprise. While most county and state employees, save Pinter's staff, enjoyed West Virginia Day, the businesses of Wharton carried on as usual. And that included the attorneys. That afternoon, Chip was to meet with Panzini and Virgil Sampson.

His client had become his nemesis. Chip knew Sampson had slashed his tires. He couldn't prove it, which made him angry, but no one could convince him that any other alternative was more probable.

After several days of comfortable and pleasant weather, an intense heat wave was predicted. Chip, sitting in his car in front of Panzini's office with the sweat dripping from his face, decided the forecast had become reality. According to the radio, the summertime Bermuda high had finally managed to build in the Atlantic. Its swirling upper level currents reached far down into the tropics and whipped warm, moist air across the eastern U.S. For all of the sunshine, the air was murky with haze, and the system was so strong that it promised no less than a week of the muggies.

He sucked in the hot air, trying to find some strength in his body, some courage. He shrugged off his hesitancy and got out of the car. He wrenched his tie loose and opened his collar. He hadn't seen Vickie since the night he had taken her out, but seeing her bothered him much less than confronting Virgil Sampson.

The bastard!

Chip wasn't afraid of him. He wanted nothing more than to thrash the man who had been making his love so difficult to realize. He feared himself, feared that Sampson would do something to cause him to lose his cool. It wouldn't take much—just a knowing leer.

Chip opened the door to Panzini's building, and the cold air rushed out to envelop him. It braced him. He looked over to Vickie's desk. She beamed at him. "Hi, Chip."

"How are you? Gosh! It's hot out there."

Vickie giggled. "I can't wait to get home to lay out this afternoon."

"Has our client arrived?"

Vickie screwed up her face. "I'll say! Boy, he gives me the creeps. He just stares at me."

Chip could understand why. Vickie wore a tight fitting knit dress which accentuated her bust. "You do look nice," Chip said.

"You haven't called me," she said, pretending to pout at him.

"I'm sorry. They're really keeping me to the grind at the office."

"I understand," Vickie said.

She always understands, Chip thought.

"Just go on in," she told him.

Chip steeled himself for the encounter and entered Panzini's office through the door in the receptionist's room. The odor reached him as he stepped into the office, the pungent scent of unwashed armpits. It conquered even the refreshing efforts of the air conditioning. And he saw Sampson, dressed in grimy blue jeans and a grease-spotted denim jacket, slouched in one of the plush chairs which Panzini kept in front of his desk.

"Afternoon, Chip," said Mario, rising to shake his hand. "You remember Mr. Sampson?"

"Very well," Chip said with deep meaning. Neither he nor his client were interested in exchanging handshakes, and Sampson's cold gaze drilled into Chip. Was the bastard smiling? The vulpine face hinted at a smirk, that leer which Chip had so dreaded. The man had probably killed two people, one an old woman. Chip was revolted. He felt dirty and guilty.

Chip took a seat off to the side, as far from Virgil Sampson as he could get. "I have to get back to the office, Mario. If we can move this along rather quickly, I'd appreciate it."

"You got a case more important than mine?" Sampson said in his rough, combative voice.

"Several," Chip retorted.

Mario turned hard eyes at Chip. "Our client advises me he wants us to move for a change of venue."

"Goddamn right," Sampson said. "I can't get no fair trial in this county."

Was Sampson referring to the fact that he was seeing an assistant prosecutor? Chip couldn't be certain.

"There are no grounds for such a request," Chip said to Mario rather than their client.

But Sampson bristled. "Goddamn it! I don't give a shit about your opinion. You're still wet behind the ears."

"I have advised our client," Mario said, "that I will make the motion. I have also told him that I doubt it will be granted. The decision's up to Pinter."

"Now you both better do right by me on that motion. I get the feeling neither of you care—"

Panzini slammed his pipe on the desk. "Stop right there! We're both being paid to represent you. I'll do my best, and so will Chip. Neither of us will take any crap from you. We don't get paid to take crap. You understand me?"

Chip saw Sampson's body tense, his jaw muscles flex. The man was ready to explode, but something stopped him. "You both damn well better get me out of this mess," Sampson said.

Chip leaned back in his chair. "From what I see, we don't have any witnesses to help us."

"I got an ace in the hole," Sampson offered.

Panzini raised his eyebrows. "If there's something we don't know, you damn well better tell us. I don't think we're gonna get your case postponed for very long."

"I got a witness who saw the knife in the guy's hand."

Chip looked to Panzini, who said, "You what?"

"You heard me."

"How come Stringfellow didn't know about this witness?" Chip asked.

" 'Cause I didn't tell 'im."

"Why might that be?" Panzini asked.

"Just 'cause."

"Damn!" Chip said. "You'd better level with us, Sampson."

Sampson jumped up. "I don't like you!"

152

"The feeling's mutual, I assure you," Chip countered, expecting at any moment to be attacked.

"Sit down," Panzini snapped.

Sampson snarled silently at Chip, then obeyed the other attorney.

"Tell us about your witness," Panzini then said.

"He's a buddy of mine. I figured we could kinda spring him at the trial—kinda surprise ever'body."

Chip buried his hands in his face. Panzini clenched his lips. It was the veteran lawyer who finally spoke. "Listen, Sampson. We're the lawyers, and you're the defendant—"

"But it's my fuckin' ass that's on the line."

"Yeah," Panzini drawled. "And if we try to pull this, your ass will be grass. Clarke Nelson will nail you to a cross. The law demands that we provide him with a list of witnesses ahead of time."

"Say we just found him," Sampson said.

"In a case like this," Panzini said, his voice rising for the very first time, "I'll bet you, Sampson, that the police already have a statement from your surprise witness if he was there that night. What did he tell them?"

Sampson's lip curled. "How would I know?"

"We damn well better know," Chip said. "What's his name?"

"Go to hell," Sampson said.

"Give us his name," Panzini then said.

Sampson fidgeted in his chair. "It's Austin . . . Maury Austin."

Chip jerked to attention. "Maurice Austin?"

"Yeah. I guess. You know him?"

Frank Keeling received the call from Art Louck just after 4 p.m. He recognized the name of the detention center's social worker. "What can I do for you, Mr. Louck? Has my client confessed to the Lindbergh kidnapping or something?"

"He wants to see you—at my urging."

"Now?"

"Yes, sir. I think you should see him."

Keeling glanced at the small clock on his desk. "Tell him I'll get out there first thing in the morning."

"He's very distraught, sir."

"Over what?"

"I'd rather not say. I just think you should talk with him as soon as possible."

Keeling sighed. "Tell him I'll get out there sometime after five p.m."

After he hung up, Keeling thought about it for a moment, then headed for the detention center. It wasn't that Frank was all that concerned over the kid. He just figured he'd better cover his ass. He interviewed Mickie Sampson in a small secure room reserved for visitors and attorneys. The lawyer noticed the boy's swollen eyes. He'd been crying, crying a lot if Frank was any judge. Art Louck had brought Mickie in and then left them alone.

"What's up, kid?"

"I wanna tell 'em all about it," Mickie said in a tight, almost hoarse voice.

"You wanna what?"

"I wanna talk to the cops."

Keeling's mind raced. "Just slow down, kid. Those people are trying to lock you up for a hell of a long time. Right now, we have something to deal with—your testimony against this other fellow. If you open up, we lose that advantage. Now, I just might convince them to let you go back to juvenile status. That means—"

"I wanna tell them!" Mickie screamed.

The boy again started to bawl, so loud that the social worker stuck his head in the door. "Everything okay?"

"Fine!" Keeling snapped. "Just get out."

Keeling placed a tentative hand on the boy's tossled hair. If Frank's firstborn had lived, he would have been—

Frank had to think. Hell! He would have been a lot older than this kid. Still Frank couldn't help thinking about his lost child, probably because of the boy's touch. "Hey, come on. Toughen up. I'm not much of a criminal lawyer, but I do know the worst thing you can do now is to talk."

"You can't stop me," Mickie said.

"I guess I can't," Frank admitted, his hand still in contact with the boy's head, "but I'm obligated to tell you the consequences of your actions. Do you want to spend the rest of your life in a prison? They'll send you to a juvenile place until you're a little older. Then you'll go to prison. I don't know a lot about prisons, but I do know a lot of those men don't do nice things to some other men. You know what I mean?"

154

Mickie nodded that he did.

"I'm trying to scare you because it's something to be scared of."

"I'm not scared."

"You're just not old enough to be scared. Look, this will keep until tomorrow. I'll come out at lunch and if you still want to do this, I'll make the arrangements. Maybe they'll let me bring you something special for lunch. You like pizza?"

"I wanna do it now!"

"No way!" Keeling said flatly.

On this point Mickie yielded. "Okay, but tomorrow I want to talk to that lady lawyer who was in court this morning."

"Karen Kinder?"

The boy nodded.

"Why her?"

"She helped my mother once. She's nice. She treated me nice."

"Now she's trying to put you away."

Mickie shook his head. "No, she's not. I can tell. She's still nice. She cares about me."

# THIRTEEN

"No fuckin' way!" Maury Austin proclaimed.

Virgil sat on the passenger side of the vehicle as they cruised up the main street of Wharton. "Maury, you're gonna tell 'em you saw the knife in that jerk's hand. You know you're gonna do it—one way or another."

"But I done told the cops I didn't see nothin'," Maury said, finding it difficult to concentrate on the heavy five o'clock traffic.

"So?"

—"Christ, Virg! They'll eat me alive. I could end up in jail."

"You might end up worse if you don't."

Maury's fright congealed like a rock in his belly. His face glistened with sweat, some of it from the unbearable late afternoon heat, some from his predicament. "Hey, man. Don't do this to me. I been a friend to you, loaned you my car whenever you wanted it. Come on, Virg."

Virgil, gazing out the open window, whistled at an attractive girl wearing short shorts who walked along the sidewalk. "Hey, you a sweet lookin' piece," Virgil called to her.

She ignored him.

"I bet your cunt stinks!" he shouted.

"Knock it off, Virg." Maury didn't need to get pulled over.

Virgil swung around and slammed his fist into Maury's shoulder. It caught him by surprise, and he jammed hard on the brake, throwing both of them forward. Maury's chest slammed into the steering wheel. Virgil caught himself against the dash. The screeching tires of the car behind them prompted them both to brace for a rear-ender.

156

Somehow the car managed to stop just inches short of the Torino's bumper. Virgil whirled around and saw the driver, a squat little man, gesturing viciously. He was laying on his horn.

Virgil gave him the finger.

"Goddamn, Virgil. I think you hurt me," Maury said, massaging his arm, his foot still jammed down on the brake. The motor of the Torino had died.

"Just get going," Virgil commanded.

Maury managed to start the car. He caught up with traffic. The ache in his shoulder continued.

"Now, them lawyers need to talk to you."

"Ah, Virg!"

Virgil balled up his fist. "I was just horsing around last time, friend."

Maury cringed. "Okay, man. I'll do it."

"Damn right you will."

Fuck ya! thought Maury. He already was trying to decide where to go. He had an uncle in south Florida, a sister up in Charleston. Florida would be better . . . farther away. Maury Austin had no intention of going to jail for Virgil Sampson.

"By the way," Virgil said, "I gotta borrow your car for a little while tonight. I gotta pay my respects to my nephew."

That evening, Mary Sampson visited her son in the detention center. Virgil had arranged for a ride. He showed up in a blue car which he said he'd borrowed. Mary knew she had no choice. She went with him.

At the center, though, the guard wouldn't let Virgil inside. Only his mother was allowed to visit, Virgil had been told. And Virgil raised mortal hell to absolutely no avail. Mary Sampson met her son in the same room that Keeling had used.

"I was wondering if you was gonna come," Mickie said.

"Had no way . . . not 'til tonight. Virgil brought me,"

Mickie paled. "He's here. He's gonna get to see me."

"They wouldn't let him in," Mrs. Sampson said. "He's waiting for me. You been cryin', boy?"

"Naw."

"You said anything about Virgil?"

Mickie's swollen eyes narrowed. "That's why you come, ain't it?"

"No, boy."

"The hell it ain't! Virgil made you come see me."

Mary dropped her eyes. "I came to see if you needed anything. Clothes maybe?"

"I been here a week, Ma. I needed clothes a week ago."

"I had to wait until I had a way."

"Bullshit!" screeched the boy.

"Now don't you talk like that to me!"

Mickie started for the door.

"Where you goin'?"

"Back to my room."

Mary rushed to stop him. "Now, you listen, boy! You listen good. You say anything about Virgil, and he'll get you. He's tol' me he would. And he jest might hurt your ma too. They ain't gonna do all that much to you. You a minor."

Mickie jerked away from her grasp. Tears seeped from his eyes. He circled the room in agitated fury. "You want me to tell 'em I killed that woman? You want me to go to prison?"

"Mickie!"

"You don't give a shit about me."

"Virgil'll get you."

Mickie moved toward her. "Not if he's in jail. That's where he oughta be. I shouldn't have gone with him that night. I didn't know he was gonna kill her. I swear I didn't know."

Mary's made-up face almost flaked off as she twisted her muscles into a mask of anger. "Hell, boy! He ain't gonna stay in no jail—never has and never will. The law's scared of 'im. You talk on him, and you and me'll suffer."

"You 'member that woman lawyer that helped you a year or so back?" Mickie asked.

Mary Sampson thought, then nodded. "Miss Kinder."

"She's gonna help me. I think maybe she can get Virgil."

Mary eyed her son. "You already talked, ain't ya, boy?"

Mickie nodded.

Her hand came up fast and hard and caught Mickie on the cheek. He staggered backward. "You're a fool, boy! You gonna get us both hurt."

Mickie, his eyes raging, screamed at his mother. "You never wanted me! You don't care what the fuck happens to me!"

158

Chip went to a fast food restaurant where he choked down a rubbery hamburger. Then he returned to the office. Earlier that day, when he had returned from the meeting at Panzini's office, he'd found a brief on his desk. It was one that he'd done for Simon King, who by then had left for the day. Scrawled across the front page was a single cryptic command.

"Rewrite," it said.

Nothing more.

Chip had become tickled, almost collapsed into an uncontrollable bout of giggling. What the hell was wrong with it? King hadn't even had the common decency to mark the errors. And, for the first time, Arthur King had assigned him work. Perhaps Chip had passed the laundry initiation. One of the King's clients, a wealthy bank president, faced charges dealing with corrupt bank practices. The King wanted the federal statutes researched. His secretary informed Chip that both the rewrite and the research were to be finished by the next afternoon.

Chip elected to do the research first. That he could handle. It was the vague directive to "rewrite" that boggled Chip's mind. Maybe Clausen—God save Isaac Clausen!—could shed some light on Simon's pleasure. He'd catch Clausen in the morning and dictate a second draft before lunch.

In law school, Chip had prided himself on his ability to perform assignments, but in school the assignments came one at a time. He was able to concentrate on one until it was completed, then move to the next. Here, he seemed to immerse himself in one project when another was dumped upon him. After two weeks, he had a dozen things going at one time, and the senior partners gave him no idea as to what took precedence.

Before he tackled the United States Code, he phoned Karen. She answered the phone giggling.

"Are you drinking?" Chip asked, incredulous.

"I've had a couple."

"Are you okay?"

"Fine. I got a friend here. I told you about Myra, didn't I?"

"The one that screws on the living room floor?"

"The one and only."

"I'm glad you have company."

"Me, too, but she's not nearly as much fun as you."

"I'm stuck working. I had a conference with Sampson today." Chip hoped his name wouldn't destroy her jocular mood.

He heard her hiss. "That scumbag. Did you say anything about—"

"No. Panzini was there. He's revolting. He smelled like he hadn't bathed in a week. He's got blackheads on his temples that look like moles."

"Yuck!"

Chip told her about the note on the brief, and she giggled some more. "We should open our own firm," she finally said.

"You are drunk."

"Not as drunk as I plan to get."

Chip hung up and reached for the appropriately colored blue and black volumes of the United States Code.

Myra, who knew nothing about Virgil Sampson until that night, hadn't planned to spend the night. She suspected that Karen was overreacting a bit. However, she did stay very late, and both she and Karen drank just enough to keep the edge on their highs.

Outside, dark storm clouds, remnants of gigantic storms to the south, rolled in to shroud the stars and the moon. Almost precisely at midnight, the first distant rumble of thunder could be heard.

Myra walked to the window. "I'd better get my ragged ass home," she said, peering outside.

Just then, a brilliant and extended display of lightning dispelled the muggy darkness. Myra gasped as a lanky, shadowy figure dashed from the jungle across the street, disappearing as the blue bright static grounded out.

"What is it?" Karen asked.

Myra shrugged. "Just the lightning. It startled me. We've had our share of storms this summer. Hey, do you mind if I stay over? I promise not to use your toothbrush."

"I'm not like you feminists," Karen giggled. "I keep a spare."

# PART THREE

"Excessive bail shall not be required . . ."
    —Amendment VI,
       Constitution of the United States of America

# ONE

At 8 p.m. the following evening Virgil Sampson sat in jail, charged with the murder of Gracie Mack.

Events had moved quickly, starting early that morning when Frank Keeling, even more hung over than usual, visited the Honorable Roger Pinter. Pinter, whose overinflated opinion of his wisdom amused courthouse insiders, was one of Keeling's chief advisers. It flattered Pinter, which Keeling recognized.

Keeling commenced the conversation with a disclaimer. "Judge, I need some advice, but it's about the Sampson boy. I wanted to tell you that up front because I don't want to compromise or prejudice you in the case."

Both Pinter and Keeling sipped from Styrofoam cups filled with steaming coffee. Pinter smiled down into the dark brew. "Hell, Frank, we'll just consider this a social call over some morning coffee. However, if you're still wanting to declare yourself incompetent, you're wasting your time."

"That's not it." Frank then told Pinter that his client wanted to talk, insisted upon it in fact. "I've strongly advised him against it. Since he's a juvenile, and since I do truly feel incompetent, what do I do?"

Pinter leaned back in his chair and studied the ceiling of his chambers. "If I was prosecutor, I wouldn't move against the kid's uncle on the uncorroborated word of an emotionally overwrought juvenile. You gotta admit, Frank. The kid's intentions are rather self-serving."

"It's also a declaration against interest," Frank said. "That gives it some credibility."

"I once had a similar case," Pinter mused. He launched

163

into a war story which consumed the better part of half an hour.

Frank Keeling listened patiently, smiling at the right times and nodding at other times. When the Judge was finished, Keeling said, "What should I do, Roger? The kid's bound and determined to make a statement."

"Hell! Let him talk. Just be sure you got a steno girl there to make a record of the statement. Be sure you make a clear record that the kid is doing this against your advice, and be sure you have the kid acknowledge that. Better yet, have the kid say that he told you he was going to talk no matter what your advice was. Get all that on the record."

"Will that cover me?"

"Like a blanket, Frank."

Keeling, knowing that Pinter was due on the bench, rose to leave.

"One more thing," Pinter said. "Require the prosecutor to get the kid's mother there. Let her express her opinion, Frank. Make that a precondition."

"I haven't even met her," Keeling said.

"Let the State worry about getting her there, like I said."

"When she's present I can advise her that I don't think the boy should talk."

Pinter nodded. "You got it."

"Yeah. That should cover me."

"Like a blanket," Pinter said.


"The kid wants to talk to you," Keeling told Karen. They were seated in Clarke Nelson's office with the prosecutor looking on.

"About what?" Karen asked. Her brain remained a bit fuzzy from the alcohol she had consumed the night before.

"He says he wants to make a full statement. I also gather that he's willing to testify."

Nelson smiled. "You understand, Frank, that we have made you no promises whatsoever."

"I know."

Karen's mouth hung open.

"To be candid," Keeling said, "I have strongly advised my client against this course of action. If he changes his mind before the statement's taken or at any time during it,

164

then I shall terminate the interview. He seems to have had an attack of conscience which I hope will disappear."

"Maybe just an attack of fear," Nelson quipped. "He's got more sense than his lawyer."

Through clenched teeth, Keeling said, "Go to hell."

"And he specifically wants to talk to me?" Karen asked.

"I gather you represented his mother or something," Keeling said.

"Yes, at Legal Aid."

"These are the conditions then." Keeling had them listed on a small piece of paper. "He wants to give the statement to Miss Kinder. There must be a court reporter present, and the statement must be transcribed completely. Furthermore, I want his mother present for the interrogation."

Nelson nodded. "No problem with the court reporter. If you want the mother, you find her."

"No way," Keeling retorted. "If you want a statement, you get her here."

"The kid wants to talk, Frank. I'd say the ball's in our court."

Keeling smiled for the first time since the discussion began. "Under the law, for any statement to be admissible, it must be taken in the presence of a juvenile's attorney. Unless you meet the condition, I might just get sick and disappear."

Nelson pondered the issue. He might get by with a voluntary statement from a juvenile without his lawyer present. On the other hand, why risk it? "Score one for the defense."

Nelson buzzed his secretary and told her to find Hemmings and have him find Mary Sampson. "Tell him to bring her here forthwith."


The interview with Mickie Sampson convened in the conference room of the prosecutor's office. Mickie eyed his mother with blossoming discomfort as the court reporter, a freelancer secured by Clarke Nelson, set up her steno machine.

Mary Sampson started to say something to her son, but Nelson stopped her. "We want the entire conversation on record, Mrs. Sampson."

Mrs. Sampson, who wasn't pleased about being dragged

to the courthouse by a cop, grew mad. "You mean I can't even talk to my boy! You're all a bunch of commies."

"Shut up," Hemmings growled.

"Put that on your record, too," the woman screeched at the young court reporter. "I don't have to take that off him. I ain't under arrest. Put down what he said to me."

The court reporter, now threading the narrow white paper into the machine, ignored the ranting of the woman.

"You about ready?" Nelson asked of her when she had finished that process.

The reporter nodded.

"Let the record reflect," Nelson said, "that the following individuals are present in the conference room of the prosecuting attorney of Custer County on this, the 21st day of June, 1983—Clarke Nelson, the duly elected prosecuting attorney for the aforesaid county; Karen Kinder, a duly appointed assistant state's attorney for said office; and Cpl. Dan Hemmings, an investigator for the West Virginia Department of Public Safety. All of the aforementioned individuals are here on behalf of the State of West Virginia. Let the record further reflect that also present are Frank Keeling, counsel for the defendant Michael David Sampson; the defendant himself, Michael David Sampson, a juvenile of the age of 14 years; and Mary Sampson, mother of the said juvenile."

Nelson paused to collect his thoughts. "Further, the record should also reflect that the defendant in this matter was transferred from the jurisdiction of the juvenile court to adult jurisdiction upon the 20th day of June, 1983. We are present in response to a request by said defendant, communicated to us by his counsel, that he be permitted to make a formal statement regarding a case style State of West Virginia v. Michael David Sampson, Case No. 83-F-270, formerly Juvenile Case no. 83-J-98. Finally, let the record reflect—subject to the objection of the defendant—that we have made no promises to the defendant, nor is he here as a consequence of any coercion or duress, and he is not now under the influence of alcohol or drugs, and further that he appears to be of sound mind and disposition."

As Nelson spoke, Mary Sampson's face had twisted into a mask of frightened disbelief. Slowly, it had dawned on

166

her what was going on. She blurted out, "You can't talk to 'em, Mickie! You're gonna ruin yourself!"

"Mrs. Sampson!" Nelson said.

The woman turned on Keeling. "What kinda lawyer are you? You can't let him talk."

Keeling shrugged. "I have advised my client that I do not favor making a statement at this time. I would also like the record to reflect that his mother, his only parent available and present, also objects to such action. I have urged that my client remain silent. I have advised him of the possible consequences of his actions. Is that true, Mickie?"

The boy nodded.

"Please give a verbal response," said the reporter.

"Huh?" Mickie didn't understand.

"Answer out loud."

"Yeah. He's told me."

"For clarification," Keeling said, "I have advised you not to give this statement, have I not?"

"Yes, sir."

"And me, too," interrupted his mother, speaking as if she were now on stage and addressing an audience.

The court reporter's fingers silently caressed the keys of the steno machine. The thin white strip of paper, cluttered with strange hieroglyphics, poured from the machine.

"I think you have more than adequately vouched the record," Nelson said to Keeling. The prosecutor then turned to the boy. "First, young man, I want to advise you that you do have a right to remain silent. That anything you say . . ." Nelson went through the classic Miranda warnings, not once but twice.

"You understand?" Nelson then asked.

The boy nodded.

"Answer out loud," said the reporter.

"Yes, sir. I understand."

"Do you have any questions about your rights?"

"No, sir."

"And you make this statement freely and of your own free will?"

"Yes, sir."

"Have we threatened you or made any promises to you?"

"No, sir."

"Finally," Nelson said, drawing in his breath for the

clinching question, "you understand that we wish you to testify in court against any other person whom you might implicate in any criminal action?"

Mickie had grown more and more agitated. He had just wanted to talk to the woman called Karen. He hadn't known all these other people would be there. He hadn't known it was going to be such a big production. "I just wanna tell what happened!" he cried. "It's like nobody wants me to. I'll talk in court. It don't matter."

"You're a fool!" his mother snapped.

"That's enough!" Nelson said to the woman. He turned to Karen. "Miss Kinder, you may take over the questioning."

Karen hitched herself up in her seat. "How are you, Mickie?"

"Okay," he said.

"Do you just want to tell us about it in your own words?"

His mother sprung to her feet. "I'm gettin' outa here!"

Hemmings rose to grab her, but Nelson cried out to him. "Let her go. She doesn't have to stay. She's served her purpose."

That surprised Mrs. Sampson. She had halted at the door. "You ain't gonna do nothin' behind my back," she said. "I'm staying!"

Nelson nodded. "You're more than welcome to remain, but I will not tolerate any more interruptions by you. Do you understand me?"

Mary Sampson glared at Nelson, and Mickie smiled, glad to see that someone had put his mother in her place.

"Just go on," Karen then said to Mickie. "If I have any questions, I'll stop you as you talk."

Mickie told it all, sometimes wiping tears from his face as he talked, but mostly relating his tale as if it were something he had watched on television. His every word was translated into strange markings on the narrow strip of paper issuing from the small machine. He told it without interruption. Nelson and Keeling made furious notes. Karen just listened, horror-struck by the sheer, coincidental insanity of it. Such a small-minded evil had caused Gracie Mack's death—and for nothing . . . for nothing but the pure hell of it.

When Mickie finished, Karen asked a few questions, but both Nelson and Keeling asked exhaustive strings of questions, many of them repetitive. Mary Sampson stared out a window through most of the session. When the steno reporter ran out of paper, she interrupted and told them bluntly that she needed a break.

The session resumed 30 minutes later. Dan Hemmings asked for permission to ask a question. Keeling objected, but Mickie vetoed his objection even before Nelson could say anything. "Has Virgil Sampson been hanging around Miss Kinder's residence?" Hemmings asked.

The question surprised everyone, Mickie most of all. "Uh . . . yes. I mean I guess he might have been. I went there once with him. He got mad when he saw her and his lawyer together at the mall."

Keeling raised his eyebrows. Nelson frowned that something like that had gotten onto the record. Karen's stomach growled.

"Did I do the right thing?" Mickie asked of Karen when the interview ended.

"I'm proud of you," Karen said. She smiled at him, and he smiled back through a light flow of tears.

"I didn't know he was gonna kill her," Mickie said. "I shouldn't have even gone with him."

The steno reporter was getting her stuff together. Mary Sampson got up and started for the door. "He's gonna get you, boy," she said to her son.

And she was gone.

Nelson shook his head.

"What now?" Karen asked.

Nelson turned to the cop. "Go secure a warrant for Virgil Sampson for murder. And try not to arrest him until after Judge Pinter's gone home. Let him sit in jail tonight before he gets bail set."

Mickie had been listening. "They gonna let him out?"

"Not if we have anything to do with it," Nelson said.

"He'll get out," Mickie said. "He always does."

A deputy had arrived to transport Mickie back to detention center. Frank Keeling, himself somewhat shaken by the boy's admission, had kept unusually silent. He left, too, without a word to anyone. Hemmings, though, held back.

"Get a move on," Nelson told the corporal.

"You know that Sampson woman's on her way to tell the

bastard about this," Hemmings said. "She shouldn't have been here."

Nelson patted the trooper on the back. "You just go do your job, Dan. We'll take care of our end. Maybe if you get your ass in gear, you can bust him before he rabbits."

Mary hurried from the courthouse with the precise intention of finding Virgil Sampson.

Not that she really gave a damn for him.

She just hoped that he wouldn't take it out on her if she warned him. Mary had a well-developed sense of preservation.

But Hemmings found Virgil Sampson before Mary did. It was one of those uncommon happenings in police work. Hemmings had gone across the street and obtained a murder warrant from the magistrate court. He stepped out of the building into the muggy afternoon heat and saw Virgil Sampson drive right by in the notorious blue Torino. And he was alone.

Hemmings rushed to his car parked some distance away to radio for assistance. Just as he got into the unmarked cruiser, the Torino passed him again. Sampson was circling the courthouse. Hemmings pulled out into traffic a few cars behind Sampson and delayed his call for assistance. Sampson circled the courthouse one more time, then headed out of Wharton. The unmarked cruiser kept a safe distance behind.

Once outside of town, Hemmings then radioed for assistance and was told that there was a cruiser approaching on the highway from the other direction. A roadblock was arranged.

Too easy, Hemmings thought. He expected the worst. Seldom was Virgil Sampson arrested without trouble.

Hemmings waited until the roadblock came into view, a lone cruiser blocking the narrow highway. Hemmings then threw on his lights and siren.

And the blue Torino pulled right off to the side of the road about 50 yards shy of the marked state police cruiser. Hemmings used his outside loudspeaker to order Virgil Sampson from the car "with your hands over your head."

Virgil obeyed. With gun drawn, Hemmings exited his vehicle and moved quickly to throw Sampson against the

Torino. He patted him down and waited for the other trooper to arrive.

"We're taking him back to the barracks," Hemmings told the uniformed trooper.

"Hey," Sampson said, speaking for the first time, "you gotta take me before a magistrate."

"Soon enough, punk," Hemmings growled.

Virgil thought about fighting at that point. He had no idea what they had on him, but he suspected. He wanted out on bail. His lawyer could tell the Judge that he had pulled over without giving the cops any trouble. So he decided to be nice—just this once.

Hemmings cuffed him, ordered the other trooper to have the Torino towed, and then read Sampson his rights and the warrant charging him with murder. He stuffed a copy of the warrant and the factual complaint upon which it was based in Sampson's pocket.

Later, as Sampson sat in a cell, he would read the factual complaint and his suspicions would be confirmed. His arrest came because the kid had talked.

Once he read that, his desire to go free would become an evil passion.

# TWO

A sharp rap on the door startled the bejesus out of Karen. She glanced at the wall clock and saw that it was a few minutes past 10 p.m. Her stomach rumbled with tension. She felt her face grow hot, then sweaty. Her knees weakened. Dressed in a thick robe and wearing nothing beneath it, she got up and inched toward the door. "Who . . . who is it?"

"It's me . . . Chip."

"Chip!"

"Yes. Open the door."

Chip? He was breaking the rules, violating the informal agreement they had struck with Nelson. She opened the door. "What are you doing here?"

"I thought you would want to know. He's in jail."

"Sampson? Virgil Sampson?"

Chip nodded.

Karen threw her arms around him. She felt reborn. She laughed and kissed Chip on the lips. He almost carried her into her apartment. "Hey, ease up!" he said. "What will your neighbors think?"

"The hell with them."

Until that moment, Karen had never realized how frightened she had become. Her mood ascended like the rising sun, all bright and cheery. Not in her wildest fantasies had she ever thought that any one thing could make her feel so good.

"I knew you'd be happy," Chip said.

"You have no conception," she said, falling onto the couch. "I knew I was scared of the grimy bastard. The worst was that phone call the other night. It's as if the jerk's psychic or something—or looking in my windows."

Chip sat down beside her. "I really thought you might have known already."

172

"The phone rang earlier," Karen said. "I was afraid to answer it."

"You got anything to drink?"

"Sure," Karen said, starting to get up.

"Sit still. I'll get it."

"There's a bottle of champagne in the fridge."

Chip snickered. "My client's in jail on a murder charge, and I'm going to celebrate with a bottle of champagne."

"Not like they said it would be in law school, is it?" Karen quipped.

"No," Chip said, "but then nothing I've encountered has had much to do with what they taught me in law school. I'll get the champagne."

He returned with the chilled bottle, carefully popped it open, and poured two glasses.

"Did he call you?" Karen asked as they sipped the bubbling liquid.

"Yeah. He tried Panzini first. Made a point of telling me that. He demanded that I get the Judge to set bail immediately. I told him I would get right on it—which might justify my visit here this evening. Does the State have a recommendation about bail?"

Karen laughed. "Certainly. If he'll cut off both legs, both arms, and his prick and leave them in the custody of the Sheriff, then I'll recommend that he be released."

"You're a hard woman, Karen Kinder."

"Did he give the officers any trouble?"

"Not a bit," Chip answered. "He made a point of telling me that. He said he thought that would help him. By the time I got to the jail, though, he was raising hell. I told him we couldn't get a bail hearing until the next morning. Then he would go before Judge Pinter. That didn't settle him down very much."

Karen's face lost a little of its joy. "The State's going to ask that he be held without bail."

"Is that done here?"

"The Judge can do it," Karen explained. "Just to be honest, Pinter's very lenient on bail." Karen started to laugh.

"What's so funny?"

"When I came here, I read about the bail which Pinter set on cases. I mean, I kinda kept up with them. I couldn't believe it. I figured in a place like this bail would be set absurdly high, and I thought how 'liberal' it seemed. Now, since the Mack case, I wonder. Any bail for that bastard would be too little." Karen swallowed the balance of her champagne, then asked of Chip, "Can he make bail?"

"Depends. He made a $25,000 bond the first time."

Karen rolled her eyes. "25,000 on a murder case. Christ, in DC it would have been at least $50,000, probably a lot more than that."

"A brother put up his house on that case. He says he has another brother who will take care of him on this one."

Karen's face had lost its joy. "Damn Pinter. He'd better set a hell of a bail this time."

Chip set down his champagne. "You know I'm going to be arguing for a low bail tomorrow. I'll, of course, call it reasonable bail."

"And I'm going for no bail."

"I hope you win," Chip said.

She grabbed him playfully. They scuffled their way into the bedroom. "Let's hurry," Chip said. "I wouldn't want Virgil Sampson questioning my manhood."

Every time they had made love the vision of Virgil Sampson haunted them. This time Karen managed to thrust his presence from her mind. Chip's muscular body played against hers. The cloud was gone, its creator locked behind metal bars—at least for now. Perhaps someone lurked outside her apartment walls, but whoever it was he or she couldn't have been any more evil than Virgil Sampson.

On this night, their passion was playful and joyful, and they relished each other's body.

Later the phone whistled.

Karen froze. "Oh, shit! Do they have phones in the cells?" Her question was serious, deadly serious.

"Let me answer it this time," Chip said.

Karen shook her head. "No. I'll do it."

She picked up the receiver, but said nothing.

"Karen?" said a female voice. "Is that you?"

"Myra!"

"Did you see the news, Karen? They locked him up tonight."

"Oh, God!" Karen sighed. "Myra, I love you deeply, and please don't be offended, but would you go to hell?" Karen hung up the phone, then picked it up again, and let it fall to the floor.

* * *

They behaved liked first-love high schoolers in court Wednesday morning. Chip sat on a bench waiting for the Sampson matter to come up. Karen occupied a chair at the State's table, disposing of a multitude of pretrial motions. Between the motions and sometimes during them, she tossed Chip a mischievous glance, fluttered her eyelids, and even once—almost—blew him a kiss. Pinter looked up about that time, and she caught herself. If any of the other lawyers noticed the strange behavior of their two colleagues, they didn't act like it.

At 10:30, an elevator door which exited into one of the court's anterooms opened. Virgil Sampson, shackled but still smiling, shuffled first into the anteroom and then, guided by a deputy, into the courtroom. All eyes turned upon Virgil Sampson, save Chip's, who looked instead at his beloved Karen. He saw her face turn ashen, her body stiffen.

Chip then looked at Virgil Sampson. Those cold, evil eyes leered at Karen, threatened her—

Chip sprung to his feet and moved quickly beside his client. In fact he nudged Sampson sharply. "Hey! Watch it!" cried Sampson.

Pinter cracked his gavel. "Quiet!"

"Sorry," whispered Chip to his client, still affronted by the foul odor which surrounded Virgil Sampson.

Karen rose under the oppressive burden of Sampson's stare. "The State of West Virginia v. Virgil Sampson," Karen announced. "Your Honor, the defendant was apprehended last night on a warrant charging him with murder. He's charged, in fact, with the murder of Gracie Mack during an apparent robbery attempt at her home. As Your Honor knows, we already have a juvenile charged in connection with the crime. Mr. Sampson appears this morning for a bail hearing."

Pinter looked to Sampson and Chip. "Step forward. Let's see, Mr. Roth, you haven't been appointed to this case."

"No, sir. However, you appointed Mr. Panzini and me to represent Mr. Sampson on the previous case. I talked with my co-counsel this morning, and he suggested that I appear with Mr. Sampson. Mr. Panzini had to be in another county. If the Court wishes to appoint another attorney—"

"No sense getting anyone else into it. Mr. Sampson, are you able to afford a lawyer?" Pinter asked.

"I ain't workin' nowhere."

175

"That wasn't my question," snapped Pinter. "Are you able to retain your own attorney? Answer 'yes' or 'no.' "

"No."

"Do you wish the court to appoint you an attorney?"

"Sure would. I'd like to have someone other than this kid." Sampson nodded toward Chip.

Pinter arched his eyebrows. "May I ask why?"

Chip looked at Karen. Her eyes reflected his own concern. What would Virgil Sampson say?

"He's wet behind the ears. Besides, we just don't get along."

Pinter addressed Chip. "Do you have anything to say?"

"I leave it to you, Your Honor."

Pinter shuffled some papers on the bench. "Mr. Sampson, if you're not happy with the attorneys I have appointed, please feel free to hire your own. However, you haven't given the slightest reason to change your counsel. Mr. Roth may be new, but he's being assisted by an able veteran. Now to the matter of bail."

Karen moved to the bench, but kept as much distance between Sampson and herself as she could. She felt his eyes on her back. "Judge, the State requests that this defendant be held without bail—"

"Bitch!" Sampson muttered.

"What was that?" Pinter asked. He'd heard something, but he wasn't certain what.

"Nothing," Sampson said.

"You're interest will best be served if you remain silent," Pinter told the defendant. "Go on, Miss Kinder."

"As I said, we ask that the defendant be held without bail. As you know, Mr. Sampson now faces two murder charges."

Pinter leaned forward. "Being accused is not the same as being convicted."

"I understand that, sir," Karen said. Pinter had the look of the wolf. She remembered the day in his office when she had offended him, when he had warned her that she had alienated him. "We have very strong cases in both instances. We sincerely question whether this defendant would appear for trial on either charge if he were released on bail. He's unmarried and has very few community ties."

Karen stifled the useless argument that he was dangerous. That had nothing to do with the matter of bail in the

State of West Virginia. Bail was not preventive. Its only function was to secure the defendant's appearance at trial.

"Is that all, Miss Kinder?" Judge Pinter's tone implied that if it was all, it wasn't enough.

"For now, Your Honor."

"Mr. Roth."

Chip cleared his throat. "Judge, my client is already free on bail on the first murder charge. He remained within the jurisdiction after his release. He submitted to his arrest yesterday without any resistance. In this instance, the State's sole evidence is the uncorroborated word of a juvenile who himself has admitted his involvement."

Pinter knew that by virtue of Keeling's visit to him the previous day. Of course, he wasn't supposed to know that. "Is that true?" he asked of Karen.

Karen glared at Chip. "We place great credibility in the young man's admission. He insisted upon making his statement in absolute defiance of the recommendation of his attorney. We know there were two persons at the scene of the crime. We can prove that with additional physical evidence."

Karen's obvious displeasure caught Chip off guard. She knew he had to argue for reasonable bail. He wanted Karen to win, but he just couldn't make it obvious. "Your Honor," he said, "the young man's anxiousness to implicate my client raises some serious questions about his motivations and credibility."

Chip looked at Karen, his eyes pleading for understanding, but Karen's image appeared not at all understanding.

Pinter made his decision. "Bail is set at $25,000."

Chip heard Karen's sharp hissing intake of air. He didn't dare look at her.

If he had, he would have noted the vanishing color of her face. She turned slowly, hoping that her quivering knees would carry her, and walked unsteadily back to counsel table. She grasped it for support and sat down.

Sampson grinned broadly. "Maybe you ain't so bad after all."

The deputy locked onto his arm and guided him back to the anteroom. Only then did Chip dare turn his attention to Karen. Her eyes drilled into him, and he saw her rage, her sense of betrayal. Most of all, he saw her terror.

They both knew Sampson would be on the streets again in a few days, perhaps on this day.

# THREE

A sharp, intense crack of lightning knocked Chip right out
of his dreams. He really wasn't certain what had awakened him until it flashed again . . . and cracked again, this
time jarring the walls of Chip's apartment.

How long had he slept?

He had tossed and turned for what seemed like hours
once he had finally gone to bed about 2:30 a.m. Throughout the previous afternoon, after Sampson's bail hearing,
he'd tried to reach Karen. The secretary in the prosecutor's office kept telling him she was tied up. When the secretary just hung up on him without saying anything, Chip
had decided to stop calling. Then, after he had gotten
home, he'd tried to call her apartment. No answer—just a
damned ringing.

Chip fumbled for the alarm clock and squinted at the lu-
minous dial. It was 5:30.

Lightning created daylight in the bedroom. A crisp crack-
le of rabid electricity filled the closed atmosphere of his
bedroom. Then came the razorlike explosion of a much-
too-close strike. Chip sprung from his bed and searched the
apartment for a fire. He found nothing. The air must have
been so charged that it snapped, crackled, and popped like
a bowl of fresh Rice Krispies.

"Screw it," he said aloud. He brewed some coffee.

He sat down to wait for the coffeemaker to finish its
task. His eyes ached for sleep, and he rubbed them and
made them worse. Physically, he was exhausted, but his
mind wouldn't stop working. Each time he closed his eyes,
his mind projected an image of Karen, her face reflecting
an intense anger directed at him, as if he had been the one
to set Sampson's bail. After the hearing, Chip had started

toward her. She had snatched up the file and almost ran from the courtroom. Her behavior turned heads, and they discussed it—how she had overreacted to the Judge's decision.

What the hell did they know!

Virgil Sampson wasn't stalking them.

Much earlier in the night, as Chip had lain awake, he had decided to wait for her at the courthouse parking lot, try to talk to her as she went to work. If he could just face her on a one-to-one basis—

Lightning flashed again, striking almost simultaneously with its flash. The light in his living room flickered, then died. The struggling noises of the coffeepot faded, too.

A bad omen.

Chip waited for the next atmospheric discharge. Instead of the lightning, he heard gusting wind, the true harbinger of the storm. It rattled the windows and whistled around the eaves of the apartment house. Large, infrequent drops of rain thumped against the window. And, finally, the lightning blinked again, followed not so quickly this time by its strike. It really began to rain, a deluge so loud that it buffered the sound of the thunder. The summer promised to be hot, punctuated by frequent stormy periods. It was off to a good start.

Chip closed his eyes, allowing the sound of the rain to buffer the anxiety which had kept him awake for so much of the night. And he slept. While he slept, the lights came back on and the coffeepot finished its job. The sun, too, rose, its summer brightness shrouded by storm clouds.

When Chip finally awoke, the skies had turned blue. The morning was very old. He had overslept.

Karen arrived at the courthouse almost two hours before Chip awoke. The sun, at that time, peeked through great gaps in the stormy cloud cover. The rain and thunder had moved off to the east in a well-defined squall line. Behind the front, the air was cool enough that Karen shivered a little as she got out of her Mustang. At least she blamed her chill on the cool air. She looked briefly at the barred jail windows and wondered if Sampson was watching her.

Like Chip, Karen hadn't slept much the night before. She had stayed with Myra. They had talked long into the night. Earlier in the evening, Karen had called the jail three times just to be certain Sampson remained there.

Nelson was waiting for Karen. "Why don't you take a few days off?" he suggested as they sipped coffee in her office.

"You think I have something to worry about, too?"

"Discretion, as they say, is the better part of valor."

"Isn't there something we can do? Appeal Pinter's decision or something?"

Nelson laughed. "Have you ever heard of our Supreme Court raising anyone's bail? Besides, for this county it's a reasonable bail. If he makes it, he'll be under $50,000."

"He'll make it," Karen said.

"Maybe, maybe not."

"Be honest, Clarke. Don't give me any false hopes. Will he be able to get out?"

Nelson stared into the darkness of his coffee. "He'll probably be out by noon."

Karen massaged her temples with her fingers. Her head ached from what she chose to believe was a lack of sleep. "There's something very wrong here. I'm an assistant prosecuting attorney. I work for an office which commands substantial police power. I'm just trying to do my job, and you—the county's chief law enforcement official—are telling me that I better leave town—that I can't be safe here."

Nelson just shrugged.

"That's shitty! Purely shitty!"

"That's life," Nelson responded. "Go down to the beach for a few days. I bet you look just divine with a tan. You can't function here with this on your mind. You've already alienated old Roger. He's spitting nails because of you."

"Screw him!" Karen snapped. "I have a job to do."

"You also have your mental well-being to protect, not to mention your life, though I doubt it would come to anything as serious as that."

"But how can we let this happen? How can we let one man, a not-so-smart man at that, intimidate the system?"

"Like you said, the system's shitty. However, he really hasn't intimidated the system—just you. He singled you out because—"

". . . because I'm a woman," Karen interjected.

"I guess," the prosecutor said.

Nelson patted her on the shoulder as he left her office.

"Do what you want to do, Karen. I'll be behind you either way."

Karen was left to her thoughts, none of which were very pleasant. She finished her coffee and was starting to review some minor magistrate court cases when the sharp buzzing of her intercom made her jump. "What is it?" she snapped.

It was Nelson on the intercom. "A Mr. Chip Roth wishes to speak to you."

"Oh! Tell him I'm not available."

"No way," the prosecutor said. "He drove this office to distraction yesterday trying to reach you. You and he both created this problem. I'm no fan of Mr. Roth, but it isn't his fault. He's just doing his job."

The intercom clicked off. The hold button flashed yellow. Karen jammed it in. "I don't really want to talk to you, Chip."

"Dammit, Karen. It's not my fault."

The edge to his voice caught her off guard. So, too, did her own reaction. Really, it wasn't his fault. "I guess I owe you an apology."

"You owe me a night's sleep. However, I'll settle for lunch."

Karen remembered Clarke Nelson's prediction that Sampson might be on the street by noon. "I think I'm going to eat here at the office today. Maybe we can see each other tonight? Maybe we can meet someplace—"

"Are we back to sneaking around?" Chip asked.

"We were foolish to think we had escaped it. Chip, I'm going to be honest with you. I don't think I can romance you at night and battle you in court during the day. Clarke might be right. Maybe if we were about to try some two-bit civil case, things would be different. I can't help myself, Chip; I find myself wondering if any of this would have ever happened had he not seen us together at the mall. Mickie Sampson told the world the other day."

"So what are you saying, Karen?"

Karen tried to shake away the cobwebs, the confusion. She knew what she should say. The trouble was, she didn't want to say it. She suggested instead, "You know that Mexican fast food place across the Virginia line?"

Chip knew it.

"Meet me there for supper around seven."

* * *

Mario Panzini phoned Frank Keeling a little before eleven that day. The call, a routine and common occurrence among attorneys, laid the foundation for the disaster which would follow. "When does that kid go for his psychological examination?"

"What's it to you?" Keeling asked, mostly in jest.

"Goddamn, Frank. Since he's accusing my client of murder, I'd like to know just how crazy the little bastard is."

"He's not the crazy one," Frank countered.

"I'd still like to know what the shrink says."

Keeling checked the note on his desk. "His appointment is June 30."

"That's pretty quick."

"We're all anxious for the results."

Panzini paused before his next question. "Would you let the kid take a polygraph examination?"

"Go screw yourself, Mario."


Simon King had left word with the receptionist that he wanted to see Chip as soon as he decided "to bless us with your presence." Chip anticipated an ass-chewing. In fact he deserved it. It was eleven when he walked into the office. However, he hated like hell having it foreshadowed by the high and mighty tone of the receptionist as she relayed verbatim Simon's message.

Chip slunk into Simon's office. "I apologize," he said before his employer could say anything.

King looked up from the brief he was reading. "Oh, you do? Do you realize that half the members of your graduating class wanted the job you got? We could can you today, have a replacement by tomorrow, and the pulse of this office wouldn't miss a single beat."

Chip stood before Simon's desk. "I'm sorry. I spent a sleepless night, and when I finally—"

"You sick, young man?"

"No, sir."

"An insomniac?"

"Not usually. It's the Sampson case. It's bothering me."

King sighed and sat back in his chair. "Have a seat, Chip." King lifted the local newspaper from his desk. "I see now that you're representing this man on two murder cases. That bastard Pinter is really shafting us with this

182

one. We have quite a bit of work coming up, which means, I suspect, that you'll be burning the midnight oil to keep up with this case and our normal work."

"I'd like to get off the Sampson case," Chip admitted. "Do you have any suggestions?"

King's eyes widened with surprise. "You want off the case? Most young attorneys would be busting a gut for a murder case. You've got *two* murder cases. From your point of view, it's an excellent chance for you to make a name for yourself. Of course, from our point of view it's a disaster. Why so glum over the case?"

"I'm having difficulties with the defendant. I can't stand him, and he doesn't care much for me."

Simon chuckled. "Hell, man! You don't have to like your clients. It's not a prerequisite. Just perform the ritual. That's all that's required."

"I know that," Chip said, "but our differences have developed into a mutual and personal aversion."

Simon fiddled with his tie, trying to loosen it without untying it. "Regardless, there's nothing we can do for you. If either Arthur or myself attempted to persuade Pinter to allow you to withdraw, it would only cement his position. Perhaps if your client expressed dissatisfaction—"

"He tried to do that. Pinter ignored him."

"Then you're stuck."

Karen called the jail at 2 p.m.

"Still here," a dispatcher told her, not bothering to conceal the amusement in his voice. It was the third time she had called that day.

"Tell you what," the dispatcher said. "If he bonds out before I leave at four, I'll let you know—save you the trouble of calling."

"Thanks," Karen said.

At 2:30 p.m., Chip received a phone call from a party who had identified himself to the receptionist as Harold Sampson. "I wanna find out how I go about bailing out my brother," a rough and unpleasant voice told Chip.

"Virgil Sampson?" Harold Sampson couldn't see the grimace of emotional pain which swept over Chip's face. "Well, Mr. Sampson. I feel obligated to inform you that

183

you might be liable for as much as $25,000 if Virgil jumps his bail."

"I know that."

"How do you propose to post bail?"

"I got a house and 20 acres of land," Harold Sampson said.

"Which you will jeopardize if you go Virgil's bail," Chip said, hoping that the man would begin to develop some second thoughts. "How much do you owe on it?" Chip then asked.

"It's worth $60,000 easy. I owe maybe $2,000 on it."

That was sufficient, Chip thought. "Whose name or names is the land titled in?"

"Just mine."

"Are you married?"

"Yeah," Sampson drawled, "but the house is just in my name." Harold Sampson, given the tone of his voice, seemed to take some comfort in the fact that his wife's name wasn't on the deed. Chip took little comfort in the fact. If his wife's name were on the title, then she, too, would have to sign the bond.

Chip cleared his throat. "The Judge will have to approve the surety. What we do, as I understand it, is to appear before Judge Pinter. You obtain a statement from the assessor's office establishing the assessed value of your property and the title holders as listed on the county land books. I'll present those to the Judge. We also will need to prepare an affidavit stating any outstanding liens against the property. If the Judge finds your property sufficient to stand behind the bond, then I assume your brother will be released."

Chip hadn't known anything about how one posted bail until that morning. Clausen had given him a crash course which, Chip had hoped, might give him some idea on how to head off a bail attempt. He was on the brink of failure.

"When can we do all this?" Harold Sampson asked.

Chip's mind raced to find some excuse for delay, but he knew it was a vain gesture. "Just about any time," Chip said, very softly.

"I'm workin' now. Can we do it after work?"

"I doubt it. The Judge leaves—"

"What about tomorrow morning?"

"Fine," Chip said, maybe a little too enthusiastically.

184

At least it would give him the opportunity to warn Karen. He decided to try one more time to dampen Harold Sampson's enthusiasm. "I'm your brother's attorney, Mr. Sampson, but I do want you to be sure you want to do this. Virgil's facing not one, but two murder charges. You know him better than I do, but if he does take off, you stand to lose an awful lot."

Harold Sampson didn't say anything for a moment. When he finally spoke, Chip heard the strain in his voice. "I ain't doin' this 'cause I want to. Virgil's no good. 'Fact, I'd almost give up $25,000 to get him to leave for good."

"I don't understand," Chip said. "If you feel this way, why not just leave him in jail?"

"Our mother," Sampson explained. "She called me and begged me to do it. I tried to talk her out of it, but she's old and ailin'. He ain't never given her nothin' but grief, but he's her favorite. I just can't tell her 'no.' I'll tell you this, Mr. Lawyer, I hope you lose. I hope they send him away for the rest of his life."

Me, too, Chip thought. "Do you want me to try to get the bail hearing set for first thing in the morning?"

"I guess," Harold Sampson said. "Might as well get it over with. Maybe the no-good bastard will die in jail tonight."

"You must really hate him," Chip said.

"You ain't just a whistlin' Dixie."

The phone clicked dead.

Chip curled his lip at the serving of Mexican food which had been slopped on his plate. "It looks like regurgitated dog food," he said to Karen, who consumed her serving with appreciative relish.

"Chip!"

"What did you call it?"

"A chili burrito dinner," Karen said, smiling at his melodramatic revulsion.

Their initial meeting at the restaurant had been a little disconcerting to them both, but Karen, able to place the issue of Sampson's bail in a less emotional perspective, broke the tension by saying, "God! I'm starving."

As they had entered the small restaurant located 12 miles south of Wharton, Chip noticed Karen scanning the small crowd. If she saw anyone she knew, she concealed it.

They had sat down, ordered dinner and were waiting for it before either even mentioned Virgil Sampson. Karen finally broached the subject. "How come he hasn't made bail?"

Chip had lowered his head. "I suspect he will first thing in the morning. His brother phoned me this afternoon, and he's probably got sufficient equity in his property to back the bail. I did my best to talk him out of it. It's Sampson's mother who's pressuring him."

Karen had reached over the table and placed her hand on his. "I behaved like a schoolgirl. I'm sorry."

He squeezed her hand in an affectionate fashion. "Forget it. I was thinking on the way here. If Hemmings paid this brother of Sampson's a visit, maybe he could talk him out of posting the bail. The guy wasn't peachy keen on the notion."

Karen had looked out the window. The sun, near to setting, threw long shadows across the two lanes which fronted the small restaurant. After their food was delivered, Karen had said, "Let's just leave it alone, Chip. If we're not careful, we're going to screw around and queer any conviction we get. And you shouldn't be trying to talk his brother out of posting the bail. You're the man's lawyer, for God's sake."

"He was really giving you the evil eye in court yesterday."

"He scares me, but I've decided to try to accept it. Nelson gave me a pistol today. I spent a good part of the afternoon with Hemmings learning how to use it. I might be able to hit a rhinoceros at point-blank range."

Chip's face turned sour for an instant. Then he rolled his eyes at himself. "I started to lecture you about a gun. Can you believe that? If I were in your shoes, if that bastard was harassing me, I'd have a shotgun. Just be careful with it."

"I thought for a minute that Hemmings was going to treat me like the fellow on *The Andy Griffith Show,* the one that they would only give one bullet?"

"Don Knotts," Chip said.

"At least I can sleep tonight."

"Can we stop somewhere for a drink?" Chip asked.

Karen's eyes sparkled. "How about my place?"

186

Chip picked at the plate of food. "Only if you have bicarbonate."

"Gotcha covered."

"Aren't we supposed to be discreet?" Chip then asked.

Karen, her mouth stuffed with tortilla chips, nodded. She washed the food down with the beer she had also ordered. "I came here with every intention of going home alone," she then said. "Your charm has overwhelmed me. Besides, this might be the last night that I can relax for awhile. I'm damned if I'm going to waste it."

# FOUR

Virgil Sampson warranted isolation, meaning he got a cell all to himself—which suited the hell out of him. He considered it a mark of success, a matter of great pride which distinguished him from the scum in the jail.

The isolation cell was situated so that the dispatcher could maintain something of a surveillance on its inhabitants, and from the cell Virgil could see the dispatcher.

"Hey, pig!" Virgil shouted.

"I ain't a cop," the dispatcher shouted back.

"That don't mean you ain't a pig." Virgil laughed uproariously at his own joke.

"Go to hell," said the dispatcher, who didn't find Virgil funny at all.

"I wanna make a call."

"Not on this shift, Sampson. You had your phone call today."

Virgil rose from the hard bunk and went to the bars. "Hey, punk! I got my rights. I need to make another call."

The dispatcher rose from his chair and walked over to the cell. He swung shut a metal door which closed off the cell in which Virgil Sampson was housed.

"Pig!" screamed Virgil.

One of these days, he thought. He thought about raising hell for an hour or so, just to get under the dispatcher's skin, but he decided instead to relax. He'd be out tomorrow. His momma had persuaded his brother to put up his house for bail.

Virgil returned to his bunk. He settled in for his night in the jail and began to daydream, imagining himself as the Lone Ranger, replete with the black mask and white horse, but armed with a machine gun instead of a .45 revolver. The image played before his mind. Astride his horse, he swept through Wharton, mowing down all those who dared defy him. And the cops, their faces dark with heavy beards, came after him. They were the bad guys, and he turned the machine gun on them, battling their onslaught heroically. In the end he rode away victorious, a million dollar bounty on his head . . .

. . . but not alone.

The lady prosecutor rode behind his saddle, her arms wrapped securely around his chest. Christ, she was a pretty thing, her blonde hair flowing with the breeze as they left Wharton together.

His fantasy descended to a somewhat more realistic and bestial level. Before it was over, he intended to pay the lady a visit—a very private visit. She'd fight him at first, but, once it was done, she'd worship him. Sometimes a fellow just had to do something rough to get the attention of a woman like her. Once she felt him inside her, she'd come around.

His thoughts assumed an erotic texture as he imagined Karen Kinder submitting to him, her streamlined body rubbing against his. Her eyes, at first wide with fear, were now closed in pleasure. He even imagined her sweet stink as she wetted herself for him. As he began to stroke, she moaned softly and dug her long nails deep into his back.

"What the shit do you think you're doin'?" a voice cried, shattering Virgil's fantasy for the moment.

He opened his eyes and saw the stricken face of the dispatcher peering through the small bean hole in the metal door. "Whacking off. What the hell do you think?"

The dispatcher's face reddened at the sight of the prisoner masturbating right in front of him. "You can't do that!"

Sampson leered at the young man. "Come in here and stop me."

"I'll call for help."

Sampson snickered, still doing it to himself. "I could use a little help. You wanna suck it?"

The small metal door covering the bean hole shut with a metallic violence which coincided with Virgil's orgasm.

Coincidentally, across town in Karen's apartment, she did writhe with pleasure, but not from the attention of Virgil Sampson. She and Chip made love wildly, as if it was the eve of some great journey for one or the other of them. After they were finished, Karen closed her eyes and languished in its sensory aftermath. Chip, lying beside her, petted her still rigid nipples. "Why can't life be like this always?" she said.

"Maybe it can be."

"Ever the romantic," she said.

"The Sampson case will end sometime."

The warmth was leaving her, sneaking away as if offended by the sudden severity of her thoughts. "Someone else just like him will come along then. The world's full of people just like him."

"Forget him," Chip pleaded. "At least for tonight."

She had tried. God! She had tried.

But he haunted her. She knew he was locked behind bars, but still it seemed as though his menacing spirit hovered just beyond the walls of her bedroom. Her fear of him had gone beyond a merely physical terror and had become instead a horror which transcended reality itself.

Clarke Nelson insisted on appearing in Karen's stead at the brief hearing on the approval of Harold Sampson's surety. Panzini had phoned Chip first thing that morning to say that he was going to be tied up. Chip would have to appear. When Chip had so informed Simon King, the junior King had frowned. "Get back here as soon as you can. We've got three divorce interviews scheduled for you this morning."

Chip stood with Virgil before the bench. Harold Sampson waited in the rear of the courtroom, silently hoping that the Judge would find something wrong with his property. Harold Sampson knew, though, that his brother would get out. Virgil possessed the kind of good luck which seemed so common to the truly evil, as if, Harold had told his wife, he'd sold his soul to the devil or something.

Pinter reviewed the surety statements and affidavit handed to him by Chip. Nelson scanned copies which Chip had provided for him. When the Judge was finished, he turned to Nelson. "Any problems from the State's point of view."

Nelson rose. "Your Honor, the State objects, not to the property, but to the amount of the defendant's bail." Nelson knew his efforts were in vain. He had planned to argue vociferously for an increase in the bail until he had read the morning paper. It devoted its editorial column to a tirade against Pinter for setting Virgil Sampson's bond so low. As a consequence of the editorial, Nelson had given up on his plea, not wanting it to seem to Pinter that he and the newspaper were in cahoots. He had a good relationship with the Judge . . . no sense jeopardizing it in the pursuit of a useless cause.

The prosecutor saw one hope. "Judge, if you like, we might discuss these matters in chambers."

Pinter tossed a wary but agitated look to the middle-aged female reporter who covered the courthouse beat. "Might be a good idea," he grumbled. "Bailiff, escort the prisoner back to my chambers."

The female reporter puffed up like an obese adder but could say nothing, not at least until the next morning's edition.

Nelson, Chip, Virgil Sampson, the bailiff, and the Judge gathered in Pinter's chambers. Nelson renewed his efforts. "I know you took a pretty good rapping by the paper this morning, and I know that makes it a little more difficult for you to reconsider the matter of the bail."

"If I did," Pinter said, "it would appear that I was yielding to media pressure and public sentiment."

Virgil, seated farther away from the Judge than anyone else, smacked a wad of chewing gum in his mouth. The bailiff stood behind him. Chip sat quietly. He planned to do nothing more than generally oppose any increase in bail.

"We have another problem," Nelson said. "We have some reason to believe that Mr. Sampson here has been attempting to intimidate a State's attorney—Karen Kinder, to be precise."

Chip's eyes widened. He sat up in his chair.

Pinter arched his eyebrows. "Just how is this being done?"

"He, or perhaps his friends, have been hanging around her apartment at all hours of the night. She's gotten a phone call or two. There's a third matter, too, Judge. We also have reason to believe that the defendant has conveyed threats to the juvenile in this case through the boy's mother. For these reasons, I ask that you increase the amount of bail to $100,000."

Virgil lurched from his chair. "Hey, goddammit! That ain't—"

The bailiff nabbed Virgil by the shirt collar and slammed him back into the chair. "Stay put," he ordered.

And Pinter, taken aback by the defendant's outburst, pounded his fist on his desk. "I won't have that, Mr. Sampson. You just sit there and be quiet. Your attorney will speak for you."

"He ain't said much so far," Virgil countered.

"I warn you—" Pinter started to say.

"Sorry, Judge," Virgil said quickly. "I just don't think it's right."

At that point, Pinter turned to Chip. "What do you have to say?"

"The arguments I made yesterday still have merit," Chip said, snatching a quick peek at Nelson. "Obviously, in the court's wisdom, it felt $25,000 was sufficient yesterday. I have heard nothing to warrant an increase."

Chip almost choked on his words. He wanted to join with the prosecutor in asking for an increase, but he was a lawyer. No matter what else, he was Virgil Sampson's lawyer.

Pinter didn't think about it very long. All that was on his mind was the newspaper. And, if Karen Kinder was being bothered, well, Roger Pinter felt no great sympathy for her. "Mr. Sampson," he said, "I'm not going to raise your bail. However, if I become convinced that you are attempting to intimidate any officer of this court or any witness in this matter, I will revoke bail, issue a bench warrant and remand you to jail without bail. Do I make myself clear?"

Virgil couldn't suppress a smile. "Crystal clear," he said.

The solemn look on the prosecutor's face said it all.

"He's out," Karen said.

Nelson nodded.

Karen shuddered. "I knew he would be."

Nelson slammed the fist of his right hand into the palm of his left. "That damned newspaper! If it had just stayed the hell out of it for a day at least, I might have gotten the bail hiked."

"I didn't know you were going to try," Karen said, truly surprised.

"I tried, but Pinter wasn't about to have it appear that he succumbed to media sentiment. The bastards!"

"What did Chip say?"

Nelson collapsed into a chair in front of Karen's desk. "As damned little as he could get by with. If he were representing me and had been so passive . . . well, anyway . . . I told the Judge that Sampson had been attempting to intimidate you."

Karen was stunned. "You told him that?"

"It was my only hope."

"And Sampson was there?"

Nelson nodded.

"Chip, too?"

Nelson hoisted a weak smile. "Yeah. The kid probably pissed in his pants."

"You had no right!"

Nelson remained calm. "I had every right. It's evidence that the man is dangerous. Don't get so upset. It ran off Pinter's back like water off a duck. He gave Sampson a stern warning."

"And probably hopes the bastard nails me," Karen said.

"You don't alienate the Judge, Karen. That's lesson numero uno in the real world."


Chip used the trip to the courthouse to clear up a title search he had been assigned. Once he completed that, he walked out of the building to find Virgil Sampson leaning against his car.

"Are you still here?" Chip asked coldly.

"Waitin' on you," Virgil answered, just as coldly.

"For what?"

Virgil mouthed a toothpick. "My brother says you tried to talk him outa goin' my bail."

Chip, his stomach full of crawly feelings, glared at his client. "I informed your brother of the consequences if you jumped bail. I was obligated to do that."

"Same thing as tryin' to talk him outa it in my book."

Chip opened the car door and tossed his briefcase into the steamy interior. "I don't read your book."

He started to slide into the car, but Virgil snagged him by the arm. Chip tried to jerk away. "I don't like my lawyer fuckin' a woman who wants to put me away."

Chip felt compelled to send a fist flying at Sampson. The

193

urge seemed irrepressible, but he held back. "My personal life has nothing to do with your case. If you continue to harass her, I'll go to the Judge myself, withdraw from the case, and tell him you told me you were going to skip town. One way or another, I'll get you locked up."

Virgil's eyes narrowed. The muscles in his clenched jaws rippled. Chip hoped that Virgil Sampson couldn't notice his trembling hands. He went on. "For now, I'm stuck with you, and vice versa. But if you cause her any grief, I'll do everything I can to get you."

The mask of hooliganish wrath melted into an evil smile. "Cool, Mr. Lawyer. That's real cool."

Virgil's eyes, dark yet scintillating, bore into Chip's, and Chip knew things were anything but "cool."

# FIVE

Virgil Sampson vanished.

He left Chip, trembling but still defiant by his car, and walked to his home where he packed a few clothes in a small paper bag. He told his mother to tell "my egg-sucking brother that I ain't jumping bail . . . just gettin' away for a few days." He kissed her, as he always did before he went anywhere, and was gone.

Karen and Chip also vanished, slipping from Wharton like uncovered agents in a spy thriller. The plan had been conjured the night before. Chip's small suitcase was in the trunk of his Toyota. Karen had left her small overnight bag and make-up kit at Myra's. A small cluster of Custer County deputies watched with some consternation as Myra's car pulled into the closed garage area of the jail. One of the officers had just started toward the trespassing vehicle when Karen appeared, told him they would leave at once, and got inside. The deputies' irritation became bewilderment when they saw the assistant prosecutor slip down out of sight as the car backed out of the garage.

Myra delivered Karen to the prearranged rendezvous and transfer site 10 miles south of Wharton. It took place in a small roadside park surrounded by a wide expanse of meadowland, a place where Chip had remembered picnicking with his parents and which provided no chance for any third-party, clandestine observation. By 5:30 that Friday afternoon, Karen and Chip were driving south to spend a weekend in Raleigh, NC. Chip had selected the city because he had once had friends who lived there.

The Toyota entered the cool tube of a tunnel which hurried traffic through the mountains of southwestern Virginia. "Can you believe this?" Karen said. "I felt like Mata Hari back there."

"Better safe than sorry. My client was waiting for me when I left the courthouse this morning."

"Oh, shit!"

Chip told her of the conversation. He concluded by saying, "My knees were knocking together, but he didn't notice."

"But he threatened you!"

"Not really. He stopped just short of it. Actually, I threatened him. I told him if he continued to bother you, I'd tell the Judge that he planned to jump bail."

"You didn't?"

They exited the tunnel, and Chip blinked in the sudden, sunny brightness. "I did, too," he said, shielding his eyes. "What difference does it make? Your boss just about let the cat out of the bag anyway."

"He told me."

A Virginia police car appeared from nowhere in Chip's rearview mirror. He glanced down at the Toyota's speedometer and breathed a sigh of relief. The speedometer wavered between 55 and 60. The cruiser wheeled around him and sped on by. "I always wondered what makes cops think they can drive faster than 55."

"Executive privilege," Karen said.

Virgil hitchhiked west, straight toward the descending sun and the state of Kentucky. His pockets were empty, except for his knife, but he had learned at an early age that hitchhiking was a good way to earn a little quick cash. Two rides after he had started, a guy picked him up who Virgil pegged as a "pansy."

Sure enough, not long after dark, the guy propositioned him—20 bucks if he could blow Virgil. An hour later, Virgil owned the entire contents of the guy's thick wallet. The car's owner lay slumped against a tree up a dark road. When he came around (Sampson hadn't hit him too hard), he'd have to walk quite a way to report the theft of his wallet and car, assuming the guy even had the guts to do it.

After all . . .

Chip blessed Mastercard for the trip to Raleigh. His card had arrived two days before. The funds from the previous bank loan had expired, and payday wasn't until Monday. Nonetheless, with the power derived from his new credit card, he and Karen checked into the luxurious Marriott just across U.S. 70 from the rambling Crabtree Mall.

They pulled into the parking lot just after eleven. Despite the lateness of the hour, the night was muggy and hot, a remnant of the searing heat which had baked the coastal Carolina plains earlier in the day. They didn't go straight to bed, though. Instead they checked into the room and then went to the posh lounge where both drank far more than they had intended—again, compliments of his virgin credit card. The lounge was chock-full of beautiful and total strangers, none of whose faces looked the least bit threatening or even interested in the loving couple who occupied a dim and distant corner table.

At 2 a.m., each supporting the other, they closed the bar and swaggered back to their room, both determined to make love. Their bodies, tired from the drive and listless from the alcohol, refused to allow it, and they plummeted into an almost immediate sleep.

The insistent rapping of a maid awakened them the next morning. Chip had forgotten to hang out the "Do Not Disturb" sign. "Go away!" Chip shouted from the bed.

"Maid!" a voice cried back, as if that made all the difference.

Chip stumbled out of bed. His head still reeled from the effects of the prior night's abuse. His mouth was parched. He made it to the door and inched it open. "We're not up yet," he told the huge black woman whose look hinted at mayhem. She went away mumbling to herself.

Chip turned, anxious to get back into bed. He saw Karen, her ivory body pink with the glow of the bed's warmth, bound from the bed and toss open the curtains. Bright Carolina sunshine invaded the room and enveloped her bareness. "It's a beautiful day," she said, sliding open the door to let the warm air enter with the sunlight.

"You'll get arrested for indecent exposure," Chip said, falling with a groan to the bed.

Karen stared down at the multilevel parking lots flanking the Crabtree Mall. The morning sun glinted off the tops of the cars which were already filling the lots. "That's my idea of heaven," she announced.

Chip lifted his head from the bed. "How in the name of God can you be so cheerful? Don't you have a hangover?"

Karen left the window and fell beside him on the bed. "I seldom get a hangover. And you snore."

Chip sat up. "I do not."

She pulled him back down to the bed. "I'm horny."

Chip tried to pull away. "At least let me brush my teeth."

"You couldn't have worse breath than me," she said.


Art Louck found Mickie reading a comic book in his cell—his unit, as they called them at the detention center. He handed Chip an envelope which had arrived in the Saturday morning mail.

Mickie took it. "For me?"

"You're Mickie Sampson."

The boy studied the sprawling scrawl across the face of the small white enclosure.

"Do you recognize the handwriting?"

Mickie shook his head. Clumsily, he ripped open the envelope and withdrew the note, written on a small sheet of yellow paper. He read the words slowly, moving his lips with obvious imprecision. When he had finished, he let it flutter to the floor.

Louck noticed the boy's pallor. "What'd it say?"

The boy looked at Louck. "It's from Uncle Virg. It says he hopes I get out soon. He's lookin' forward to seeing me."

Louck snatched the note from the floor. Mickie had stated the note's contents very precisely. The social worker shook his head. "It's not really a threat."

Mickie fell to the bed and covered his head with his pillow.


Hemmings received a call from one of the other troopers after his Saturday evening supper. "A fellow by the name of Harold Sampson called here for you," the trooper told Hemmings. "He wanted your home phone number . . . said it was urgent. I told him I would call you and give you the message. Then you could call him if you wanted."

"Did he say what he wanted?" Hemmings asked.

"No, sir."

"He went Virgil Sampson's bail. Maybe I'd better call him."

Hemmings phoned the number the other officer gave him. A gruff, impatient voice answered. "Mr. Sampson, this is Cpl. Hemmings."

"Yeah! Glad you called me back. My brother's left town."

Hemmings measured his words. "That was one of the risks you took, sir, when you went his bail."

"He said he was comin' back. Leastways that's what he told our mother. I thought a guy out on bail couldn't leave town."

Hemmings sighed. "The only thing your brother has to do is make his court appearances. If he does that, he complies with the conditions of the bail. That's the way it is."

Harold Sampson grew irritated. "Somebody shoulda told me that. It ain't right! I mean I got a lot ridin' on him. He oughta have to stay right here until his trial."

"I'm just the investigating officer," Hemmings replied, himself becoming somewhat bothered. "I suggest you call the prosecuting attorney. He's the one—"

"You're a cop, ain't ya?"

"But you're your brother's jailer, Mr. Sampson. You round him up and turn him in, and that'll get you out from under the bond."

Sampson's naturally coarse voice grew more strident, more indignant. "I ain't no fuckin' cop. Virgil's crazy. He's mean. He'd just as soon shoot me as you! I sure as hell—"

Hemmings's patience was exhausted. "Look, fella! I'm not even working tonight. I returned your call, but I'm not about to listen to any more crap. You knew what you were doing. If you get burned, I'd say you shoulda seen it coming."

"A hell of a lot of fuckin' good you people—"

Hemmings quietly hung up the phone.

Chip and Karen started back toward Wharton at 1 p.m. Sunday afternoon. As soon as his car pulled into the westbound lane of U.S. 70, Chip sensed the sudden shift in Karen's mood. They had spent a joyful Saturday shopping at the mall. On the previous night, they had again closed down the Marriott's lounge and had then made love until almost dawn. They had awakened just in time to beat the checkout time. Throughout all of it, Karen had been up and happy and bubbling—until they started home.

She turned silent as Chip navigated the roller coaster of a highway connecting Raleigh to Durham and points west. Chip leaned forward to measure the progress of the sun. "Maybe we can get to I-77 and start north before it gets too low," he said, trying to make conversation. "It's murder if it gets too low while you're heading due west."

"What time will we get home?"

Chip checked his watch and did some quick mental calculations. "Given the Sunday traffic, probably around six unless we stop for a while somewhere."

Karen just nodded.

"Are you that scared?"

"I try to be brave," she said, "but he scares me. It's his eyes. There's nothing human in them." She turned to stare toward a rolling, well-kept cemetery on their left. "He's death, Chip. He's a grave maker."

But, when Chip and Karen finally got back into Wharton that evening, Virgil Sampson was miles away. He sat on a barstool in a beer joint in southeastern Kentucky. Virgil still owned a good part of the bankroll he had removed from the guy who had given him a ride. He had abandoned the vehicle the previous day after the engine developed some trouble.

As Karen had in Raleigh, Virgil enjoyed his current anonymity. No one in the dark, rank confines of the humid bar knew him. People weren't staring at him, pointing him out as the guy accused of two murders. They talked to him just like he was one of them—hillbillies whose pitiful lives depended upon the ups and downs of the coal fields.

The nasal whine of George Jones issued from a garish jukebox. Shrill, female laughter came from the shadowy corners. Virgil swiveled around on the barstool, his eyes trying to see into the corners. Virgil ached for a woman. More precisely, he ached for that female lawyer, but that would happen in time, in Virgil's own good time.

The Kinder chick knew it. They all knew it, especially that punk kid of a lawyer who's laying her.

That was the best part to Virgil. He didn't even have to be back home to worry her, to make her scared of even the slightest sound of the night.

Virgil laughed.

A woman, big and hefty with tits that came to settle on the scarred surface of the bar, hoisted herself onto a stool beside Virgil. "Hey, cowboy. What's so friggin' funny?"

"Hey, momma!" Virgil cried. "I dig them jugs of yours."

She leaned away from him, an instant caution in her heavily made-up eyes. "Ain't you a fast one. Tell you what. You buy me a beer, and let's just talk for awhile before we get too personal."

Virgil laughed some more and bought her a beer.

It was so easy for Virgil. It always had been. Women just kind of came to him . . . maybe because of his smell. He always smelled like a hard-working man.

Or maybe it was his eyes. Some women had told him they liked his eyes.

The lawyer bitch would come around once he got ahold of her. For now, the woman beside him, with her great big tits, would do just fine.

# SIX

Vickie Carmichael recognized the overpowering nature of her physical attributes. She dressed to enhance her bounty. On the evening before, a humid and windless Tuesday night, she had escaped the heat of her small house by driving out to Pine Ridge Mall. In the air conditioned coolness of J.C. Penney's, Vickie had purchased a new dress which swooped low on her chest. She had gone across the aisle and purchased a bra which lifted her mammoth breasts right out of the low-cut dress. It would be Hemmings's theory that her provocative dress had gotten the secretary into trouble, but Karen would suggest otherwise . . . not that their theories really mattered.

If Vickie—who knew Virgil had an appointment that Wednesday—had known a little more about the man, perhaps she might have worn something else that morning. On the other hand, Virgil Sampson may have done what he did no matter what she had worn. Vickie realized her mistake as soon as Virgil entered Panzini's outer office. At once, he ogled the fluffy, tanned mounds of flesh erupting above the bodice of the sundress.

"Nice tits," he said aloud, leering, almost drooling.

Vickie blushed all the way down to the delicate mounds of soft skin. "I'll tell Mr. Panzini that you're here," she said, trying to put as much ice into her tone as she could.

Sampson licked his lips. His body odor reached out to Vickie, and she recoiled as she reached to buzz her employer. She kept her eyes on Sampson. Dark, prickly stubble shadowed his cheeks and neck. His hair lay in greasy strands on his head.

She received no immediate response from her boss.

Vickie jumped from her chair and hurried into Panzini's office. "What's your hurry?" Virgil called after her.

In just a second, the lawyer came back out with her. "In my office!" Panzini snapped to Sampson.

Panzini saw the sudden flash of rage which crossed his client's face. Just as quickly, the fleeting displeasure vanished to be replaced by an affected grin. "Sure thing," Virgil said, his voice projecting total innocence. He turned and swaggered down the hall and into the front door of Panzini's office.

Panzini used the other door and met Virgil just as the client entered. "Let me tell you something," the lawyer said. "I gotta represent you, but by God you're not comin' in here and making obscene remarks to my secretary. You understand me?"

Virgil shrugged off his sin. "Didn't mean no harm. Besides, women dress that way so us men'll notice. I just noticed."

Panzini seldom lost his poise, but on this day a fit of outrage grabbed him. "Just who the hell do you think you are?" the lawyer said, prancing back and forth behind his huge desk. His darkly complected face reddened with anger.

"Easy!" Virgil said. "I done said I was sorry."

Panzini saw no apology in Virgil Sampson's eyes. If anything, the foul-smelling bastard was mocking him. "You're not sorry. You don't know what the word means."

Virgil could only take so much tongue-lashing. It just didn't set well with him. The urge to react rocketed toward the surface, and he hoisted himself from his chair. Panzini braced for the attack.

"Ah, the shit with ya!" Virgil said, sinking back into his chair. "I don't fight old men, but I'll tell you this, lawyer man. You got a smart mouth."

Panzini waited for a moment, just to be sure. Then he sat down, suddenly thankful that Sampson hadn't come at him. He'd never been much of a brawler. "Mr. Roth is on his way. I'd prefer to wait on him before we get into this matter."

Virgil had phoned early that morning to tell Panzini that he needed to see him, adding that it was "very important."

"You want I should wait outside," Virgil offered.

"Hell, no! Just stay put."

Virgil smiled broadly.

As Chip entered Panzini's office, he noticed that Vickie seemed very pale, very agitated. "What's wrong?" he asked.

"That bastard!"

"Panzini?"

Vickie shook her head so vigorously that it made her bursting boobs jiggle. "No! That Sampson bastard. You wouldn't believe what he said to me."

Chip, too, had noticed the dress. "I can just imagine," he said.

"He smells so raunchy I almost puked."

"I'll just go on in," Chip said.

Panzini relaxed a little as Chip walked through the door. "Chip! Good to see you." Panzini rose and offered Chip his hand. Virgil just nodded at the younger lawyer, and once again Chip didn't offer to shake Virgil's hand. "What's up?" he asked of Panzini.

Panzini hiked his shoulder. "Who knows? Our client called me this morning and said he just had to see us."

Virgil was quick to correct Panzini. "I called to talk to you. It was your idea to call in the kid, here." He tossed Chip a look of contempt which Chip openly returned. The young lawyer surprised himself with his courage, knowing that his behavior was like the taunting of an uncaged but vicious animal.

"So . . . what's up?" Panzini said to Virgil.

"I wanna talk a deal."

"You what?" Panzini asked.

"I wanna cop some kind of plea," Virgil explained.

Panzini looked to Chip, who was no less surprised than the veteran lawyer. "What kind of deal?" Panzini asked.

"I'll plead guilty to killin' the old woman," Virgil said, "but they gotta drop the other one. And no first degree murder either. I won't plead to first."

Chip laughed. He just couldn't help himself. "You're crazy, Sampson. Nelson won't buy any kind of pleas. He thinks he's got you on both counts for first degree."

"The kid's telling you straight," Panzini added. "We're obligated to mention it to him, if that's what you want, but it's a waste of time."

"Hold it a minute," Chip said. "I don't understand. You might slip out of the Mack case easier than the other one."

"At least we only have one eyewitness to rattle in that case," Panzini also said. "On the first one, there are half a dozen witnesses. What's your angle, Sampson?"

Virgil lowered his head. "That kid . . . Mickie . . . I kinda got a special feelin' for him . . . like he was mine. I wanna help him outa this mess. He deserves a break."

"Sure," mocked Panzini. "You're just brimmin' with peace and love and good thoughts. Somebody might buy that bullshit, but not me. I bet as young as he is, even Chip here ain't gonna buy that sob story."

Virgil eyed both lawyers, again smiling. "Okay. I'll level with you both. You know if that fuckin' little bastard talks, I'm a goner. They'll nail me on a first degree murder."

"But it doesn't make sense!" Chip persisted. "Why try to deal on the ugliest charge? Any court would be more likely to burn you on the Mack case than on the other one."

"I got my reason," Sampson said.

"Let's wait until after the kid's psychiatric examination." Panzini suggested. "Shit. They might decide the kid's a real nut."

Virgil tensed. "When they gonna do it?"

"Tomorrow afternoon at the hospital."

"Just talk to 'em," Virgil persisted. "You tell 'em I'm doing it for the kid. So long as they don't send him up to do hard time, the rest I'll be willing to talk about. Anything but first degree murder."

"Like I said," Panzini emphasized, "we're obligated to pass your message along. Just don't count on it. I'll show you out." Panzini rose from the chair.

Virgil frowned. "I know the way."

"I'm not worried about you getting lost," Panzini retorted.

When Panzini returned to his office after showing Sampson to the door, Chip said to him, "He's after something."

Panzini agreed. "He don't give a damn about that kid, but I can't figure what he's after."

Chip rubbed his chin. "Maybe he figures that if they buy the deal, then they'll release the kid before the matter comes up. That would give him a chance to get to the kid."

"Maybe," Panzini mused.

"I'll talk to the prosecutor's office," Chip offered.

Panzini eyed his partner in the case. "And, I gather, you're gonna suggest that possibility to them."

"I thought I might mention it."

Panzini laughed. "Go right ahead and talk to them."


Within an hour, Chip sat in Nelson's office with Karen and the chief prosecutor. Both of them listened to him with amused smiles. "So Sampson's worried about the kid?" Nelson said when Chip had finished.

"So he says."

"Bullshit!"

"He's our client," Chip explained. "We felt obliged to present it to you. At first, we planned to wait until after the kid's psychological, but there really seemed no reason to."

Nelson propped his feet up on his desk and leaned back in his chair. "You tell your client that there won't be any plea bargains in this case. We're going after him on both charges." He looked at Karen. "Any sign of him around your place?"

"None at all."

"According to Hemmings," Nelson told them, "our boy left town this weekend."

Karen and Chip exchanged sudden glances. Nelson picked up on it. "Of course we have no idea where he went," he said.

Karen blushed, but Chip shook his head. "Don't worry about it," he said to her. "We planned a masterful escape."

Still, Karen worried.


Even as she left work that afternoon, Vickie's encounter with Sampson remained chillingly vivid. She blamed it on the dress. It was probably too late to return it, so she vowed to herself to sell it at a yard sale or to destroy it. No matter that it cost her good money, of which she had little enough.

The June sun remained high and bright at 5 p.m. The heavy heat felt good to her as she moved toward the municipal lot in which she rented a space for her aged Volkswagen. Vickie had been cold all afternoon, which she chose to blame on the air conditioning. She spoke to other secretaries who were also leaving their jobs in the handful of other offices in the same area.

Vickie, as she exited the lot, noticed the blue car behind her, but she gave it little thought. She was in a hurry to get home. It was early enough for her to lay in the sun for an hour or so after she got home. Not that she expected to get very much sun so late in the day, but she wanted to try to hold the tan she had gotten during her vacation.

Her house, located a few miles north of Wharton, had been left to her by a grandmother. During the divorce, her former husband had tried to get the house, but the Judge had just laughed at that portion of her husband's prayer for relief. The house sat far back in a tall grove of pines and the privacy of its backyard allowed Vickie the luxury of nude sunbathing. On this day, though, she chose to wear a bright orange two-piece. She chilled a little as she exited her house, but once she was spread out on her stomach, the rays of the sun vanquished her chill and brought a sheen of sweat to her already dark skin.

Since it was so late, Vickie used no lotion. She reached behind her back and unfastened the thin tie strings on the bikini's top. Bees buzzed around her as she adjusted her body upon the huge towel which she had spread on the lumpy ground. She rested her chin on the back of her hand and studied an ant as it threaded its way through the jungle of grass. She was thinking of how badly the grass needed to be mowed when a lonely cloud . . . or something . . . cast a shadow across her body.

She started to look around, but the voice stopped her.

"I shaved for ya," said a masculine voice.

Vickie gasped. She flipped over, forgetting even to grab the bra to her swimsuit. Virgil Sampson smiled down upon her, at the massive breasts which jiggled like extra firm gelatin.

He was on her before she could scream. The sharp point of a small knife pricked her throat. "Don't holler," he rasped. She gurgled a little, and her fear became a choking, swelling knot in her chest. Roughly, she was hauled to her feet. One arm was locked around her throat. In its hand was the knife. The other hand came around to cup one of her breasts.

"In the house!" Virgil commanded.

"What will they do to me tomorrow?" Mickie asked of Art Louck.

207

"I can't tell you exactly," Louck said. He had brought Mickie his dinner and sat with the boy as he ate. Since the juvenile was charged with murder, he was being isolated from the other inmates.

"Does it hurt?"

Louck laughed. "It's a psychological examination, Mickie. A doctor will ask you some questions, kind of talk to you, but I don't think he will do anything that hurts."

"But it's at the hospital," Mickie said. He equated the hospital with previous experiences, all of which had involved some degree of discomfort.

"The psychiatrist has his office there."

Mickie was just picking at his food. "I ain't crazy. I'm tellin' them the truth."

"Take it easy," Louck said. "No one is saying you're crazy. Your lawyer requested the examination. It might help you."

Mickie dropped his spoon into his tray. "It'll help me if I'm crazy. I'm not crazy."

"Well, don't worry about it," Louck said. "Things will work out." Mickie seemed agitated, his mood very unsettled. "What's wrong, Mickie?"

"How come my uncle's outa jail and I'm not?" he said.

"Who told you he was out of jail?"

"My mother. She came to see me today."

Louck threw up his hands in exasperation. He had tried to get the detention center director to prevent Mrs. Sampson from visiting her son. Her visits did nothing but upset him. Louck hadn't been at the center that afternoon, and obviously the center's director hadn't abided by Louck's wishes—which wasn't all that unusual.

"Please go," Vickie pleaded. "Leave me alone."

She had mounted only token resistance as Virgil Sampson had wrestled her into the house. He had shoved her around the small house until he located her bedroom. There, he had thrown her down on the white bedspread.

"But I shaved for ya," he repeated for the second time, using the hand without the knife to rub his face. Dark streaks of stubble had eluded whatever kind of razor he had used, and the striped pattern of his beard created a demonic mask of his leering face.

Vickie started to babble, to cry, as he leaned down. With

208

a single flick of the blade, he sliced away the thin strip of material on one side of the bikini panties. He ripped away the material. The point of the knife cruised through her dark but fine pubic hair, its touch like the caress of a snake against her skin. She whimpered but held as still as she could as its cold edge slipped into the folds of flesh which protected her femininity.

"Please!" she cried.

Virgil rose from the bed. For an exhilarating moment, Vickie thought that he was leaving—until he started to unbuckle his pants. Her eyes bulged, and she screamed as loudly and shrilly as she could.

His jeans, stiff with grease and dirt, crumpled slowly toward the floor. He dived on top of her and began to knead her breasts. Drool dripped onto her nipples. His sharp knees pushed between her soft thighs, and he entered her.

Vickie thought of the knife. Where is it? Could she reach it?

An abrasive flash of pain caused her to shriek as he forced himself deep inside her. She twisted her head first to the left, then to the right, searching for the knife, dodging his foul lips as they sought hers. Sampson grunted away above her.

Blessedly, her conscious mind fled from the terrifying and revolting reality, retreating behind the shroud of a faint.


Maury Austin had waited until Virgil disappeared into the house's backyard. Just like Virgil had wanted, he waited a little longer, just to be sure Virgil didn't come back out. The minutes passed slowly, and it was pure agony. Maury knew what Virgil was doing.

It was part of Virgil's plan for Maury to leave. Virgil said he was going to take the girl's car. So Maury drove off—in a hurry. He had told Virgil he was going straight home, but that was a lie. The Torino's gas tank was full, and a small suitcase lay concealed under some greasy blankets in the car's trunk. Maury headed for I-77. He was going south.

Time had come to put a good many miles between Virgil and himself. He had planned to leave earlier, but Virgil had showed up at his house—almost caught him dumping the suitcase in the trunk. Maury didn't really want to leave, but he'd decided it was best.

And that decision had been made much earlier—before he had become an accomplice to a rape.

Virgil tossed a glass of cold water on the girl's face. She came alive screaming. He slapped her into silence. She resisted him not at all as he wrapped her in the white bedspread and pushed her out the back door to her small gray Volkswagen. He tied her hands with a piece of rope he had in his hip pocket and gagged her with his grimy handkerchief. Just to be safe, he concealed her beneath the white bed covering. She gagged at the handkerchief's foulness, but Virgil slapped her two or three more times. She turned silent.

The car keys were in her purse. So too was about $25.

Not a bad screw, Virgil thought, as he struggled to become familiar with the VW's stick shift. He patted the two tens and a five which he had jammed down into the pocket of his shirt. Better yet, he'd gotten paid for it.

# SEVEN

Virgil just cruised the county for several hours. In the back seat, his captive grunted against the bindings. Around 8 p.m., he glanced down and saw that the gas tank was almost empty. And he was getting pretty fucking tired of listening to the bitch groan. He'd hollered at her several times, but she hadn't stopped. Now he needed some gas, and he couldn't have her making such noises in the back seat.

He pulled the small car into a secluded parking lot at the rear of a vacant warehouse just south of the town limits. It was almost dusk. Virgil got out of the car and searched for any possible witnesses. Seeing no one, he uncovered the girl. Her eyes bulged at him. Her face was deep red and soaked with sweat. The gag, too, was soaked with both sweat and saliva.

Virgil hit her once before he removed the handkerchief. "You make any noise, and I'll cut off one of them tits," he threatened. "You unnerstand me?"

Vickie Carmichael's eyes fluttered with fear.

"You unnerstand!" Virgil cuffed her once more and then lifted up one of her breasts. Furiously, Vickie nodded that she understood.

He removed the gag. Vickie gasped for fresh air.

"Now, lookee here, bitch." He squeezed the breast which he still held. She gasped in pain. "I gotta get some gas in this car of yours. Now, you make any noise, and you're dead. You unnerstand?"

"Please! Just let me go," Vickie wailed. "You can have the car. I promise I won't tell anyone."

Virgil chuckled. "Shit, girl! You think I'm dumb or

211

somethin'? I got your car, and I got you. I ain't done with you yet, not unless you cause a stir at the gas station."

"Oh, please—"

This time Virgil jammed the wet handkerchief into her mouth, having already balled it up. He pushed it in deep. She struggled against him. "That oughta keep you quiet," he said, taking time to run a finger around her large nipple. He then checked the restraints, decided they were fine, and covered her again.

Chip, sitting alone in his apartment, checked the time and then hurried to the telephone. He'd promised to call Karen about 10:30 each night. That way she would be pretty sure that it was him calling. He allowed the phone to ring twice, then hung up and redialed. It was their prearranged signal, and Karen grabbed the phone on the first ring. "You must have been right on top of the phone," he told her.

"I was going to take if off the hook," she told him.

"What? Has something happened?"

"Not really. Myra just left and I wanted to take a quick shower. I'm kinda behind schedule tonight. What would you have thought if you had called and it had rung and rung with no answer?"

"The worst," Chip admitted. "God! I want to see you. I don't think I can wait until the weekend."

"You just saw me this afternoon."

"I mean 'hold you-see you,' " Chip said.

"Not a good idea," she told him.

"I have an idea." Chip had spent the better part of the evening contriving his plan. "I'll drop by the courthouse tomorrow and give you the key to my apartment. You'll probably get off before I do, and you can come to my apartment and wait on me. I'll fix us a good dinner."

"What if he follows me to your apartment?"

"That's not likely."

"How do we know what's likely or not likely? Let's reverse it. You come by here and pick up the key to my place. You can get there before me, before he's even likely to be watching my place. If he would follow me, then he wouldn't know you were inside."

"I probably can't get away that early," Chip said.

"Ah, come on. You can sneak away by 4:15 or so."

212

Chip's hissing demonstration of exasperation made Karen smile. "This is ridiculous, sneaking around like this. Besides, he might see me leaving your place."

"I doubt you'd leave until very early the next morning," Karen said, her voice heavy with suggestion. "Of course, you would have to find some place to stash your car."

"I'll be glad when we're shed of the bastard."

Karen added her agreement, then said, "I haven't seen a thing of him. Maybe the Judge's warning did some good."

"The son of a bitch is up to something. You can count on that," Chip said.


Virgil got horny again around midnight.

One for the road . . .

. . . then.

What then? What after he was done with her?

At least she had wised up. She remained quiet throughout the evening, shifting sometimes as he turned sharp corners, but his threat had kept her quiet. Of course, hogtied like she was and with the hanky stuffed in her mouth, what else could she do but be quiet? At least he had talked to her, kept her company during the evening.

So . . . what to do with her afterward?

Maybe the second time around she'd warm up to him. It had happened before. Maybe she was playing hard to get. He had known women like that. Of course, the chick in the back seat had class. She was a tougher nut to crack, he decided. After all, she wasn't one of those beer joint bimbos he usually settled for.

"How about it, hon? You ready for a little more lustin'? After that, maybe I'll let you go . . . if you make me feel real good this time. 'Course, maybe you won't want to go."

He got no answer. He didn't expect an answer.

Virgil headed the Bug out of town and about five miles out the interstate. He exited onto a state route which ran alongside a small creek at the base of a valley. That particular hollow was scarcely populated. Back in his younger days, he and his buddies had discovered an old logging road which led to an abandoned mining operation. They used to go there and drink and fight and sometimes fuck when they found a girl or two.

The night was moonless. Lightning winked in the distance. The instability of high summer was upon Custer

County, and the late evening continued to bring brief but sometimes violent thunderstorms. Virgil squinted at the dark roadside and had a difficult time finding the old logging road. He drove by it.

"Fuckin' bitch!" he cursed just as he passed it. "Hang on, girlie. Gotta turn around."

The VW wheeled around as pretty as it pleased on the narrow road. "Nice car you got here."

He turned into the road. "Might be a mite rough," he cautioned. "Don't get scared."

The road proved to be more than a little rough. It was tortuous, its two tire tracks so washed out that Virgil once or twice was sure he was stuck. The car conquered it though. He bounced up the steep grade in first gear. The car came to a stop in a weed-choked meadow which fronted the mouth of the abandoned mine.

"And here we are," he announced.

Virgil stepped from the car and stretched. His muscles ached, and his throat was parched. "Wish I'd got some fuckin' beer for us."

Crickets chirped. An owl hooted at him from the darkness. Virgil looked up and saw that the sky was cloudy. Otherwise, in the total darkness of the wilderness, the night would have glittered with stars. A breeze hinted at the coming rain, and the faint flashes of lightning and distant thunder confirmed the wind's rumor.

Virgil pushed forward the driver's seat and leaned into the back seat. "We better hurry, hon. I'd hate to have to try to screw you in the back seat of this oil can." He pulled the blanket from her just as an extended atmospheric discharge brightened the western sky. Her eyes, red and cloudy, stared back at him. Her face appeared deep purple.

"God! You all right?" He pulled the slimy rag from her mouth.

"Hey!" He shook her violently.

She didn't budge.

"Goddammit!"

He touched her face. The warmth he had savored before was gone, replaced now by a rubbery coolness. Furiously, Virgil searched his pockets for his lighter. He flicked it and used it to illuminate her face. Vickie lay there, her mouth still open, moisture glistening around her lips. The tanned duskiness of her face had assumed a bluish hue, and her eyes, dull and flat, were shot with the crimson tracks of broken blood vessels.

"Shit!" he proclaimed, realizing that she was dead.

"Damn you!" He smacked her discolored face. Her head lolled away from the blow, resisting it not at all. "Bitch!"

He yanked her body from the back seat and flung it into the high weeds which covered the narrow plateau. "You fuckin' bitch!" he railed. And he kicked her again and again, smashing her face. As he punished her for her selfish act, the rumbling thunder intensified. The formless flashes of lightning turned into angry, jagged streaks. The tall clouds, driven by their own energy, raced overhead. The first drops of rain thumped on his head.

"I kinda liked you," he said to the dark shape in the grass. "I mighta let you go. I mighta . . . really. But you had to die, damn you. Damn you!"

He aimed a final, vicious kick at her head, then hopped back into the car. He reached the paved road just as the rain started.

When Vickie failed to get to work on time, her angry employer dialed the number of her house. It wasn't uncommon. Vickie often overslept. He expected to hear a sleepy voice answer in confusion, then turn to apologetic panic as she realized her sin. Often Panzini had warned her about it. Her phone rang and rang. He gave up, figuring she was on her way to work.

"Damn," he muttered. She never picked a good morning to pull her tricks.

Panzini was due in court at 9:30 for a divorce hearing. His client was already probably waiting for him at the courthouse. Women going into divorce hearings, especially for the first time, needed a little tender, loving care, and he hardly was going to have time to pat her hand. He scribbled out a note telling Vickie where he was and locked the door behind him, thinking to himself that this would be the morning the million dollar suit came to his office . . . . . . to find the door locked.

This time was it, he vowed. He'd set her straight one last time, and the next time she was late—kaput! Enough was fucking enough!

Tad and Homer often skipped school—on the average of
215

about once a week, in fact. Usually, they headed up to the old mine where they could puff a little dope without fear of being caught. Not that being caught worried them all that much. Both had been to juvenile court before, and both knew nothing would be done to them for having a little grass. The bad thing about being caught was the loss of their stash. Pot was hard to come by, and the idea of some pig taking it home with him—to smoke for himself—now that steamed both Tad and Homer.

Homer, tall and lanky, strode quickly through the high grass on the meadow. The sun shone brightly, but the vegetation remained damp from the soaking the night before. Tad, appropriately named because he was such a tad of a boy, followed in the path created by his companion. They already had shared a joint as they hiked through the woods toward the mine, and neither felt much pain.

Homer hummed an off-key, nasal version of Conway Twitty's most recent hit and was moving right along to his own music when he tripped over something and sprawled in the smothering, itchy grass. Tad, a couple of yards to the rear, broke out laughing.

"Goldamn you!" Homer cried, scrambling to his feet, ready to thump Tad for laughing at him . . .

. . . but first he glanced down to see what had tripped him.

Tad stopped giggling when Homer loosed a squall that made the birds take to the sky. Homer had discovered Vickie Carmichael, who never would oversleep again.

Panzini phoned Chip from Judge Pinter's office. "I need you to go to that psychological on the Sampson kid today."

"I didn't know we could go," Chip said.

"I just talked with Keeling. He's got no objection. I had planned to go, but apparently my secretary has decided to take the day off. She didn't show this morning, and I just called my office. She's still not there. I gotta keep my office open this afternoon."

Chip glanced at the stack of work on his desk. "Christ, Mario! I don't know whether I can make it. I'm swamped."

Panzini clucked at him. "Tough, kid. Look, I'm not going. It probably won't be all that important anyway, but I'm asking you to go. You do what the hell you want."

Panzini hung up.

"Bastard," Chip said.

Homer and Tad stalled for more than two hours before they phoned the police. At first, they decided not to call the cops. It would cause them both a world of trouble. Tad would get yelled at for playing hooky. And Homer, his dad would beat him. All his dad ever wanted was an excuse. Besides, they both were stoned.

Once they started to come down off their high, both had grown jumpy. "We'd better do somethin'," Tad said.

Homer, though, shook his head. "No, man! No way."

"That woman's dead, Homer! Somebody kilt her. We gotta tell somebody."

The boys were in a run-down old barn near Homer's house. They had bolted from the meadow after their discovery.

"My dad'll whup up on me," Homer said.

"We could just call and tell 'em. We wouldn't have to tell 'em who was callin'."

With that, Homer concurred. They went to find a pay phone—just in case the cops tried to trace the call.

# EIGHT

Art Louck and a single deputy sheriff accompanied Mickie
Sampson to the Wharton General Hospital. On the fourth
floor of the hospital, in a small corner area created to serve
as a minimally secure mental ward, Chip and Frank Keeling waited in the outer offices of Dr. Natassi Darwha,
WGH's resident psychiatrist.

Chip and Frank talked shop as they awaited Mickie's arrival. Chip found, to his mild surprise, that he liked Frank
Keeling in spite of the stale odor of alcohol which always
seemed to shadow the older attorney. Keeling evidenced a
compassion which Chip so far had discovered wanting in
most of the veteran members of the legal profession.

"I always shied away from criminal work," Frank was
saying. "I just never liked dealing with that kind of person. I've had my share of profitable personal injury cases.
The mainstay of my income is real estate work, estates,
and divorces—as long as they're not too messy. I'm on retainer to the Wharton Sanitary Board. Their fee covers
most of the rent."

The man's openness led Chip to ask, "Doesn't it get boring?"

Keeling chuckled. "I don't know why I became a lawyer. I find the whole profession boring, even the criminal side of it. You're young, Chip. Maybe you'll see the
light. Lawyers flourish off humanity's misery. Maybe
that's why most lawyers are pompous, arrogant ass-
holes who simply come to accept the premise that it's
okay to bilk people in trouble. Perhaps their arrogance
and pomposity are just shields against their guilt. It's a
lousy line of work."

* * *

Three stories below, the gray cruiser bearing Mickie Sampson pulled into the emergency room entrance. The hospital demanded that cuffed prisoners be brought through the emergency entrance. They didn't like the idea of shackled, handcuffed men being led jangling through the main lobby.

Of course, Mickie neither was shackled nor cuffed. The deputy, an aging veteran of the department, had forgotten the keys to his cuffs that morning. Worse, his back bothered him, and he wanted to avoid bending over to secure the ankle shackles. The deputy rarely transported prisoners, and to him the kid seemed pleasant enough, even if he was charged with murder. Still, the deputy had asked Louck's opinion. And Louck, young and liberal and much concerned with juveniles' rights, confirmed the deputy's opinion. No restraints were needed.

They both were wrong . . . either for good or bad.

The boy walked between them from the cruiser toward the emergency room door. The sun glared into the faces of all three. Mickie saw his uncle leaning against the corner of the building before either Louck or the deputy noticed him. Not that it would have made any difference, since neither Louck nor the deputy knew Virgil Sampson on sight.

Mickie had noticed the shape of his uncle before he recognized him. The sun burned bright and Mickie was within five yards of Virgil before he realized who it was. The boy emitted a weak yelp and stopped.

Louck looked down. The deputy continued on for a few paces before he reacted. Mickie's face whitened as his eyes met those of his uncle. Just as Louck prepared to ask what was wrong, Mickie broke and ran, scampering away from the two men with the youthful grace of a gazelle.

"Holy shit!" cried the deputy, fumbling for his never-used revolver.

Louck started to give chase just as the deputy unholstered his .38. The social worker saw the gun being pointed at the fleeing figure of the boy who, by then, had reached the other side of the lot.

"Halt!" the deputy yelled.

Mickie never even looked back.

"God, no!" Louck got to the deputy and struck the gun just as its blast shattered the air. The bullet whined off the asphalt parking lot.

The deputy, just a few short years away from a retirement to which he had dedicated his miserable career, saw his future racing across the highway and into a small patch of forest which bordered the city park. His heart raced; his blood pressure soared. He whipped Art Louck across the bridge of his nose with the gun. Louck collapsed to the ground, blood spewing from his crushed nose.

The boy was out of sight. No matter to the deputy—he emptied the remaining five chambers at the forest.

Chip and Frank, startled by the shooting, reached the window in time to see the deputy lower his gun. Chip saw the social worker kneeling, his face obscured by blood. "My God! Someone's been shot."

Nurses, orderlies, and doctors, most of the latter of foreign descent and jabbering away in puzzled confusion, poured from the emergency room. Not a one stopped at the injured man. They all wanted to know what had happened first. Chip watched it from four stories above. He didn't see Virgil Sampson, now smiling, very pleased with himself, walking casually toward a small gray Bug parked nearby.

The phone in the Sheriff's department rang just as the stymied dispatcher accepted a radio report from the deputy at the hospital.

"Hold the line," the dispatcher said to whoever was calling. On the other end, Homer danced a nervous jig inside the phone booth. The boy just knew they were tracing the call to the ragged phone both in which he stood. Tad waited outside, asking what was happening.

The jail dispatcher jotted down the sketchy information on Mickie Sampson's escape. He signed off the radio, shaking his head at the incompetence of the veteran officer, and then answered the phone. "Sorry for the holdup. Can I help you?"

The voice sounded young, nervous. "I gotta report a killin'."

When it rained, it poured, thought the dispatcher.

"You mean you all let the damned kid get away!" Hemmings shouted to the dispatcher.

"Hey, I didn't let him do a damned thing. I'm sitting be-

220

hind a desk, calling you because the sheriff told me to."
The dispatcher had taken enough "shit" for the day.

"Have you mounted a search?"

"Not yet. The Sheriff said call you first thing."

Hemmings viciously crumpled the case report on which
he had been working. "Well, for Christ's sake, get some of
your men out there. Search the park! I'll get some troopers
out there."

"We also have a report of a body," the dispatcher added,
almost as an afterthought. "The Sheriff said you were the
one to be called."

Hemmings sucked in air. "Who called it in?"

"Some kid. Hung up before I could get his name."

Hemmings thought it over. "I'll check out the body. Give
me the directions." He would have rather supervised the
search for the kid, except for the fact that the kid was probably long gone already. The alleged body was his first pri-
ority. Other officers could handle what would amount to a
fruitless on-the-scene search for the Sampson kid. Nelson
always insisted that Hemmings handle possible murder
investigations before less experienced officers "urinated
on the evidence," to quote the colorful prosecutor.

He decided to call Nelson.

And, as Hemmings told an incredulous Nelson about the
escape and the body on one incoming line, Chip—still at
the hospital—was on another line telling Karen about
Mickie's escape. "And the cop shot at him?" Karen asked.

"Hell, yes! The center worker knocked off his aim. He
smashed the guy in the face, then let a barrage fly at
Mickie Sampson."

"Jesus!" Karen wondered if he might have struck the
boy.

"Now that stupid cop wants to charge the social worker
with aiding and abetting an escape. Can you believe it?"
Chip was incensed. Karen had never heard him so agitated. "If your boss," he went on, "allows that to happen,
I'll defend the social worker myself. The hell with the King
and his court."

"It won't happen," Karen said, not really sure.

"I talked to the social worker. He thinks the kid saw
something that made him run."

"Virgil Sampson?" Karen asked.

221

"Who knows?"

"What's going on now?"

Chip, calling from a pay phone beside the double doors to the emergency room, saw police cars—the lights flashing—filling the parking lot. "Reinforcements are arriving. You'd think John Dillinger had been resurrected."

Officers cradling shotguns exited the cruisers. They fanned out and crossed the road and started toward the woods into which Mickie had vanished. Chip gave Karen a brief play-by-play.

"Let's hope they find Mickie before his uncle does," Karen said.

"Hell, the way they look," Chip proclaimed, "he'll be lucky to live regardless."

Clarke Nelson entered her office and motioned for her to hurry up with the phone call. "I've got to go, Chip. Clarke needs me."

"Tell him about the social worker."

"I will. I promise."

"I'll be there after awhile for the key."

"Okay. I'll be here."

Clarke motioned at her furiously. "Hold on," she told Chip.

"I'm sending you out in the field," Nelson informed her.

She frowned, not understanding.

"If you'll get off the damned phone, I'll tell you about it."

Karen told Chip she would leave the key with the secretary, adding that she would be out of the office that afternoon.

"Have you heard?" Nelson asked as she hung up.

"About the kid? Chip just told me."

"That's one problem. We got another one. Hemmings is coming by to pick you up. We have a possible homicide. He's heading out to the scene. I want you along."

Karen blanched. "Aw, Clarke. That's all I need."

"Just get going."

"Did you hear about Louck, that social worker?"

"I hear he helped the kid get away."

"That's not what happened!" Karen snapped.

"Ohhhh! You were there?"

"Chip said—"

"I don't give a damn about Chip's opinion. Get moving," Nelson retorted.

Chip returned to Art Louck's side. The worker sat on a cart in the emergency room. Finally, someone had decided to treat him. A nurse was pasting a heavy bandage over his nose. The deputy, now just as interested in hauling Louck before the bar of justice as he was in apprehending the kid, hung around within hearing distance.

"How do you feel?" Chip asked.

Louck snorted back some of the blood and mucus which still clogged his nose. "Like the victim of police brutality," he said, tossing a defiant glance toward the deputy.

"Don't worry about it. You did what was right."

Chip's comment brought the deputy into the conversation. "Okay, lawyer. Scram! He's goin' with me."

"Not quite," said the nurse.

The deputy ignored her. "You can still beat it. If he's your client, you can see him at the arraignment."

"I cannot believe that you insist on charging this man. You had no cause to shoot at that boy!"

"Hell, for all I know, they both was in on it from the start. He's the one that told me I didn't have to cuff the boy."

" 'Cause you forgot your keys," Louck shouted.

"Shut up!" ordered the deputy.

Chip threw up his hands. "You're crazy," he told the deputy.

The cop's face twisted into a vision of pure hate. "I'm ordering you to leave! You give me any hassle, and I'll arrest you for obstructing an officer."

Chip put up his hands. "Take me! I dare you! I'm telling you now. This man's my client. I'm staying with him as long as I can . . . as long as he is being treated just to be sure you don't do anything else to him."

The deputy's face reflected an instant of uncertainty. He looked at the nurse whose sympathies weren't on his side. "Ah, shit!" he said, and stepped back.

"I don't know why he ran," Louck said to Chip. "Something happened out there. He just kinda hollered and went white. Then he ran like hell."

"Did you see anything?" Chip asked.

"Nothing. I didn't see a thing. I certainly hope they—"

223

He nodded toward the glowering deputy. ". . . don't kill him."

"Me, too," Chip said.

Neither Karen Kinder nor Cpl. Hemmings knew Vickie Carmichael. If they had known her, they still would have had problems recognizing her. The bones of her pretty face had been ravaged, the skin and muscles separated from the bone. Again, Karen was sick. The mutilation was bad enough, but something had chewed on her . . . some creature of the night who had scented death and took her—a human being—for common carrion. The absence of blood, which had been washed away by the night's deluge, compounded the grotesque scene.

Hemmings and another trooper, the only duty officer besides Hemmings spared from the search for Mickie Sampson, worked in expanding circles looking for evidence in the frustrating jungle of tall weeds. Karen sat inside the cruiser, its engine going and its air conditioner refreshing her, settling her anguished stomach.

The victim, Karen intuited, had been pretty. She was certainly built very well. In death, the white pulchritude of her breasts, her legs spread wide, created an image of sexual ravishment which revolted Karen in an even more primeval fashion than the robbery-murder of Gracie Mack. The body was not quite as mutilated as that of Gracie Mack, but the act seemed even more unwholesome, if that was conceivable.

Maybe Karen felt as she did because she was a woman? Rape is an act which possesses level upon level of meaning to most women. Sometimes, the act of forcible sex can provide the framework for erotic fantasies. Karen herself was not immune to such fantasies, but she wanted them to remain what they were—fantasies and nothing more. Karen's overwhelming image of true-life rape was a nightmarish vision of spiritual and physical violation. Giving herself to a man was an act of trust as much as love, a demonstration of mutual respect, and no matter how much one questions it or begs it or worries at it, rape is a manly crime against women, a one-sided proposition altogether.

Of course, Karen only assumed that the woman had been raped before she had been killed. Had she resisted?

The cruiser door clicked open, startling her. "Feeling better?" Hemmings asked.

"You scared me. I'm feeling a little better."

"It looks like two people were here after the rain. Probably the ones who reported it. She definitely died before the rainstorm."

"I'm surprised anyone found her."

Hemmings nodded. The wailing cries of an ambulance reached them.

"Can we go now?" Karen asked.

"We gotta wait for the photographer," Hemmings said.

Karen just shook her head. "What a way to make a living."

# NINE

Sometimes things happen with nerve-racking slowness. Other times, one event feeds quickly upon its predecessor, and, like the unraveling of taut rope, the mystery unfolds in a twisting frenzy, sweeping those around it into its violent vortex. That Thursday afternoon, the events found perspective in a mad rush as Virgil Sampson's evil engulfed all those who had become so familiar with him.

By early afternoon, Mario's anger had been replaced by a gnawing worry, a gut feeling that this time her absence was more than her instability. He phoned the Sheriff's Department just moments after the department's dispatcher had taken a radio message that the unidentified body of a woman was on its way to the hospital. The time between Panzini's phone call and the radio message was so short that the dispatcher, not normally very quick, wondered if there was a connection.

The long shot paid off.

A much shaken Mario Panzini met the ambulance at the hospital. Karen and Hemmings had followed the vehicle into town, and, as Karen stood back, Hemmings unzipped the body bag right there in the hospital parking lot so Panzini could attempt to make an identification. The darkly pigmented face of the lawyer turned ashen at the sight. He stared at Vickie Carmichael for a very long time before his revulsion turned to a gagging realization that the decimated human being was his secretary. He broke down. Several minutes passed before he could tell Dan Hemmings and Karen Kinder just whom they had found.

A cruiser was immediately dispatched to her residence. The officers reported back to Hemmings that there appeared to have been a mild struggle inside the house. The victim's vehicle, its description provided to them by her employer, wasn't at the residence. Nor were her car keys.

Meanwhile, Panzini, still ashen but also growing ever more angry, told Hemmings and Karen about the prior day's visit of Virgil Sampson.

"Did she have boyfriends?" Hemmings asked.

Panzini shook his head, then caught himself. "Wait a minute! Chip Roth took her out once not long ago."

Karen sucked in air, realizing now with whom he had been that night. Hemmings gave her an off-the-shoulder stare. Still, Virgil Sampson, possibly driving a gray VW, became the subject of an all-points bulletin . . . a BOLO, a "be on the lookout for."

Chip, sitting in Karen's living room, glanced at the wall clock. It was already past six p.m., and still Karen was not home. He resisted an urge to phone the courthouse. He didn't want to seem to be checking up on her. When 6:30 arrived, if she still wasn't home, then he would make the call.

As if in response to his non-verbalized thoughts, he heard the sound of a car. He started for the window, then stopped. He didn't want to be seen. For all he knew, Sampson lurked somewhere outside. Chip had parked his car several blocks away in the parking lot of a fast food restaurant.

A car door slammed shut. Chip waited. A key clicked into the door lock, and the door opened, spilling bright sunlight into the dimly lit room. Karen came in.

"You're here," Karen said in a joyless voice.

"What's wrong?"

Karen closed the door. She pulled open the curtain to allow the westerly sun to brighten the room. Then she plopped down on the couch. "Sampson killed again," she said.

Chip braced himself. "Mickie?"

"A girl—someone you know."

Chip walked over and sat beside her. "Someone I know?"

Karen looked at him. "Vickie Carmichael."

For an instant, before his brain cells whirred into action, the name prompted no signal of recognition—just a momentary lapse because it was so incredible. When the realization struck him, it chilled him down to his soul.

227

"Oh, my God!" He got to his feet, his knees without confidence, and walked unsteadily to the window.

"He brutalized her—raped her, according to the preliminary medical examination. He abandoned her body on some godforsaken mountainside. According to Mario Panzini, you'd been seeing her."

It came out not like an accusation, but rather like a misunderstood fact.

"Seeing her?" Chip turned, his mind not functioning with any clarity.

"That's what Panzini said."

"Just once—the night you called me."

"You and Sampson seem to have the same taste in women," Karen observed

The comment, made so casually, struck an angry chord. Chip spoke in a rush of fury. "What the hell does that mean?"

Karen dropped her head into her hands. "I don't know. I don't why I said it. I'm sorry I said it."

Chip's rage evaporated. He went to her, sitting beside her, placing his arms around her. "I took her home and came straight here. That's all there was to it. Have they got any leads on Sampson's whereabouts?"

"Nope. He's probably in her VW. Hemmings says they'll find him now—unless he's already left the county."

"So they can let him out on bail again," Chip said.

"One thing's certain," she said.

"What?"

"You're off his case now."

Chip nodded. "But I doubt he's off ours."

Mickie had heard all six shots. One of the bullets whizzed right by his left ear. Each time the gun had boomed, his young, pounding heart had hitched. Mickie had expected to die, but he had to run . . . he just had to . . . with Virgil standing there, waiting for him, smiling death at him.

Once he made the cover of the thick woods, Mickie had fallen to the leaf-covered ground. And he had cried a little, just long enough to catch his breath. Then he had gotten to his feet again and ran to the other side of the woods where he had crossed a deserted softball field. He had jumped a small creek which ran behind a townhouse complex.

A large metal shed sat behind the townhouses. Its door hung open. Mickie stopped running. He slipped into the building which contained maintenance equipment for the newly constructed complex.

In spite of the oppressive heat which grew unbearable in the late afternoon, Mickie had remained there, huddled in a dark corner on a pile of fertilizer sacks, wondering what to do. He wanted to return to the detention center, but they were shooting at him. They'd probably shoot him on sight just because he ran away. At least he was able to stop crying. A painful loneliness, not his fear, caused his tears. There was no one he could turn to. Not even his mother. Everyone was against him, just like always, because his name was Sampson.

The boy slipped into a fitful sleep. As he alternated between dozing and consciousness, the answer to his dilemma came in a disjointed nightmare. The only friendly face in his dreams belonged to the lady lawyer. Virgil chased him in his dreams. The cops shot at him. Even his lawyer turned him away from his door.

But Miss Kinder. She smiled at him and told him it would be all right, and Mickie felt safe until . . .

Mickie came awake with a frightful start.

Until what?

His dream was over, its conclusion denied to him, but he knew what he had to do. He had to go to the lady lawyer's apartment. Only once had he been there—with Virgil. He thought he could find it even though it was several miles away, all the way across town in fact. If he kept to the back streets, to the dark alleys, Mickie decided he could make it. Then she could call the cops and tell them what happened, and they'd take him back to the safety of the detention center.

Outside the building, the sun set in a threatening aura of bloody color. Mickie opened the door, anxious to escape the smothering heat of the metal building. His stomach growled with hunger, but he paid it no attention. In the fading twilight, he began his trek across Wharton, trying to follow the darkest trails, always watching for police cruisers, for that single shadow that might be Virgil Sampson.

Virgil Sampson, too, awaited the night. After leaving

the hospital, he had driven the VW to a desolate, almost forgotten state park located on the northern edge of Custer County. While he doubted that anyone would find the girl's body, he knew they would be searching for her, for her car. He stayed in the park until nightfall. When he drove back to Wharton, he did so carefully, sometimes taking curvy and rough back roads to avoid the main highways.

A single score remained to be settled. Virgil planned, in his own mind, "to kill two birds with one stone." He liked the sound of the cliché. Just as he reached the town's city limits, he pulled off onto a side street which would deliver him to Karen Kinder's apartment. Brazen now, he sped right by her apartment and saw, through drawn curtains, the faint glow of a light. Her car was parked in its customary space. Nowhere did he see the car belonging to his punk lawyer.

Virgil wanted her. The brief session with the wop's secretary had left him unsated. Karen Kinder would sate him; then she probably would die too—two birds with one stone.

Virgil parked the VW a block down the street, not caring that the bug blocked the driveway to a house. He hiked back toward Karen's apartment and concealed himself again in the thick foliage across from the apartments. He wanted to wait for a little while. In his belt, he carried the .44 magnum. Its weight made him feel comfortable. If she would just open the door, then he would have her. The huge gun insured him of that. He'd lead her back to the car. Together they would leave Wharton—forever.

And she would live for as long as she was good to him—maybe even as far as North Carolina.

# TEN

Inside Karen's apartment, the sound of subdued passion mingled with the muffled throb of the stereo. Karen and Chip lay on the thick rug which covered the floor. Empty glasses, which had once contained a deep, rich burgundy, rested on a nearby table. Dishes, smeared with the remains of Chip's modest but tasty dinner, also cluttered the coffee table.

Chip nuzzled between her legs. She groaned in both pleasure and appreciation. "You haven't done this before," she said.

"I was bashful," he mumbled.

"Ummm . . . you make me tingle."

Chip ascended to her lips, kissing her, letting her taste herself. When they parted, he said, "Actually, I'm stalling, trying to build up my strength." If they made love again, it would be the third time that evening.

She pressed a finger to his lips. "Stall all you want. I love the way you stall."

Chip reached for his wineglass. "It's empty. How about another glass?"

"Sure." Karen started to get up.

"I'll get it," Chip said. "You lay there. Or maybe put on another cassette."

They were both nude, now totally comfortable with each other. Chip padded into the kitchen, and Karen got to her knees and began to search through her small but varied collection of tapes. She withdrew a Kris Kristofferson and slipped it into the system. The singer's gravelly voice began to sing about a woman called *Bobby McGee*.

"You like him?" Chip asked as he returned.

"I love him," Karen said. "You kinda look like him. Has anyone ever told you that?"

Chip giggled. "Christ, no! I like his songs, as a writer I mean, but he's not much of a singer."

"He grows on you," Karen countered. "He's got such a sincere quality in his voice."

Chip sat her glass on a table and ordered her to lay back. He tipped his wineglass and allowed a little of the deep crimson fluid to seep out onto her stomach. She started to jump up, but he stopped her. The wine puddled in her belly button. "What are you doing?"

"It's called creative love-making."

"I'd call it 'kinky' . . . but nice. It tickles."

Mickie was sure he knew where Miss Kinder lived, but somehow he had ended up on the wrong street. Rather than go around the block, through the bright circles thrown by the street lights, Mickie cut through the woods which led to the next street over. He figured he'd just ended up one street off. He moved through the trees as quietly as he could, confident now of finding a safe refuge.

Virgil heard the sound of movement, coming straight toward him. Someone—he didn't know then who it was—was coming through the woods. Virgil crouched low, withdrawing the bulky pistol from his belt. A half moon had just started its ascent and hung like a great bisected orange just above the eastern horizon. Its glow did little to lift the dark cover of the small forest, and Virgil could just barely discern the shadow which invaded his domain.

The intruder was 10 yards away from him, now starting to move a little away from him. The shadow belonged to a small person . . . perhaps a—

Virgil slipped down even lower, but only to try to get a little better view of the person. The small figure halted at the fringe of the woods and looked over at Karen Kinder's apartment. Virgil studied the silhouette, a sudden hope in his mind. The possibility had came to him moments earlier, and the manner in which the person stood now seemed so familiar. Virgil's suspicions were confirmed as the small boy moved out from the cover of the woods and onto the berm of the street.

Damn!

It was Mickie.

Virgil suppressed a laugh, thinking to himself that he was born to good luck—more birds to stone!

Car lights swept across the street. Mickie dashed back into the woods as a car drove slowly by, a long car which stopped down the street a block away.

Mickie watched as it just sat there for a moment. Then the passenger side door opened, and a woman got out and walked from the car and up a sidewalk to a house. The car pulled over to the side a little farther down the street. Its taillights flickered off; its engine died.

And Mickie waited . . .

. . . Virgil too. Still crouching farther back in the cover, he heard the shutting of the car doors, but he could see nothing of what was transpiring farther down the street.

The man, who had just parked the long car, exited it and studied the little Bug which blocked his driveway. With all of the room on the street to park, it puzzled him why someone would decide to park right in front of his driveway.

His wife, more angry than he, came back out of their small house. She carried a flashlight.

"I've never seen the car before," he told her.

"I just can't believe how inconsiderate people are," his wife said. She used the flashlight to illuminate the VW's license plate. Her husband memorized the number. "You oughta call the police."

"I don't know," the man said, looking around the neighborhood. "I'd hate to cause one of our neighbors any trouble."

"Always spineless," his wife chirped. "By God, I'll call them." And she marched into her house.

Mickie heard the voices down the street. As still and quiet as the hazy night was, the sounds carried, but not so well that Mickie could understand the spoken words.

When the voices became silent and the light of the small electric torch vanished, Mickie hurried across the street. He hoped he remembered the right apartment number. Glancing furtively over his shoulder, he softly rapped on the door to Number 13.

233

Neither Karen nor Chip heard the gentle knocking. Kris now sang about *Blaming It on the Stones*. They didn't hear much of what Kris was saying either. They were making love.

The tapping repeated itself, this time a little louder.

Karen, her face reflecting the passionate pleasure of the moment, opened her eyes and listened for a moment. "Chip! Someone's at the door."

"Shit!" He withdrew from her and fumbled for his pants. He pulled them on, deciding not to even bother with his shirt. Karen darted to her bedroom for her velour robe.

"I'll get it," Chip said as she returned. The knocking came again, this time rather insistent.

"I'd better—" Karen started to say.

"No way!"

"Then be careful."

Karen lifted her pocketbook from a chair. From it, she pulled the shiny pistol which Hemmings had given her. She tucked it in the pocket of her robe.

Chip cautiously opened the door.

"Mickie!"

Karen, seeing the boy standing in the doorframe, gasped and withdrew the gun from the robe. She tossed it on a chair and rushed to him. "What on earth—"

"Can I turn myself in?" the boy asked in a weak voice.

Chip pulled the boy inside, quickly closing the door.

Virgil, having moved to the fringe of the woods, saw the door open, saw the shirtless figure of Chip Roth, and saw his nephew go inside.

". . . Four fucking birds," Virgil said aloud, this time allowing his satisfaction to express itself in actual laughter. He was going to do away with the lawyer, with his stoolie nephew, screw the blonde fox, and then probably get rid of her. To his way of thinking that made three people, but four birds.

In the house down the street, the woman, now fuming at her meek husband as well as over the VW which blocked her driveway, dialed the number of the Wharton City Police. She had never phoned the police before. Thus, never did it occur to her that she lived just outside the city limits of Wharton. To her, police were police.

"There's a car blocking my driveway," she told an official-sounding voice at the city police station.

"Do you know who owns it?" the voice asked.

"If I knew that, I'd be calling them, not you. I got the license number," which she reeled off.

"Where do you live?"

The woman gave the address.

After a brief pause, the voice said, "But that's outside the city limits. We don't have any jurisdiction. You'll have to call the Sheriff's Department."

The woman understood nothing about jurisdictions. "Why can't you all do something?"

"Because you don't live in the city!"

"That's splitting hairs," the woman argued.

"Look, just call this number," said the frustrated voice. Even more angry, the woman dialed the number.

"Custer County Jail," another officious voice declared.

"But I wanted the Sheriff's Department!"

A sigh. "This is the Sheriff's Department."

"There's a car blocking my driveway," the woman said.

"Is it on private property or public right-of-way?" the dispatcher asked.

The woman looked for help from her husband, but he was paying her no mind, already entranced by the television. "How should I know?" the woman said. "That's your job!"

"Ma'am, if it's on private property, then you have to call a towing service and have it moved. If it's on the street, then we'll check it out as soon as we can."

"It's on the street," the woman said.

"What's the address?" the voice then asked, resigned to the fact that it was a complaint—albeit trite—which would require a response . . . sometime.

She told him the address.

"We'll get there as soon as we can."

"But it might be gone by then!" the woman cried.

"Fine. Then that solves your problem," the dispatcher snapped.

"People who do this should be given a ticket or something. I have the license number."

235

What the hell, thought the dispatcher. It was easier to take the information than argue.

She gave it to him, adding, "It's a Volkswagen, white or gray. I can't tell in the dark."

The description rang a bell with the dispatcher. He'd just seen something on a Volkswagen which matched that description. "We'll get there as soon as we can," he told the woman. When he hung up, he scanned the message board which hung above his desk.

"And you're sure it was your uncle?" Karen asked after the boy had completed his explanation. They sat in the living room. Chip had donned his shirt but remained barefoot. Karen was still in her robe. The boy sat on the couch, eyeing the gun which had been shoved by Chip into the crevice of the chair in which he sat.

"Holy shit!" exclaimed the dispatcher.

No wonder the description had seemed familiar. He grabbed the radio mike. His closest unit was the evening shift commander who was a good 10 miles from the suspected location of Vickie Carmichael's stolen Volkswagen.

By radio, the shift commander told the dispatcher to see if the State Police had units any closer, and also ordered that he notify Cpl. Hemmings.

Karen got the boy a soda pop and made him a sandwich. Chip continued to talk to him, hardly able to wait to see the look on the face of the deputy who had pistol whipped Art Louck.

Once the boy had his pop and sandwich, Chip lifted the gun from the crevice in the chair. "We better do something with this," he said.

"Just stuff it down where it was for now," Karen said.

"It makes me nervous," Chip answered.

"I'm going to call the police now," Karen told the boy as Chip shoved the gun almost out of sight into the deep crack separating the chair seat from its plush arms. "They'll take you back to the detention center."

"They won't shoot me?" the boy asked, his words muffled by the food in his mouth.

"Of course not!" Karen said.

Just as Karen rose to go to the phone, someone else

knocked at the door. Chip looked at Karen who looked to the door. Mickie froze. Karen moved to the door. "Who is it?"

"Police!" a voice cried.

Mickie almost choked on the food in his mouth.

"Don't worry," Karen said. "They won't hurt you in here."

This time she went to answer the door.

# ELEVEN

The dark shape of the gun jammed into Karen's chest. Then she saw the wicked face of Virgil Sampson. What should have been a scream came out as a pitiful whine. Chip bounded out of his chair just as Sampson shoved Karen back into the room and stepped inside. "Tonight's really my night," he said, smiling at Chip, who had frozen at the sight of the gun.

Mickie paled, swallowing the wad of sandwich. "Uncle Virg!"

"Hiya, kid. Glad to see me?"

"What do you want?" Chip said. He eased over to Karen and put his hands around her quivering shoulders.

"That's a stupid question," Virgil said, waving the gun at them both. "I came for her. Looks like I'm getting ever'thing on a silver platter tonight."

The intruder moved closer to Karen and fingered the lapels of the robe. "Nice." He glared at Chip. "Get away from her!"

Chip shook his head. Virgil drew back the gun to strike Chip, but Karen pushed Chip away. "Do as he says," she said.

"Smart girl," Virgil said. "Looks like you two been fuckin'. Tell me, is she as good and tight as she looks?"

Chip had inched away from Karen, but Sampson's vulgarity made him stop. "You bastard!"

Virgil leveled the gun squarely at Chip's forehead. "You're gonna find out what it's like to die tonight. It don't matter to me when. So just keep up playing hero, and I'll waste you now."

"Like you did Gracie Mack," Karen suddenly said.

Virgil looked at her. "Sure, just like I did to the old

238

woman. Right, Mick? You were there. Used this little baby right here. It does the job. Right again, Mick?"

"Leave 'em alone, Virg. I was the one that told on you. Take me with you, but leave them alone. Please."

Virgil smiled. "You sure ain't got your ol' man's yellow streak, do you, kid?"

Hemmings was home when he got the call about the VW. He told the Sheriff's Department dispatcher that he'd contact the state police barracks, which he had. Two troopers had been dispatched to meet him. The search for Mickie Sampson was ongoing, and for now it took precedence.

Hemmings then hopped in his car, flipped on the siren, and sped toward the location given to him by the Sheriff's Department. He expected to find nothing more than Vickie Carmichael's abandoned car.

"On the couch," Virgil ordered, "all three of ya."

Karen and Chip sat on each side of the boy. Their captor saw the two glasses of wine on the table. "That stuff any good?" he asked. He swallowed the contents of one of the glasses.

"I wish it had poison in it," Karen said.

"Mean stuff!" quipped Virgil. He downed the other. "Ain't as good as Strawberry Hill."

Karen saw the vicious glow in his eyes. She knew he was on the verge of something . . . nothing good, she was sure.

He pointed the gun at Karen. "Stand up."

Karen didn't move.

"Goddammit! I said stand up." He moved the gun until it was again directed at Chip. "I ain't got a thing to lose here, woman. Now you best do as I say."

So Karen, her stomach now nauseous, got up.

"Take off the robe," Virgil commanded.

Chip started up.

"Try it!" snapped Virgil. "Come on! Just give it a try. You're a piece of yellow shit, lawyer. Tell me, you shit, what would you think if you had a lawyer and you saw him drooling all over the lawyer that was tryin' to put you away? You tell me what you'd do! I asked you that once before. You never gave me no answer."

Chip remained silent.

"Tell me!" bellowed Virgil.

Karen hoped someone was next door. Surely they could hear Sampson's loud, angry voice. Maybe, just maybe, they'd call the police.

Still Chip kept quiet. Suddenly Virgil cackled. "See! You get my drift?" He looked back at Karen. "Now strip!"

Then they all heard the sirens, distant but coming closer.

"Back on the couch," Virgil told Karen.

Karen almost collapsed with what she knew to be premature relief. Virgil eased over to the window and peeked out of a small crevice in the curtain. He saw blue lights turn a corner far down the street and stop about a block away, right where he had parked the VW.

Chip took the opportunity to take Karen's hand, reaching across the boy to do so. Mickie wondered if he had a chance to get to the gun that was stuffed down in the chair across the coffee table from him. If he got it, could he use it? Mickie decided that he could.

"They'll get you," Chip told the gunman.

Virgil glanced back. "Not until after you're all dead. 'Sides, I might just get away with three hostages. Like I told you, tonight's my night. You might just call it Sampson luck."

Virgil looked back out the window just as another car with a blue light stopped where the first was. He couldn't tell what was going on, but he figured they might not even find him. It was a long shot—that they wouldn't find him, but he really did feel lucky.

Hemmings circled the car. It definitely belonged to Vickie Carmichael, and he ordered it secured until it could be checked out.

"I guess he just abandoned it here," a youthful trooper said.

"Maybe." Hemmings looked around the neighborhood. He walked to the rear of the VW and lifted the engine cover. A gentle warmth radiated from it. "It's still a little warm. He's not too far from here. Get on the radio and cancel the search for that kid. Order all units here."

Virgil left the window. For one horrible moment, Mickie thought his uncle was going to sit down in the chair which concealed the gun. Instead his uncle's gleaming eyes searched the room. "You got anymore of that wine?" he asked.

"On the kitchen counter," Karen said.

"Go get it, kid."

Mickie stood.

Virgil walked to him and placed the sturdy barrel against the boy's chest. "You try anything and this here pretty woman that you like so much just might get a hole put in one of her pretty tits. You unnerstand?"

Mickie nodded and started toward the kitchen.

Virgil spoke to Karen. "He thinks you're nice. Guess that's why he came here. That's sure why I came here. Now, let's get back to what we was doin'. Stand up and take off that robe."

Chip sat stewing, frightened, yet so mad he could—

He wanted to smash Virgil Sampson, kill him with his bare hands. The emotion was strange to Chip.

Karen rose this time without hesitation. She allowed the robe to fall to the floor. Just as she did, Mickie came back into the living room with the large bottle of burgundy. He stopped in his tracks as he saw Karen standing naked before his uncle. "Bring it here!" Virgil commanded.

Mickie handed him the bottle. It was open. Virgil lifted it to his lips and drank. "You oughta keep this cold," he said to Karen.

"I hope you choke," she said.

"Karen!" snapped Chip. "Take it easy."

"Yeah," drawled Virgil, studying her nude body. "Take it easy. You got nice titties—small, but nice. Now that chick last night, man, did she have a pair of knockers!"

"And you killed her," Karen said.

"Didn't mean for that to happen," Virgil explained. "See, she kinda choked on her own juices. I got mad that she died on me, kicked her around a little, but she was dead by then."

Virgil walked over to Karen. Mickie stood beside her as if he intended to protect her. With the hand with which he held the gun, he gave the boy a single shove that sent him crashing across the coffee table. Virgil then brought the gun up to touch one of Karen's prominent nipples.

"Cold?" he asked.

Hemmings walked down the street toward Karen's apartment, his hand on the butt of the gun he carried in a shoulder holster. The young trooper and his older partner were going down the street the other way. When Hemmings got in front of Karen's apartment, he performed a classic double take. Only then, when he saw Karen's car in front of her door, did he realize where he was. The implication struck him like a freight train.

"Goooddammmnn," he growled.

He turned. His two companions were much too far down the street to be of any help at that moment. Too far to shout.

Alone, Hemmings inched toward the door.

Virgil, still holding the gun in his right hand, massaged both of her breasts with his left. He kneaded the firm mounds of flesh roughly. "You're right, kid. She's nice."

Chip could stand no more. He went straight for Sampson, rocketing off the sofa. Virgil's fist, clutching the gun, caught Chip squarely on the chin. The blow, augmented by the weight of the gun, sent pain arrowing up the left side of Chip's face. Something snapped in his jaw, and he tumbled back, almost landing on Mickie who still lay on the floor following his confrontation with his uncle.

Someone knocked on the door, then pounded on it.

Virgil whirled around, releasing Karen in the process, and aimed the gun at the door's center. He pulled the trigger, and the concussion sounded like a blast of dynamite in the confines of the apartment. The huge bullet punctured the wooden door, exiting in an explosion of splinters within an inch or so of Hemmings who, because of his training, stood off center of the door.

Hemmings backed away from the door and fired a shot into the air to attract his partners. More sirens approached.

"Sampson!" bellowed the state police corporal. "You're surrounded. Surrender! Toss out your weapon."

Virgil went back to Karen and grabbed her by the throat, shoving her ahead of him to the door. "Stay out, pig! I got the girl right in front of me. You shoot—you kill her!"

Lights flashed on throughout the apartment complex.

Doors opened. Heads popped out. Hemmings ignored them until the door next to Karen's opened. A frightened face peered out. "Get back in there!" commanded the officer.

The door slammed shut.

"You got no chance, Sampson. Let her out!"

"Fuck ya! I got three chances. You just come and try to get me, and you'll see more'n one body comin' out that door."

The other two troopers joined Hemmings. A string of police cars squealed around corners at both ends of the block. As they screeched to stops and officers jumped out, Hemmings commenced shouting orders. The cars formed a barricade in front of Karen's apartment.

Barricade!

The word gave Hemmings goose bumps. Hostage situations seldom resolved themselves without injury or death. And no police officer in Custer County, including himself, had much experience in such situations. They had all had training, but without experience the training meant little. He had no intention of letting Virgil Sampson go. Of that he was certain, no matter the consequences. Of course he might get overruled.

Inside, with Karen still in front as a bullet shield, Virgil moved to the window and peeked outside. Blue flashing lights flooded the apartment with an eerie, flickering illumination. Virgil reached for the light switch and threw the inside of the apartment into darkness.

Chip, just coming to, touched his jaw. The shooting pain made him cry out. Virgil turned at the sound, but chose to ignore the injured lawyer. Mickie, thankful for the darkness in the apartment, inched ever closer to the chair which contained the gun.

Cautiously, Virgil slammed the barrel of the gun through the window. At the sound of glass, the shotguns and pistols and rifles outside of the apartment jerked to attention.

"Don't fire," screamed Hemmings.

"Hey, pigs!" Virgil shouted. The abrasive volume of his voice, the fetid breath of his lungs, caused Karen to babble. She felt the pressure of her bladder, and she knew what was going to happen before long. At least, she thought, her mind having assumed a surreal aspect, she wouldn't dirty any clothing since she was still stark naked.

"Pigs!" Virgil cried again.

Karen voided, feeling the warm fluid trickle down her legs.

"You better talk to me," Virgil continued. "I got me three prisoners in here."

Hemmings looked to another officer. "Three?"

The trooper shrugged. "So talk to him."

"You're full of shit!" Hemmings shouted back.

"Like hell! I got the woman. I got that screwy lawyer of mine, and I got my nephew. We was havin' a party 'til you s.o.b.'s came along."

Hemmings's face, cast slate-blue by the lights, glistened with sweat.

"You hear me?" Virgil said.

Hemmings cleared his throat. "We hear."

"I ain't got no time to fuck with you guys. I'm gonna start wasting them. The lawyer goes first. Then the kid. I'm gonna wait five minutes. If you guys ain't cleared out, you gonna hear a gun shot. Scratch one lawyer! Be doin' the world a fuckin' favor. After another five minutes, you gonna hear another shot. Scratch one nephew. Be doin' myself a favor with that 'un! Then—"

Viciously, Virgil jammed the gun into Karen's rib cage. She wailed with pain. Chip tried to get to his feet, but his head floated away from him.

"Then," Virgil repeated, "I'm coming through the door whether you're gone or not with this here good-lookin' piece of ass right in front of me. You wanna save me all that trouble you kin leave now. Just leave the keys in one of them unmarked cruisers, and be sure the radio's workin'."

"You might as well give it up, Sampson," retorted Hemmings.

"Hell, I got ya'll by the balls, and you know it. And I got this pretty thing by the tits. You don't believe me, just ask her."

"Are you all right, Karen?" Hemmings shouted.

"Yes," she hissed.

"Louder," Virgil ordered.

"Yes! We're all right. And he has got all three of us."

"Way to go," Virgil whispered in her ear.

Chip pulled himself up to the couch, managed to mount his feet without making much noise. Again he launched himself at Virgil Sampson. He had to do something, even if that something was stupid and suicidal. Virgil heard him, and the gun came around and exploded. Virgil hadn't even bothered to aim. Chip spun and crashed to the floor.

Karen shrieked and started to fight against him. He cuffed her on the ear with the gun. "Stop it!" he ordered. "Or the kid's next."

Karen sobbed but ceased fighting.

"Forget the lawyer!" shouted Virgil. "He played hero. That cuts your time by five minutes."

"Okay," Hemmings answered. "Give us a few minutes."

"You got five!"

Virgil caught sight of Mickie out of the corner of his eye. The boy stood beside a chair. "Come on around here, kid. Get ready to open the door."

Mickie looked down at the lawyer and saw the blood blooming around the wound high on his chest. In the dim and eerie light of the room, Mickie couldn't tell if the lawyer was alive. He leaned down toward the chair.

"Move it, you snot-nosed little rat!" Virgil said.

His uncle kept his eyes glued to the window, anxious for some sign that the contingent of cops were giving in. Mickie reached down in the chair and withdrew the .38. He had no idea if it was loaded. The action was tight, too tight. He decided that he'd have to cock the hammer—which would alert his uncle.

"I said 'move it,' kid." Mickie tensed, ready to try it if Virgil turned . . . if Virgil gave him a shot. Then to the cops, Virgil cried, "Three minutes!"

From the darkness came a low, liquid moan.

"Chip!" cried Karen, stunned that he was even alive. She pulled against Sampson who throttled her around the throat. Outside, car doors started to open. Engines fired up.

Virgil kept his eyes on the action outside. "Get ready to open that door," he said to Mickie. The boy had come up close behind him.

Virgil heard the sharp metallic crack of a gun's action. "What the hell—"

He turned his head and his nose touched the cool metal of the .38. Karen collapsed.

Mickie Sampson jerked the trigger.

# EPILOGUE

Clarke Nelson surprised Chip when he came to the hospital. Karen, who had been sitting with Chip, was also shocked to see the prosecutor amble into the room.

"How's it going?" he asked of Chip.

Chip's jaw had been dislocated, not broken, but still the doctors had wired him up with some contraption which almost precluded speech. "I'm healing," Chip mumbled.

"What'd he say?" Nelson asked of Karen.

"He says he's doing okay."

"Good." Nelson sat down in one of the two chairs in the room. Karen was perched on the edge of Chip's bed. "I figured you'd be here," he said to Karen.

"Where else would I be?"

"Maybe in the office doing some of the work that's piling up."

Karen bristled. "If that's why—"

Nelson laughed at her anger. "Easy. Just kidding. I just came by to see how he's doing."

"It's only been 18 hours. He's still sore," Karen said. "He's just lucky that big bullet grazed him. It still just about ripped off his arm."

Chip fought to form his words. "How's Mickie?"

"What?" Nelson asked.

Karen, too, was uncertain of what Chip had said.

"How's the kid?" Chip repeated, this time a little more clearly.

"He's back at the detention center."

Chip closed his eyes.

"Does he have to be kept there?" Karen asked.

"I'm afraid so," Nelson said. "He still faces the murder charge. And, of course, we'll have to present the case to the grand jury on his shooting Virgil Sampson. That's standard practice in any death like this. I can assure you he won't be tried for that."

"Generous of you," Chip tried to say. "Nice of you," he said, which came out very clear.

Nelson shook his head. "I guess you two want me to just let the kid walk away."

"He needs help," Karen said, "not prosecution."

"We'll see." Nelson rose to leave.

"What about Louck?" Chip asked.

Nelson just couldn't understand Chip.

"He asked about the social worker," Karen said.

This time Nelson smiled proudly. "I convinced the deputy to reduce the charge from aiding an escape to obstructing an officer."

"You what?" Karen said, incredulous.

"We'll take a misdemeanor plea," Nelson said, basking in the glow of what he thought was a nice gesture.

Karen's anger surged out. "You're a bastard, Clarke! The kid ran for his life."

Nelson, by then at the door, sighed. "Jesus, Karen! You're on our side. No one saw Virgil Sampson but the kid. For all we know, he just decided to make a break for it."

Karen advanced on Nelson. Chip, helpless and virtually muted, watched wide-eyed. "Just why the hell would he turn himself in then?"

"He's a Sampson, Karen. Don't ask me to explain a Sampson."

"I quit," Karen said.

"You what?"

"You heard me. I quit."

Nelson frowned. "And just what are you going to do?"

Karen looked back at Chip who seemed as taken aback by her declaration as the prosecutor. "First," she said, "I'm going to marry Chip Roth—just as soon as he can say 'I do.' Then, after a brief honeymoon, he and I are going to open our own practice of law. And we've already got two clients—Art Louck and Mickie Sampson."

Nelson opened the door. Chip tried to sit up in his bed, but the streaking pain drove him back down.

"You might open offices," Nelson said, "but you'll have some trouble representing either of those two individuals. It'd be a conflict."

247

"So what's one more conflict?" Karen shouted. "Now scram Mr. Prosecutor. I'll see you in court."

Clarke Nelson shrugged and vanished out the door.

She returned to Chip's bedside. "We'll starve," Chip managed to say.

Karen, understanding his mumbled words, patted his hand. "There are much worse fates."